THE
WRONG
MOVE

Jennifer Savin is an award-winning journalist and currently Features Writer at *Cosmopolitan*. She has a particular passion for undercover investigations, which have seen her do everything from exposing predatory landlords who target vulnerable women, to sharing a cramped bedroom with a stranger while reporting on the housing crisis. *The Wrong Move* is her debut novel.

You can follow Jennifer on Twitter @JenniSavin and Instagram @savcity

THE WRONG MOVE

JENNIFER SAVIN

EBURY
PRESS

First published by Ebury Press in 2020

1 3 5 7 9 10 8 6 4 2

Ebury Press, an imprint of Ebury Publishing
20 Vauxhall Bridge Road,
London SW1V 2SA

Ebury Press is part of the Penguin Random House group of companies
whose addresses can be found at global.penguinrandomhouse.com

Penguin
Random House
UK

www.penguin.co.uk

A CIP catalogue record for this book is available from the British Library

ISBN 9781529104509

Typeset in 12.5/15.65 pt Garamond MT Std
by Integra Software Services Pvt. Ltd, Pondicherry

Printed and bound in Great Britain by Clays Ltd, Elcograf S.p.A.

Penguin Random House is committed to a sustainable future for
our business, our readers and our planet. This book is made
from Forest Stewardship Council® certified paper.

MIX
Paper from
responsible sources
FSC® C018179

For everybody who lived (and loved) at 17 Wakefield Road

Prologue

The sunlight dazzled that afternoon. Two women thanked their cab driver and mounted the steps of their shared flat, skin still laced with sweat and salt from the night before, mouths dry. Both were desperate to crawl under the covers of their respective beds and cocoon themselves, blocking out the slithers of Sunday dread that were already beginning to creep in. Neither were ready to start thinking about work or real life again just yet.

'I know I say this every time,' started the taller one, 'but I can't keep partying like that; the day after is too much of a killer.'

The other, with smudged eyeliner, murmured in solidarity and began fumbling in her bag, searching for keys. Her neck was stiff from sleeping on an unfamiliar sofa. Hot rays beat against their backs as the key turned in the lock. For anyone else, this would be the perfect summer's day. For them, it was too early. Too bright.

The cool air in the hallway felt unusually still. It was gone lunchtime; surely their other flatmate would be up and about by now? Boiling the kettle and sliding bread into the toaster, singing along to music playing from her phone. It wasn't like her to sleep in so late.

They headed upstairs and the woman with the smeared make-up knocked on the door of their flatmate's room. She waited a few moments for a reply. There was none. Hesitantly, she let herself in, just wanting to check that everything was okay. The sour stench of vomit hit instantly. It was all over the sheets and in her flatmate's hair, undignified clumps of it clung to her chin and lay scattered across her chest. She noticed her flatmate's ashen face, the body lying there lifelessly. She shook her, then urgently tried to scrape whatever was blocking her flatmate's airways using her finger, took her wrist in one hand. There was no pulse. She let out a high-pitched scream and her friend ran in, stood for a moment in stunned horror then grabbed the phone from her bag and started to dial an ambulance. But she could see it was too late. Their flatmate was dead.

CHAPTER ONE

Flat-hunting had proven to be a thoroughly arduous task, on a par with training for a marathon or having a tooth – no, *several* teeth – extracted, by an incompetent dentist. In fact, Jessie Campbell decided, either of those options would be preferable to viewing yet another flat that was riddled with damp, or falling in love with a room listed on SpareRoom or Gumtree, only to realise it was three times over budget. Even the ones that she'd actually visited in person and liked seemed to end in disappointment. It was always the same: she'd reply to a 'flatmate wanted' advert, make small talk in the kitchen with the current tenants, before judging whether or not all of her belongings could fit into the available bedroom. So far, after a month of intensive searching, Jessie had made an offer on four different places and heard nothing back from any of them. Nothing. Despite politely following up twice. The rejection was worse than being vetoed after a job interview, given that it was based strictly on the twenty minutes of personality she'd been allowed to display – not her skillset or lack of experience – all the while trying to work out how much cupboard space she might get in the kitchen.

Jessie had posted her own 'room wanted' adverts too, to minimal response, and then spent an afternoon emailing all of the Brighton letting agents that came up on the first page of Google, with a list of her requirements. A good-sized double bedroom in a friendly flat-share, £600 (bills included), happy to live with males or females, but no students, please. Within minutes, her phone had started buzzing non-stop with calls from unrecognised numbers. Did letting agents not sleep? And how did they keep managing to convince her to view so many rancid places? Jessie always felt as though she were snooping without permission when viewing a bedroom still obviously in occupation, barely daring to do more than peer around from the threshold.

One of the dives she'd been shown by an agent, on Upper Lewes Road, had an actual gaping hole in the floor covered by a sticky Persian rug. Another, a basement flat near Preston Park station, smelled of burnt rubber and was so cramped that when Jessie sat on the bed, she could touch the walls either side. Then there was the rundown townhouse by Hove Lawns, where a plump landlord resembling Henry VIII had given her a wink and said that he often crashed on the sofa whenever he had business in town. Truly repulsive. She'd seen plenty of properties with black mould scattered across the ceilings in hazardous constellations too, all of which made her ache for the flat she'd spent the past three years lovingly curating with a man she'd believed was her future. A flat that had once upon a time seemed so perfect.

Ian, the balding letting agent from Happy Homes (or was it Moving On Up? They'd all started blending into one), seemed to be the nicest of the bunch. Almost trustworthy, if he weren't working on commission. His favoured lilac shirts were a little on the baggy side and his shoes always meticulously shiny, reminding Jessie of a child on their first day of school. Endearing, really. The car he drove her around to viewings in was always pristine too and smelled of freshly cut pine, thanks to a tree-shaped air freshener hanging from the rear-view mirror.

It was a calm October afternoon, just after lunchtime when they pulled up outside 4 Maver Place. The flat was part of a large Edwardian house conversion, split over three floors – the top one of which was occupied by neighbours who let themselves in via another entrance down a small side alley.

'From what the current tenants have said, the neighbours pretty much keep to themselves,' Ian told her. 'A bonus, if you ask me.'

It was in a superb location – only a short walk from the seafront – and the rent was below the market rate for Brighton, a city growing notoriously more expensive with every passing year. Ian had reassured her that the three housemates already residing in the property (he always said 'property', never 'flat') were also young professionals in their twenties, just like her.

'One male and two females,' he'd chuckled. 'The poor bloke!'

Jessie tried not to let herself get too excited, looking up at the red-brick building with its blue front door and sweet little balcony, but she couldn't help the fizzing in her stomach. Hope mixed with desperation. Something was telling her that this, the twenty-third flat she'd seen, might just be the one.

Ian did his customary rat-a-tat-tat knock before letting them in. Jessie followed timidly behind him and blinked at the hallway. Magnolia, nothing special, but not as shabby as some of the other flats she'd seen over the past month. When they reached the open-plan kitchen-lounge at the end of the hallway, it became apparent there was somebody home after all, despite there having been no answer to Ian's banging on the front door. A young woman was sitting at a round pine table, engrossed in her phone. She jumped at the sight of them, then removed her headphones before introducing herself as Lauren. She had bleached-blonde hair chopped into a sharp bob, tucked behind pierced ears, impeccably straight teeth and red lacquer nails. In the centre of her face was a perfect, dainty turned-up nose.

'Sorry, I was in my own little world then.' She held up the phone. 'In a bit of a YouTube rabbit hole.'

She smiled, pushing her chair back with a loud scraping sound.

'Tea?'

Ian laughed and gave a grateful nod.

'That'd be great, thanks. We've been running about all over the place today.'

Jessie nodded too, taking in the room. The lounge area had two squashy, burnt-orange sofas and a rickety book-shelf, creaking with artistic tomes from museum gift shops and dog-eared paperbacks. A shoddy coffee table stood before the TV, with a few cardboard beermats pilfered from a nearby pub in use instead of proper coasters. She watched as Lauren stirred the milk in, and spotted a tiny tattoo of a delicate pair of feathered wings on her wrist. She decided the tattoo made this potential house-mate, Lauren, instantly cooler than her. Jessie had never been able to brave getting one herself. Not because of the physical pain, but because she was too terrified that she'd end up regretting it. Feeling confident in her decisions wasn't a strongpoint of hers. Lauren, on the other hand, came across as the type of girl who spearheaded the con-versation at parties, regaling a hooked crowd with her wild tales, gesturing animatedly with a rolled-up cigarette in hand. The type of person who both drew Jessie in and unnerved her a little. At parties Jessie was usually the one quietly stacking plastic cups into neat piles and making sure nobody knocked anything onto whichever laptop the Spotify playlist was coming from.

After handing over steaming Sports Direct mugs to Jessie and Ian, Lauren leaned back against the faux granite kitchen counter clutching her own mug, making idle chit-chat. She'd seemed excited at the prospect of having Jessie move in, especially after discovering they shared a few basic interests.

'I'll have to take you to my favourite yoga studio sometime in that case, it's just down the road,' Lauren had smiled, when Jessie mentioned she enjoyed taking the odd class.

By odd class what she had really meant was that she'd been a handful of times, in an effort to de-stress, and found the posture names like 'passive pigeon' and 'humble warrior' a bit ridiculous. But finding a new flatmate was like dating (something else she would need to get used to all over again) – any vague interests you had quickly became fully fleshed-out hobbies in order to make you appear more of a well-adjusted, easy-to-live-with individual. She had a strange urge to impress Lauren, whether or not she decided to move in. Ian slurped down a final mouthful of tea.

'Shall we do the rest of the tour, then?' he asked, putting his mug in the sink.

Lauren went to wash it up immediately, along with her own and Jessie's, then trailed them upstairs.

The bathroom was unremarkable but not unpleasant, despite rust-coloured grout lining the tiles above the taps, something Jessie had come to view as par for the course. A typical array of Aussie Miracle Moist shampoos and conditioners fought for space around the bath and the toothbrushes lived in a mint-coloured plastic beaker perched on the edge of the sink. Next door to the bathroom was Jessie's room (in theory) if she decided to take it.

She'd felt Lauren's eyes on her, as Ian opened the bed-room door and motioned for her to step inside. Jessie had been careful to inspect the space without looking overly judgemental, taking in the grey carpet and peering inside the white double-door wardrobe. It wobbled, but at least it had a mirror inside, and enough space for all her coats. There were two drawers built into it, which could hold her underwear, pyjamas and gym gear too. The rest of her clothes would have to live in boxes under the silver double-bed frame, just as they'd done when she was at university. That was the last time she'd moved in to a flat with strangers. Those boxes would be a daily reminder that life had taken a step backwards.

At least the previous tenant had already cleared their personal belongings out of the space, leaving nothing but a few ghostly dents on the carpet where heavy furniture once sat. A small nod to the cycle of renting life.

'How long has it been empty for?' she asked.

'Only a week or so,' replied Ian, before Lauren had a chance to. 'And we have plenty more viewings lined up for tomorrow. If I'm being completely honest with you, Jessie, I don't think this room will be available for long.'

Jessie readied herself for another of his sales pitches.

'It's the best size you're likely to get for your budget,' he continued, looking at her with earnest eyes. 'Plus, there's so much more communal storage space down-stairs too. It *will* get snapped up, so don't take too long thinking it over.'

As much as she hated to admit it, she knew Ian was probably right. Jessie ran her finger across the window-sill, gathering dust along the way. Whoever the former tenant was, they hadn't done the best job with cleaning.

'I'll take it,' she announced to the room, as if not only informing Ian and Lauren, but all of the Argos budget furniture and heavy damask curtains she'd inherit too.

Ian's face split into a grin.

'An excellent decision.'

CHAPTER TWO

A week later, Jessie stood on the doorstep of 4 Maver Place, with her suitcase and a couple of carrier bags by her feet. After that initial viewing, she'd hopped back into Ian's car and been driven to the cheerily named Happy Homes letting agency, to give them her reference details to check. Yesterday, her reference cleared, she'd signed the contract for a six months (minimum) tenancy and received a set of keys. They came complete with a plastic keyring displaying the Happy Homes sunshine yellow logo of a grinning house, the windows of which looked like kind eyes – hopefully a good omen of things to come, of the fresh start that she so desperately needed.

Jessie held the keys in her hand, but it didn't feel right clicking them into the lock and marching on in as she was yet to pay her share of a gas bill, had never left an IOU on a fellow housemate's milk or spent a night on one of those sunken sofas, cramming pizza into her mouth and watching *Friends* on a loop. Perhaps knocking was a better idea?

She prodded the carrier bags with the toe of her boot as she waited for someone to answer. A dark shadow slowly approached the frosted pane of glass in the centre of the blue wooden door, before pulling it back. It was Lauren.

'Hey, newbie, come on in!' She looked down. 'Is this all you've got with you?' she asked, reaching for the suitcase.

'There's more in the van I've hired,' Jessie said, nodding her back head in the direction of where she'd parked across the street. 'It's lovely to see you again.'

'And you! I was so pleased when you said you'd take the room,' Lauren replied, immediately putting her at ease. 'Here, I'll give you a hand.'

Together they carried Jessie's possessions from the van up into her new room. She was relieved to see it looked just as she'd remembered it and hadn't shrunk over the past week while her referencing forms were being processed. Jessie's mum had seemed pleased with the photos she'd sent her of Maver Place too, which strengthened her belief that she'd made the right choice. The extensive searching had all been worth it. And although Jessie had liked the comfort of coming home to her parents every night after a long day of flat viewings and job hunting in Brighton, she knew that leaving her hometown of Chesterbury, over 100 miles away, was for the best. There were too many ghosts there for her to be happy.

'Thanks so much for helping me move my stuff. I think I'll have to leave properly unpacking it all until tomorrow – I'm pretty knackered now.'

Lauren nodded in understanding.

'I honestly can't think of anything more exhausting than moving. I totally get how you feel.'

'Somehow it always seems to take so much longer than you remember, too,' said Jessie, conscious of sounding overly negative.

Lauren laughed.

'God, yeah! I guess you don't feel like cooking, and neither do I. How about we order a Thai?'

She was already fishing her phone out of her back pocket to pull up the website of a local takeaway joint.

'Sofie and Marcus aren't back for another hour or so, but I'm not sure I can wait that long.'

Although she would have preferred pizza, Jessie would never dare say. Thai would do fine.

'Sounds good to me,' she said with a smile. 'I'll run to the corner shop and grab some Prosecco while we wait, to say thank you for all your help.'

'That's so sweet of you. I need tobacco, I'll come too.'

As the big hand of the kitchen clock pushed past the 12 and the small hand hit the eight, the two new flatmates spooned curries from plastic boxes onto mismatched plates. Not that she could have known, but Jessie's plate had been hand-painted in deep purple swirls by Sofie Chang, the woman who occupied the bedroom next to Lauren's, directly opposite her own.

The glasses of fizz helped cement the occasion and Jessie began to feel herself relax, slowly making herself at home. It was an odd situation, knowing that although they now shared a postal address for the foreseeable future, neither she nor Lauren could say for sure whether or not a friendship would form between them or if they'd just be polite to one other in passing. As possible as it was that in two months' time they'd both be sitting around the same table saying, 'I can't believe we've only known each other a few weeks, I can barely remember life without you!', it was equally possible that their communication would be limited to a WhatsApp group chat that revolved around paying council tax and debating whether or not it was worth paying for a monthly cleaner.

Suddenly, Jessie had a sense that they were no longer alone. She noticed a figure standing in the doorway of the kitchen, almost … lurking, silently observing the scene of domesticity before him. He wore black ripped jeans and a washed-out T-shirt, bearing the grainy image of an unidentifiable 90s grunge band. After a nervous cough, the man who Jessie presumed must be Marcus, dropped a heavy canvas bag down by his Doc Martens and stepped forward, giving a nod as he did so.

'Marcus, this is Jessie,' said Lauren. 'Or do you prefer Jess? Sorry, I haven't even asked.'

He peered out from behind the side-swept fringe covering his eyes.

'Either is fine,' Jessie smiled. 'Great to meet you, Marcus.'

'Likewise. Looks like you're settling in well.'

Without another word, Marcus busied himself with searching through the cupboard closest to the fridge, then took out a packet of instant noodles. It looked as though there were Post-it notes on some of the cans in the cupboard, but Marcus closed the door before she was able to get a proper look.

'Microwave free?' he asked and yawned, running kettle water over coils of ramen.

'Go for it, mate. How was the shop today, then?' Lauren asked, without looking up from the prawn cracker she was loading with sticky rice.

'Ah, you know. Same as it ever is.' He stared over at her for a few seconds, then opened the microwave.

On their walk back from Singh's off-licence, cheap booze in hand, Jessie had asked more about Marcus and Sofie, the other flatmates. Lauren, only too pleased to answer, had dutifully informed her that Marcus worked in a music shop down one of the winding streets in the North Laine area, which specialised in selling vintage guitars. Jessie knew the one, it had a green exterior and a neon sign above the door saying 'Basement Beats'. In the past she'd occasionally stopped to check out the vinyl on display in the window, but couldn't recall ever having seen Marcus behind the counter serving customers or teaching a child how to tune their first bass. She struggled to imagine him doing either – he didn't exactly radiate the vibe of somebody who'd tell you your receipt was in the bag and wish you a great rest of the day.

Marcus began banging the bottom of a glass ketchup bottle over his packet noodles, before adding a squirt of mayonnaise and a sprinkle of pre-grated Red Leicester on top. Jessie visibly shuddered and shot a puzzled glance at Lauren, who merely shrugged. Jessie smoothed her features back out, hoping that Lauren wouldn't think she was judgemental. But she couldn't help it – every movement these new flatmates made had the chance to take on a second meaning.

Lauren savoured another bite of her prawn cracker, noticing the cheese Marcus had left scattered across the faux granite worktops. She made a silent bet with herself that he'd saunter back to his room without tidying it up.

'I'm back!' called a sing-song voice from the hallway. 'But only for a minute, just grabbing some stuff. Henry's here too.'

The voice was reminiscent of a children's TV presenter who Jessie couldn't quite place the name of. In reality, it belonged to a woman with a heart-shaped face, blessed with high cheekbones and a light dusting of freckles, who managed a healthy eating café. Her blue tie-dye leggings fitted so perfectly they looked as though they'd been sprayed on. Jessie recognised the logo on them; a new ethical label that all the fitness bloggers had been going mad for lately. Something to do with being made from recycled water bottles?

'You must be Jessie. I'm Sofe – welcome to the madhouse.'

She immediately engulfed Jessie in a hug.

Jessie attempted to twist her body round to reciprocate but found the back of her chair was in the way. Sofie didn't seem to notice, or if she did, didn't say, and continued wrapping her arms around the new face in her home.

'Did you guys order from Blue Elephant? You know that's my favourite,' she said and fake-pouted, as a tanned man wearing a long-sleeved rugby shirt slid his arm around her waist.

He was classically good-looking in a double-barrelled surname sort of way, with broad, weighty shoulders.

'Sorry, I was going to message but I knew you wouldn't be back for a while and poor Jessie here was about to die of starvation. Moving is hungry work, right, babe?' Lauren used her fork as a pointer and aimed it at her newest flatmate.

Jessie didn't like that she had been made the scapegoat – the reason that Sofie hadn't been told about their dinner – but quickly forced herself to nod in agreement. Lauren surely hadn't meant it as a dig; she was reading meanings into things again. It never did any good being oversensitive or making rash judgements, she had to remember that. It was hard not to, given that she'd just made the leap to move in with these people. But, she reminded herself, *this* Jessie was different to the old Jessie. New Jessie didn't forage through every conversation looking for the words that made her feel upset or afraid.

'It's cool. We had leftover sandwiches at my work and I'm staying out tonight anyway. I brought back some brownies that were going spare; they're vegan.'

Sofie, obviously unbothered, produced a pink-and-white striped paper bag from her patchwork rucksack and placed it next to the takeaway containers on the table.

'You'll have to pop into the café when you get a chance, Jess,' she continued. 'It's just at the bottom of St James's Street, and we run an open mic night in there every fortnight too, which is always fun. Plus, the drinks are cheap.'

The thick-jawed man leant across the table and helped himself to a brownie.

'She even sings at it. Rather well, unlike me, who got kicked out of the school choir for letting the side down,' he laughed, kissing the top of Sofie's pastel-pink head, complete with dark roots poking through at the crown.

Even Marcus smirked. It was clear that, whoever this man was, he knew how to work a room.

'Henry Goldsmith-Blume, by the way.'

He thrust a colossal bear hand at Jessie to shake, the vicelike grip matching his booming oak-tree baritone perfectly. They seemed a slightly odd pairing. He clearly came from money and radiated an air of assured authority, learned from childhood. Sofie, on the other hand, in her millennial New Age gear and rows of gold hooped earrings, didn't seem to be the type of woman who'd be especially fussed about inheriting a stately home in the Sussex countryside. But Henry's arm remained firmly around her taut, caramel waist and she nestled into it.

'Anyway, I hate to be rude, but we've literally just popped back so I can grab some contact lenses for tomorrow – I'm blind as a bat,' Sofie said, rolling her eyes, as if to demonstrate how inconvenient they were. 'But let's definitely make plans to all hang out together soon, okay? Lauren can you add Jessie to the group chat?'

Without anybody realising, Marcus had slunk back to his room, the only bedroom on the ground floor, food in hand. The hum of bass-heavy music tiptoed out of his speakers and under the door but fell short of the ears in the kitchen. He knew they wouldn't be paying much attention to his whereabouts anyway. Nobody ever did.

A short while later, from the balcony where she was inhaling smoke, Lauren listened to Henry's car purr as it moved away from the kerb outside. She could see Sofie sitting in the passenger seat, jabbing away at the radio, trying to find a station playing the sparsely worded house music she loved so much. Turning back towards the flat, Lauren watched through the window as Jessie made a start on the washing-up, for which she was grateful. Her dream of flat-sharing with somebody else who was as into cleaning as she was might finally be coming true. She smiled and ashed her roll-up out on the bare brick wall and flicked the butt into an old Heinz baked beans can, already half-full with yellowing ends. She had a good feeling about this already.

Later that night, Jessie sank below the covers in her newly rented bedroom and stared at the unfamiliar patterns on the ceiling, waiting for her body slip into a soft and drowsy state. Her life lay in boxes, bags and piles around the room. It had been a very long day and soon enough, her thoughts quickly wrapped themselves around one another and the exhaustion of moving kicked in. She felt truly weary. But as she neared the brink of sleep, a sound yanked her back into a state of alert. Some kind of shuffling. Or was it a scraping? The noise seemed to be coming from downstairs. It came again, muffled and almost rhythmic. Jessie's heart rate quickened as she strained to decipher what it was that she was hearing. It wasn't a sound she could identify as ever having come across before. Was Marcus dragging something across the floor? His bedroom was almost directly under hers. She continued listening, then after a minute, the noise stopped just as suddenly as it had started. Unnerved, Jessie pulled the covers over her head, the way she used to as a child, and took a few deep breaths. All houses sounded different, had their distinctive creaks and whistles that appeared at night, and took a bit of getting used to. That's all it would be. Besides, she'd always been the anxious type, prone to succumbing to the tricks that her mind loved to play on her, she knew that. Didn't she?

CHAPTER THREE

The next morning, a chink of light drifted through a gap in the curtains and settled over Jessie's eyes. They flickered, then opened. For a moment she couldn't quite place where she was, her surroundings were unfamiliar and it took a couple of seconds for her brain to catch up. It was the first official day of her new start, a feeling she paused to bask in for a few moments.

She forced herself out of bed and pulled on a pair of jogging bottoms, with the intention of heading to her old gym along the seafront and re-registering as a member. She liked being able to watch the waves (which appeared either a glittering blue or dull brown depending on the weather) dashing up the pebbly shore and then retreating while pounding the treadmill. It helped to distract her mind away from any burning feet. She checked her phone. The time read 8.14am, still early for a weekend. But after a few deep yawns and stretches to help her adjust to being back in the land of the living, Jessie shuffled out of her bedroom and into the bathroom next door. The flat was quiet. She guessed Lauren and Marcus must still be asleep. It was a peculiar feeling, being in her own home but feeling like she had to creep around like a cat burglar. Through bleary eyes, Jessie laced her toothbrush with a slug of Aquafresh and began to clean her teeth, almost on auto-pilot. Forward, back. Up down, repeat. Spit.

She then clipped her fringe back and carefully pushed cleanser deep into the groves on either side of her nose, then washed away the residue. Apart from the sound of the running tap, the flat was silent. Jessie flipped her head up and moved closer to the mirror to inspect her skin for any blemishes; her entire body jumped when she realised there were four eyes, rather than the expected two, staring back at her. She let out a sharp yelp.

'Sorry,' muttered a pallid reflection in the mirror, just over her shoulder, before quickly retreating back into the shadows of the not-quite-light hallway.

In the second it took her to turn around, Marcus had gone. Jessie touched the mirror, as if to reassure herself that it really was just her face in there now, as his footsteps faded away, back towards the direction of the stairs. How long had he been there? Watching her. Studying her. Perhaps she'd noticed him just as he'd appeared and he hadn't been watching her at all, making for an unnecessarily awkward encounter? An awkward encounter with a housemate who she was keen to get along well with. Jessie pushed the door firmly shut and slid the bolt across, feeling uneasy. In her half-awake state she hadn't realised it wasn't properly closed, which was unlike her. Flat-sharing, having lived with a partner and then family for so long, would take a bit of getting used to. It was such a peculiar set-up: living in close quarters with complete strangers, who could walk in on you during intimate moments. Sleeping in a bed that was never truly just yours. The lay-out of the flat, its smell, everything about Maver Place, her home, was alien. Including the other tenants.

Pushing the incident with Marcus from her mind momentarily, Jessie cautiously headed downstairs to the kitchen in search of breakfast. She'd picked up a few choice items during her Prosecco pilgrimage with Lauren yesterday and settled on a pre-workout strawberry yoghurt. Her shelf in the fridge was neatly ordered in comparison to the others'. Sofie's appeared to be mostly made up of cans of Diet Coke and half-eaten tubs of humus, one of which was several months out of date, suggesting she wasn't often around, but there was still a Post-it stuck to it saying 'Do Not Throw Away!'.

Jessie slid her carton of semi-skimmed milk back into the fridge door, next to the cartons of various nut and oat alternatives. Lauren had scribbled her name on one with a smiley face while Marcus had gone for a simple under-lined 'M' in thick black marker pen on his. A quick count told her that there were more varieties of milk stuffed in there than flatmates.

By the time she'd reached the last spoonful of yoghurt, Jessie had decided she would give Marcus the benefit of the doubt. It was probably a simple mix-up as they got used to their new routines. Perhaps she should actually apologise for hogging the bathroom? Maybe now he'd be late for work at the shop and it was all her fault. Why else would he be awake so early? She had no idea whether or not any of her housemates worked on a Sunday and made a mental note to ask Lauren when she saw her later. Zipping up her grey fleecy hoody, Jessie tried to shut the front door quietly, so as not to disturb the neighbours, or Lauren, who she presumed was still asleep.

She made her way along the garden path, enjoying not having her headphones in for once, just hearing the hum of traffic in the distance. It was the epitome of a crisp autumn morning, her favourite time of year. It became colder the closer she neared to the seafront, thanks to the wind bouncing off the water. She drew the hoody a little tighter and upped her pace, hoping that the gym would still be relatively empty. Despite having lived in Brighton several years ago while at university, the size of the seagulls there never ceased to amaze her. They were like cats with wings, circling and squawking overhead, forever angered. Jessie approached the gym door and made a beeline for the reception desk. The automatic doors groaned shut behind her.

Back in the flat, Marcus, who had the day off work, stirred a saucepan full of baked beans while Lauren sipped a coffee at the table. She idly folded over the corners of a fashion magazine's pages whenever she spotted an item of interest. The photography studio she assisted in was often used for editorial shoots by the publication, so she always made sure to pick up a copy. She loved feeling the glossy paper between her fingertips and seeing the models, who she'd run out to buy lunch for, pouting back at her from the pages, their bodies twisted into human origami positions. It gave her a thrill of pleasure knowing she'd played even a tiny part in it all.

'Got much going on today?' she asked, cutting through the silence.

Marcus shrugged.

'Just hanging out with the band. We're hoping to get a new song finished.'

'I look forward to hearing it,' Lauren replied, eyes still on the models. 'But you'll be back in time for dinner? I'm thinking of doing a little welcome meal for Jessie.'

'I'll keep you posted.'

'Sure. If it sways it, I'll make lasagne.'

Marcus nodded but said nothing, preferring to concentrate on pouring his beans over two precise squares of toast, which he'd cut the crusts from. He topped the dish with one clockwise spiral of ketchup and another anti-clockwise one of mayonnaise, his signature finish.

'I just think it would be nice for us all to make a bit of effort and make her feel welcome,' said Lauren, closing the magazine and rising to her feet.

She looked at the stray crusts on the floor by the bin and made a mental note to message Marcus about them later, not wanting to confront him in person.

After hitting her 10-mile target, Jessie slowed the treadmill and wiped the sweat from her eyes with the back of her hand before stepping off. She'd made good time today. Over the past few months, working out had become her saviour when it came to dealing with anxiety, stress and misery. Taking up regular exercise, although basic, was one of the best pieces of advice that her counsellor had offered throughout their now concluded sessions. Hitting targets helped her to regain some control and feel good about herself, like she was worth something, after believing otherwise for so long.

She headed to the changing room and retrieved her phone from her bag. There were two notifications: a text from her mum asking how her first night in the new place had gone, another showing she'd been added into a WhatsApp group chat. The chat was named 'Flatmates!' with several house emojis next to it. She clicked on the app and saw that Lauren was typing. She checked who else was in the group and saved the numbers for Sofie and Marcus, whose contact details she hadn't yet stored in her phone.

Jessie was immediately curious to see what photos they had all chosen for their WhatsApp profiles, the small circle icons offering a peek inside their respective, yet newly joined, worlds. Who knew what she could learn from the one image they'd chosen to represent themselves with. Jessie hadn't managed to find her housemates on social media yet and Ian had only given her Lauren's number as a point of contact. Lauren's picture showed her wearing a cropped red leather jacket, glass of wine in hand and laughing, eyes closed. The photo was slightly blurry – perhaps whoever had taken it was laughing along too. Lauren obviously wasn't fazed at the thought of being snapped off guard, preferring to be fully absorbed in socialising.

Sofie's photo, on the other hand, was more staged; she'd gone for a sunset selfie taken on holiday. Somewhere with palm trees in the background. Her tanned skin glistened against the peach melba sky and her trademark boho earrings were just visible through beachy waves. At the time she'd favoured turquoise hair over her current pastel-pink tones.

Marcus, on the other hand, had chosen not to include a photo of himself on his profile. Instead, he'd gone for the artwork used on one of his favourite punk albums, depicting an oozing human heart being squeezed by a woman's freshly manicured hand. The nails looked sharp, like enlarged cat claws, and were the same cartoon red as the organ. Jessie zoomed out of the image and clicked back onto the chat to read Lauren's message which had just come through.

Hey housies! Dinner tonight at 7? I'm going to make Mama McCormack's famous lasagne to welcome our newest recruit. Don't be late.

The phone vibrated again.

Also, I'll make the vegan version for you Sofe

A few seconds later the top of the screen indicated that Sofie was typing a response. It was prefaced with heart-eyed emojis.

Yessss, thanks, babe! Henry will come too

Jessie noted that Henry hadn't actually been invited and wondered whether he and Sofie were one of *those*

27

couples. The ones who said 'we love Italian food' or 'we hate living autonomous lives.' Jessie knew the type only too well, given that until very recently she had been a part of one herself. Now, she couldn't wish to be further away from Matthew if she tried. Although it was a relief knowing he was back in their shared hometown of Chesterbury and didn't know where she was, the hundred-odd miles of distance between them didn't feel wide enough.

Marcus sent a thumbs up into the group chat, Jessie sent two back.

Sounds great! Let me know if I should bring anything

What could possibly go wrong?

CHAPTER FOUR

On her walk back to the flat, Jessie called Priya, her closest friend, and one of the reasons why she'd chosen to move back to Brighton. While Jessie had returned home to Chesterbury after graduation (upon Matthew's insistence), Priya had stayed and was living with her girlfriend, Zoe, in a flat overlooking the remains of the West Pier. It was comforting to know she had a somebody who cared for her near by, especially after everything she'd been through this past year.

Priya picked up after a few rings.

'All right?' she dragged each syllable out.

Jessie suspected the call might have woken her up.

'Morning, I'm just walking home, not all that far from yours, actually.'

'Why, where've you been? Not traipsing back from a one-night stand already, are you, Jess? Bloody hell, you've only been back five minutes.'

Jessie found herself moved by the sound of Priya's laughter, having not totally realised how much she'd missed hearing it. Things between them had been strained over the last few years, and she felt a smile spread across her face now, knowing she finally had her best friend back. They'd met almost six years ago, when Priya had been waiting outside the same university lecture theatre as her, wearing sunglasses, and caught Jessie glancing over at her quizzically. Priya had offered her half a Kit Kat and explained that the indoor sunglasses were because she had a tequila-induced headache. It turned out the pair lived on the same floor in halls.

'I won't even dignify that with a response. You, of all people, know the idea of anything like that is so far from what I need now,' Jessie said and laughed too. 'You, on the other hand, sound like you've had a big night?'

She hung up the call when she arrived back at the flat, needing both hands to recover her keys from the bottom of her gym bag. Once inside, Jessie headed into the kitchen and saw a piece of paper had been taped to the swing bin. Upon closer inspection, it read *'Dear house, it's really easy to use a bin. Please stop starting one on the floor next to it instead.'* The note hadn't been signed. She raised her eyebrows and turned to raid the fridge, hungry from her workout. Reaching for the yoghurts, she noticed one was missing. Odd. And cheeky, too – whoever it was that had helped themselves had a nerve. She'd barely moved in and had only been gone a few short hours. Surely one of the unspoken rules of flat-sharing is that you have to at least be friends with a person before you start helping yourself to their food? Maybe she should start marking her territory by leaving notes on her things too. Jessie texted Priya to gauge how outraged she was entitled to be and was disappointed when the response simply read: *It's a yoghurt, hardly the crime of the century – don't go falling out with people in your first week over dairy products!* Priya was right, though; it was annoying but definitely not worth causing a scene about.

The rest of the day passed with relative ease and Jessie spent it unpacking her belongings and finding places for everything. She lined the windowsill with her photograph collection, her favourite being one of her and Priya taken at a day festival last summer, their cheeks daubed with glitter, ciders in hand. She had only been able to go because Matthew was away that weekend. On a training course, he'd said, although who knew how true that was.

After several hours of unpacking and organising, Jessie flopped down onto the bed and watched the sun dip outside the window. Her eyes grew heavy. By the time she woke to the sound of Lauren clattering around the kitchen and singing, the sun had fully disappeared. She was singing an old 80s pop song, one that Jessie had heard her parents playing in the car before. Lauren could hold a tune, even though she probably wasn't trying all that hard. She seemed like the kind of girl who was good at most things.

Jessie stood up and debated what to wear for dinner later on, keen to get her outfit just right. She wanted her flatmates to like her, to think she was cool and worth getting to know. They all looked, like a lot of Brighton residents, as though they'd rolled straight out of art school or stepped off a catwalk. In comparison, she felt plain and safe. Even her haircut, with its blunt, eyebrow-grazing fringe, had been the same since she was a child. Her bravest move was getting caramel highlights woven through the dull brown on Priya's insistence a couple of years ago. Matthew had barely acknowledged it, bar a disapproving grunt.

Now she could feel her anxiety levels rising at the thought of having to be outgoing around people she didn't know very well. What if they ran out of things to talk about? Or she said the wrong thing? After rifling through her newly organised wardrobe, Jessie threw on a floral tea dress that she'd brought in a vintage shop, hoping someone might at least ask where it was from and she could slip that titbit of information in. Personality in a garment. She headed downstairs, acutely aware of the shuffling her black tights made on the brown-carpeted hallway, a shuffling which then turned to squeaking when the carpet met the black-and-white kitchen tiles.

'Looking lush, babe!' said Lauren, giving her a quick glance and fanning her face with an oven glove. 'I've opened a bottle of shiraz if you fancy a glass?'

The windows were steamed. Drops of condensation raced down each, giving the kitchen an intimate feel. Jessie smiled to herself wryly. What letting agents would describe as 'cosy' in reality meant 'cramped' and that the TV and fridge were in the same room.

'Love one, thanks!' Jessie replied, helping herself. 'I meant to ask earlier, do you have a number for the girl who lived in my room before me? The key for my lock is missing.'

Lauren stopped humming.

'Er, for Magda? No, sorry I haven't,' she said, looking a little awkward. 'How's the wine?'

'Oh, it's good …' Jessie paused, then tried again. 'Would Sofie or Marcus have it?'

'Well, Marcus will probably have beer. And Henry will bring over a far more expensive bottle of wine for him and Sofe.'

'Oh no, I meant Magda's number – do you think either Sofie or Marcus will have it?'

Lauren made a face which suggested she was thinking before speaking.

'To be honest, Magda wasn't the easiest to live with and things didn't end all that well.'

Lauren fidgeted uncomfortably.

'There were some clashes between her and Marcus. She'd often complain about him playing his music too loudly, that sort of thing. I was trapped in the middle, playing peacemaker, seeing as Sofie is hardly ever in.'

Jessie sipped at the wine. Lauren looked concerned that she might have put her foot in it. It was a tricky topic to discuss, former housemates and why they left, without incriminating yourself in the process.

'I swear we're all nice and it's a really laid-back flat,' she said to Jessie. 'And you fit in so well already, it's like you've always been here.'

On cue, Marcus glided into the room, palming his fringe down flat. He slowly cracked open a lager and enjoyed letting it hiss, something to take the edge off. He wasn't looking forward to this flat dinner but he'd do it for Lauren, of course.

'Who's hungry, then?' Lauren asked, pulling a tray of garlic bread from the oven, flinching as the edge of it nicked her wrist.

'Definitely me, it smells amazing,' replied Jessie. 'Thanks so much for organising this, it's really nice of you all. Are Sofie and Henry still joining?'

Before she could get an answer, the thud of the front door came from down the hall and in walked the odd couple, Henry striding a few paces ahead of Sofie. Almost imperceptibly, Marcus's shoulders stiffened. Henry represented every boy at school who'd ever teased him for being too skinny, too pale or too weird. Henry's type was the reason Marcus had spent every lunchtime locked away in the music rooms, playing the same chords repeatedly until his fingers hardened.

'Looking lovely this evening, ladies! I come bearing wine,' Henry said, producing a bottle from behind his back with flourish.

Lauren and Jessie shared a knowing look.

'Where's the corkscrew around here?'

Sofie shrugged. She spent so little time in the flat she'd be hard-pressed to say where most things were kept.

'I think it's in the cutlery drawer,' said Lauren. 'But let's be real, I'm a screw-top kind of girl, so it's been a while since I've dug it out.'

The round pine table had been set with apricot-coloured paper napkins. Jessie thought it a sweet touch on her new housemate's part – it was clear that Lauren enjoyed playing hostess and had gone to a lot of effort with arranging this meal. She was grateful for it. It was also clear that the wine Henry had decided to bring along was probably worth more than the battered dining table itself, just as Lauren had predicted.

'On the old cat's piss eh, Marky Mark?' Henry gave a jovial headshake at Marcus's can of lager, looking him up and down.

Today's band T-shirt had holes in it, making Marcus appear as though he'd been swallowed whole by a paper shredder, then spat back out in time for dinner. The meal wasn't Henry's idea of fun either. He'd have given anything for a slab of steak, so rare it was still almost twitching on his plate, and someone to swap tales of rugby initiation tasks with. Sports chat was something he'd tried initially with Marcus, but he had been met with a deafening silence.

'So it would seem,' Marcus replied coolly. 'Sadly, I don't have my own wine cellar to pick and choose from.'

Lauren placed the stoneware dish of lasagne down on the table and motioned for everybody to take a seat. Sofie held back for a second until Henry had chosen his spot, then placed herself between Jessie and Lauren.

'It looks delicious.' Jessie nodded earnestly.

'I can't wait,' agreed Sofie, rubbing her hands together in anticipation. 'Work was insanely busy today and this is the first time I've sat down. We sold clean out of the new almond energy balls I made.'

After everyone had helped themselves to a serving, poured a glass of either very expensive or decidedly cheap wine (bar Marcus) and swallowed their first few mouthfuls down, conversation turned to the landlord of the flat.

'He's fairly absent,' Lauren said through a mouthful. 'In fact, he actually lives in Germany. I've only met him once and that was years ago, when I first moved in. So, we're talking around 2014.'

'I've never met him,' Sofie chimed in. 'I found the flat through Happy Homes, the same as you, Jessie, in the spring of 2016. If there's ever been a problem, though, Ian's been all right enough to deal with and gets things fixed pretty quickly.'

'Did you know each other before living here?' Jessie asked Lauren and Marcus, switching her gaze between them as she spoke.

Marcus's eyes remained firmly fixed to his plate, as though he had a bell jar placed around him and couldn't hear.

'I guess so,' he said eventually, monotonously.

'Well, you know what Brighton's like,' Lauren added. 'It's a small city, everybody knows everybody, one way or another.'

Talk then turned to how Lauren and Sofie had gone to the same life-drawing class for years, only realising they vaguely knew one another a few weeks after Sofie had taken up residency in the flat.

'Are you all unpacked and settled in now, Jessie?' Sofie asked.

Jessie noticed Henry leaning on his elbow and looking over in her direction.

'If you ever need a hand moving anything else in or want a lift to IKEA, feel free to call me,' he said. 'I'm good at flat pack furniture and … all other kinds of bedroom-related activities.'

He gave a guffaw and drained his glass, then looked at Sofie, expecting her to be laughing along too.

She wasn't. Instead, she frowned slightly and thought back to the day that Henry had spectacularly tried – and failed – to build her a bookcase. She'd ended up batting him away and doing it herself in half the time. His bravado always cranked up a notch when he drank wine.

Henry cocked his head to one side. The sound of scraping cutlery filled the silence. Lauren widened her eyes at Jessie in confused solidarity and reached for the cheaper bottle of wine.

'Why does every single wine on the planet seem to say it's great paired with fish or pasta?' Lauren turned the bottle round and read the label. 'No matter where it's from or what it's like.'

They all forced a laugh, glad for a change of subject. Henry's boomed over everybody else's.

'Have I ever told you about the summer I spent studying wine in France?' he said, refilling his glass, then swirling and studying the contents.

'Yes – and let me guess, you're about to again?' Sofie muttered.

'Thanks for this.'

Marcus stood up and carried his empty plate over to the sink, adding it to the pile.

'Plenty left for seconds if you'd like?' Lauren offered, her voice a little too high, but Marcus shook his head.

'There's some band stuff I need to be getting on with. See you later.'

With that, the party wound down to four. Okay, so it hadn't been the great bonding session she'd imagined, but Jessie felt happier than she had done in a long time. Even if Marcus was difficult, Sofie and Lauren seemed like the type of girls she would love to be friends with and intent on getting to know her. Henry probably hadn't meant anything by offering to help either, she was just on edge, as per usual, and reading too much into things.

A short while later, Henry ordered a taxi back to his place, Sofie dutifully following, too tired to explain that she'd prefer to sleep in her own room for a change. Jessie volunteered to do the washing-up again, to say thank you for dinner, and Lauren headed out to her usual spot on the balcony to smoke. She exhaled and looked down at the street, to where Henry was holding open the taxi door for Sofie. At that exact moment, Sofie glanced up at the balcony. For a split second, their eyes met, then Henry ushered Sofie inside. There was something about him that just didn't sit right.

CHAPTER FIVE

Despite a small smattering of nerves, on the whole, Jessie was quietly confident about her impending job interview. She wasn't a complete novice when it came to working for the NHS, having done plenty of temp administrator shifts throughout university – well, something had needed to pay for all those weekend trips back to Chesterbury to visit Matthew. As much as he'd insisted he couldn't cope without her, he rarely made the effort to drive down to Brighton, claiming that Jessie's student accommodation was too shabby and that Priya obviously didn't like him. He was spot on about the latter.

She strode purposefully towards the gated entrance of Tulip Court, an unimposing building primarily used for psychiatric outpatient appointments and substance-abuse therapy groups. The area, Woodingdean, was a little out of town and not one she was overly familiar with. Reaching the reception desk, Jessie gave her best winning smile and smoothed down the black suede skirt she'd decided made her look most employable earlier that day. She'd teamed it with a black blazer on loan from

Lauren and pinstripe shirt, with plain pointed court shoes which were not too high, professional-looking and easy to walk in. Jessie had been grateful when Lauren offered to help her with choosing an outfit, along with soothing any last minute pangs of self-doubt. It felt as though the two of them were already forming a real bond and, in fact, she was already looking forward to dissecting the interview with her later. It was good to know she could make new friends and that people *did* like her. Jessie was almost beginning to feel more like her old self. Almost.

The receptionist looked up from her computer.

'Can I help?'

'I have an interview at half past one, I'm a few minutes early I know.'

'Name?'

'Jessie Campbell. It may be under Jessica?'

The woman ran a polished fingernail along a list of names and ticked one off.

'Perfect, take a seat. Someone will be with you shortly.'

Jessie helped herself to a plastic cup of water and chose a seat next to a tank of brightly coloured fish. That apart, the waiting room was the definition of clinical, with off-white walls and threadbare blue chairs, foam innards splaying out, ready to be picked at by nervous patients. All the magazines on offer were at least three months old, the covers curled. Her eyes rested on one with an unflattering picture of a celebrity wearing a spotted bikini, shielding her eyes from the sun, on the cover.

'Jessie? I'm Pamela, head of the administration team. Pleasure to meet you.' A woman in her fifties with ashy blonde hair, that she clearly had blow-dried on a regular basis, extended her hand. Jessie took in her accompanying cranberry jumper, complete with diamanté V-neck and could tell that Pamela was the sort of woman who smelled faintly of Olay face cream. The type who chatted endlessly at her husband about their upcoming week in Tenerife, while he desperately sought solitude in a newspaper. Who gave her neighbours home-made coffee cakes over the fence in exchange for gossip. Jessie extended a hand back and stood up.

'Thanks so much for calling me in; it's nice to be back on NHS soil.'

After asking a series of standard interview questions, that Jessie answered with relative ease, Pamela leant back on her chair. Her body language grew looser. Jessie took a sip of the water that another member of staff had dropped off at the beginning of her interview. Whoever she was, she had given a small, encouraging thumbs up after placing the drink on the table, before backing out of the room.

'So, I can see from your CV that you've spent the last few years in Essex. What is it that's brought you back to Sussex?'

Jessie paused. How honest were you meant to be in this type of scenario? Probably best to just keep it vague.

'I wish I'd never left, really,' she replied, in what she hoped was a positive and convincing voice.

It was the truth too.

'I always loved living here and it felt like the right time to come back.'

This seemed to satisfy her prospective new employer who, Jessie suspected, was just being nosy, albeit in a friendly sort of way. They'd got on well throughout their half hour together in the small, windowless meeting room. Pamela seemed to particularly warm to Jessie when she'd mentioned her love of writing lists as a way of keeping organised.

'I'll be in touch very soon. Let me show you back out, my love.'

With the rest of her day free, Jessie decided to walk home. It was a bright Tuesday afternoon, the schools hadn't yet finished for the day and the streets were quiet. The interview had left her riding high on a wave of newly accrued confidence; she had a sneaking suspicion that Pamela would indeed be calling her with an offer in the not too distant future. To celebrate, Jessie diverted via the shops on London Road, to treat herself to a new lipstick as an inexpensive pat on the back. A congratulations present for getting through her first face-to-face interview. As she waited, phone in hand, for the traffic lights to signal it was safe to cross, Jessie saw the flash of a man's khaki jacket disappearing into a coffee shop on the opposite side of the street. Suddenly the air felt too shallow to properly inhale; her grip tightened involuntarily on her phone and her blood ran cold. She stood rooted to the ground, as though the tarmac beneath her had turned to quicksand, desperately trying to remember what it was that her counsellor recommended she do whenever she felt a panic attack coming on.

It *couldn't* have been him. It was just a coincidence. Plenty of men wore parka jackets similar to Matthew's. Besides, he couldn't do anything to her in broad daylight in the middle of the street. Could he? She began to slowly count down from 100 to zero until her breathing slowed, and reminded herself that she was safe now. It was just taking a while to adjust. Perhaps she ought to hurry up and register with a new GP, to ask about increasing her dosage of sertraline, which she'd been prescribed to help manage her anxiety. The silver foil tray of calming Tic Tacs that she took religiously each night before bed, which she sometimes popped a few extra of when she struggled to sleep. They helped to block his face out. That and wine.

By the time she reached zero, Jessie was ready to start making her way home. Forget the lipstick. Reaching for the front door, she was relieved to see her hands had stopped shaking. Stepping inside, she wanted nothing more than to curl up with a book and detach her mind for a few hours, before getting back to emailing out her CV. She wasn't especially passionate about the potential of resuming her life as an admin assistant but had no idea what else to do. Anything that paid her rent and provided some kind of structured routine would do for now. To cull the silence and odd creaks caused by the wind, Jessie flicked the communal radio on and hummed to herself as the kettle boiled. A mint tea would be the perfect reading companion.

It was the first time she'd had Maver Place all to herself. She tried singing aloud, gradually getting louder, testing the waters. Even though she'd been living here for a week now, things like not immediately knowing which drawer the cutlery was in still made Jessie feel like an outsider. The walls stared as she opened the wrong cupboard searching for teabags. That one must be Sofie's, all bags of seeds and organic grains she'd never heard of, stacked in messy piles. Some red lentils had spilled out of the packet and there were several jars of home-made kimchi and jams in there too. The Post-it notes, that Jessie had spotted over Marcus's shoulder the other day, listed all the ingredients and the date they'd been made on. A few were over a year old and still untouched. She sniffed at one and reeled. Definitely off. Still, there was something thrilling about looking through someone else's cupboard, finding out more about the relative strangers she now lived with. Another tempting thought made itself known. Jessie glanced over her shoulder, even though she already knew the rest of her flatmates were out, then headed to the hallway. Their bedrooms would tell her so much more than any cupboards could.

Sofie's seemed the safest one to start with. It appeared she was always out, rarely popping back for longer than twenty minutes to shower, change and go to Henry's, or to the café for work. Ever since the dinner party, Jessie had found herself wondering what Henry's home might be like. She'd heard from Lauren that his parents' place was pretty spectacular, with a lake in the back garden, and that he personally had a spacious two-bedroom flat by the seafront. No wonder Sofie preferred to hang out there.

Jessie padded along the corridor, her mug left abandoned on the kitchen counter. She paused at the bottom of the stairs, which Marcus's room was to the left of. Actually, there'd be no harm in just cracking the door slightly open and looking inside on her way upstairs. Her hand hovered over the doorknob, which had splatters of gloss paint from the door on it. It was typical of the flat – slapdash and done without care. Jessie pushed down on the handle but was met with resistance. Locked. It reminded her that she needed to replace the lock on her own bedroom door too.

Sofie's room, however, opened right away. The thin bamboo blinds were dropped part way down the window, but plenty of light still entered the room. A tie-dye hanging had been pinned to the ceiling and several others, many of which were silk, hung on the walls, making Jessie feel as though she'd stepped inside a sewing box. It was a playful set-up. The dreamcatcher above the bed had small shells and feathers cascading from it and along the windowsill lay mounds of incense ash, plus one entirely burnt-down stick, which had been jammed into a blob of Blu-Tack. Unlike her own bedroom, with its grey worn-in plush carpet, Sofie's bedroom had cheap vinyl panels that looked like wood underfoot. She'd cosied the place up with a shaggy rug too. It'd be easy to look inside and see whether Sofie stored any secrets in her sock drawer.

A hand met Jessie's right shoulder.

'You shouldn't be in here.'

Heavy cigarlike fingers pressed their way into her flesh and her stomach clenched. Jessie couldn't tell whether Henry's grip was deliberately hard or if he was just unaware of his own strength. Either way, he was right. She shouldn't have been in Sofie's bedroom without permission.

'Oh God, I'm sorry,' she managed to whisper, still not turning around to meet his eyes. 'I've lost my phone charger and just wondered if Sofie had a spare.'

Jessie knew her cheeks had lit up crimson; she could feel the heat radiating from them and trickling down her neck as though someone had poured warm water over her head. She willed herself to face him. His expression was largely unreadable. She swallowed and waited.

'Don't worry, I won't tell Sofie you were snooping. Actually, I'm glad I caught you alone,' said Henry, glancing back into the hallway. 'There's something I want to speak to you about.'

'I should go,' Jessie said, turning to leave but finding Henry was blocking the doorway and her chance to escape to the safety of her own room.

'That skirt looks great on you,' he started, looking her square in the eyes. 'Is that your thing then, short skirts? Only you had one on at dinner the other night too.'

'It's … I had an interview today,' she stuttered.

Why wasn't he moving out the way?

'I noticed you checking me out the other night, Jessie,' he continued, a smirk spreading across his lips.

'Anyone home?'

They both heard the footsteps growing louder as someone mounted each step. The figure stood still when they reached the landing. It was Lauren, whose eyes narrowed at the sight of Jessie and Henry standing together in Sofie's bedroom.

'Everything okay?' she asked, tilting her head to one side.

'All fine. I'm just grabbing some bits for Sofie and was asking for Jessie's advice on what dress to bring her,' Henry replied, without missing a beat. 'She asked me to choose a "nice going-out dress" and you know I'm crap at that sort of thing.'

'Didn't want her to end up in a rugby shirt,' Jessie added quietly.

Henry grabbed a duffle bag from under Sofie's bed and started to fill it wordlessly. Lauren nodded hesitantly.

'No, we definitely wouldn't want that.'

Jessie breathed a barely audible sigh of relief and headed back downstairs, attempting to brush off the imprint of Henry's hand on her shoulder as she went. She flicked the switch of the kettle again and, as it juddered to a boil, Lauren ambled into the room. She'd changed into an oversized striped jumper, her bobbed hair pulled into a low, scruffy ponytail.

'Can I tell you something?' Lauren asked, pulling a mug off the drying rack.

'Of course,' Jessie replied, her curiosity piqued.

'I think they're such an odd match, him and Sofie,' Lauren whispered conspiratorially, her eyes cast upwards. 'I just can't work it out. Honestly, I think he's a bit of a private school buffoon.'

Jessie filled both their mugs with teabags and hot water, then leant back against the counter.

'Mmm, they do seem an unlikely pairing I guess?'

'Yeah, I mean, she smokes tofu and he smokes *actual* vintage cigars. Go figure?'

They laughed and took sips of tea, both temporarily lost in thought – Jessie over Henry's comments about her skirt. Maybe she hadn't imagined him flirting with her the other night after all. But if she now lived with his girlfriend, how could she ever avoid bumping into him again in future? The front door slammed shut.

CHAPTER SIX

'We'll see you on Monday at nine o'clock, then. Have a lovely weekend.'

As Jessie had predicted, she hadn't had to wait long for Pamela to call and offer her the job. No longer would she need to rely on her savings and the goodwill of her parents when the first lot of rent for Maver Place was due. She couldn't believe how quickly the time had flown, realising that she'd already lived there for a couple of weeks. All her boxes were unpacked now and she'd done her first load of washing, borrowing Lauren's clothes horse to dry everything out on. Although the flat hardly had her dream décor and that run-in with Henry had left her slightly disorientated, Jessie was starting to get into a routine and feel at home at Maver Place. As Lauren worked sporadic hours, dependent on what shoots were happening at the studio, on the days that she was also free they'd slipped into the comfortable habit of making one another avocado bagels for breakfast, then watching trashy reality shows together or going for a walk.

After texting her parents the good news about the new job, Jessie also texted Priya, who replied suggesting celebratory drinks later that evening. It would be the first time Jessie had sampled the Brighton nightlife since she'd moved back and she was keen to visit some of their old haunts to see how much – or how little – they'd changed. Each new experience she crafted was, hopefully, helping to nudge Matthew further out of the forefront of her mind. The new plan was to focus only on positive thoughts and new memories so that there would be no room left for any of the old ones that kept her awake at night, before the double dose of pills kicked in. Well, that and the constant scuffling sounds that travelled up through the floor from Marcus's bedroom, which she'd noticed got louder the later he arrived home. Earlier that morning she had counted five empty lager cans in the wicker basket they used as a recycling bin. One had leaked, leaving a sticky brown puddle in its wake. She'd really have to figure out a way of saying something soon.

Jessie had arranged to meet Priya at The Mash Tun, a two-storey pub they'd both liked and frequented on a regular basis during university. It had enough cosy corners for a private conversation and was near to a few decent chip shops, meaning come kickout time junk food wouldn't be far away. Buttoning up one of her trademark printed tea dresses, Jessie stared hard at her reflection in the mirror. This person was employed and lived in a happening city with new friends. She was getting closer to becoming somebody she recognised again, the person she'd forgotten that she even used to be. The person she was before Matthew. Not the small, scared-looking version of herself that she'd grown accustomed to, that he had prodded her into, then crushed. She smoothed some anti-frizz serum through the ends of her hair, applied a final slick of eyeliner and slipped her arms through a light trench coat. The weather outside didn't look too cold, but it would soon be dark and dropping a few degrees.

On her way out, she passed the kitchen and stuck her head round the archway, finding Lauren sitting in her usual spot at the table, sketchbook laid out before her, drawing charcoal in hand.

'I had some good news earlier,' smiled Jessie, peering in further.

'Go on, I'm all ears!'

'I am once again officially employed. You're looking at the newest member of the Tulip Court admin team.'

As soon as the words left her mouth, Jessie knew how dull they must sound to Lauren, whose own job meant she spent the day surrounded by big-name photographers and models, strutting around in big-name designer outfits. But Lauren's reaction rivalled that of being told she'd just won the EuroMillions – her face broke into a huge grin as she smashed her hands together giving a frenzied round of applause.

'Yes, Jessie! Amazing news, told you that blazer was a lucky charm.'

They both laughed.

'Are you off out to celebrate then?'

'Yeah, I'm going for drinks with my best friend Priya.'

She hesitated before continuing.

'You're welcome to join us. It won't be a big night, we're not going to any cool clubs or anything. You know, nowhere that you'd be interested in.'

Lauren gave a warm smile.

'That's a lovely offer, thank you. But I'm hoping to have a catch-up with Marcus tonight, about him helping to clean up a bit more, so I'll have to pass. How about we raise a few glasses tomorrow evening instead?' Lauren suggested. 'We can do a nice dinner and watch a romcom or something.'

As curious as Jessie was about Marcus and his odd behaviour, she didn't feel able to grill Lauren about it just yet – what with still being the new girl around the flat and wary of saying the wrong thing. Coming across as bitchy towards another flatmate wasn't something she wanted to risk.

'I'd love that. Catch you later then.'

Lauren raised a hand goodbye and turned back to her sketchpad.

'Maybe drop me a line on your way home to see if I'm still up?'

At the end of the street, Jessie saw Marcus step off the number 46 bus. She called out a hello and he nodded but continued walking determinedly in the direction of the flat.

As she neared the pub, Jessie's phone buzzed with a new email alert. Hopefully it would be Pamela sending over her contract, so she could see how many days of holiday she had. Jessie clicked onto her inbox and felt her stomach plummet. The new message wasn't from Pamela. Instead, it was sent by 'Truth Teller'. Truth Teller? What did that mean? She looked at the subject line and jerked her head away from the screen: *You make me sick* it read. Scrolling further down, Jessie saw it wasn't the only email. There were others. Lots of others, a flurry of over ten messages, all sent within the last few minutes and bearing similar subject lines. *Thought you could get away with it? I can't believe your lack of respect. People must pay for their mistakes.*

Her throat tightened. It could only be one person. She had blocked his number, the same day that she'd finally managed to escape, so this was clearly the next best thing. Jessie shuddered. The messages were a loud and clear signal that Matthew was still thinking about her. That he was angry. That maybe his threats, of what would happen to her, if she were to ever leave, weren't idle.

She didn't want to read the emails, or entertain those thoughts. Life was only just getting back on track and tonight was meant to be a celebration. But she couldn't help it. Jessie blinked back the tears of frustration that had gathered without her realising, then began meticulously blocking the email address and deleting all of the messages, then emptying them from her trash folder. Maybe it was just a weird virus or some kind of spam, she tried to reassure herself. She and Lauren had been using dodgy streaming sites to watch old episodes of *Sex and the City*, after all. It was probably just that. Besides, Matthew hated anything tech-related anyway, so would he really go to all that effort? Needing to feel in control of something again, Jessie fired off a message to Ian at Happy Homes, asking if he could please arrange replacing the lock on her bedroom door. She put her phone back in her pocket gingerly, not wanting to touch it, and forced herself to stand a little taller.

She spotted Priya, slouched against a wall outside The Mash Tun, absentmindedly tapping away at her own mobile and deliberately ignoring a group of workmen who were trying to engage her in conversation.

'Oh thank Christ, you're finally here!' she said, waving.

Jessie apologised and hugged her friend, then steered Priya towards the bar, where they both ordered a house white wine. The pair edged their way through the crowd towards an empty table at the back of the room and toasted Jessie's new job. She made a silent vow not to think about Matthew and the messages, or let either of them ruin her night. This was her new life, where *she* got to choose how she felt.

'It's so nice to be back in town and have things clicking into place.'

Priya twirled a strand of her long dark hair around one finger.

'And how's the new flat going?' she asked, genuinely interested. 'Hopefully you're not living with a psychopath any more?'

'So far, so good,' Jessie nodded fervently. 'Although one of the housemates, the only guy – his name is Marcus – seems a bit lazy and … odd.'

By the time Jessie had explained the unusual sounds keeping her awake at night and Marcus's strange eating habits, failure to clean up after himself and lack of eye contact, she had Priya hanging on to her every word. One glass of wine soon turned to two, then three.

'This always happens with us, Pree!' she laughed, getting up. 'I knew we should've just ordered a bottle – I'm going to get one now.'

Jessie made her way unsteadily to the bar, taking wild guesses as to what the time might be. Probably around half nine. She'd deliberately left her phone back at the table. Spotting a gap in the queue of waiting customers, she slotted herself in neatly and waited, tapping her debit card against a box of straws to an imaginary beat playing in her head. The alcohol was moving gently through her veins, loosening all her tight screws as it went. Those messages were just spam, that's all, she repeated to herself. It was a busy night but the harassed bar staff were still high-fiving and cracking jokes as they passed one another. Jessie watched a barmaid wearing a tartan dress chop a lime, then push the segments into a plastic box with the edge of her knife.

'Who's next?' she asked, wiping her hands on the lower half of her dress.

'Me!' a woman edged Jessie out the way, thrusting a banknote over the bar.

Once she'd finally been served, Jessie walked back to the table and deliberately placed the ice bucket down with a thud, ready for a rant. The sound of the bucket made Priya jump. She had picked Jessie's phone up and was fully engrossed in whatever was on the screen.

'What are you looking at?' Jessie asked, unscrewing the bottle of chardonnay. 'That's *my* phone!'

Priya shrugged, clutching it to her chest.

'Stop it! Don't be a witch, what have you done? You've not been on my emails, have you?'

'No! Why, should I have?'

'Tell me what you've done!'

'Okay, don't be mad at me but I just downloaded Tinder,' Priya grinned. 'And I've made you a cheeky little profile, because it's about bloody time you met someone nice for a change.'

'Oh Christ, no!' Jessie wailed. 'That's so desperate. I don't want to meet up with some random from the Internet.'

'And yet, you've quite happily moved in with three of them?' Priya retorted.

Jessie paused for a moment. Flatmates were different somehow. They just were.

'How did you even manage to unlock my phone?'

'You passcode has the same number of letters as "Jessie" so it really wasn't hard,' Priya snorted, making her blush. 'Everyone uses apps to meet people nowadays, it's normal. Besides, look at this guy – he's already matched with you and he definitely doesn't look like a loser. Even I'd say he's pretty fit, actually.'

Jessie snatched her phone back and stared. The profile belonged to a man named Rob, a couple of years older than her at 26. His cherry-picked photos showed that he was slim and good-looking, with dark hair, blue eyes and a dimple on one cheek. Priya was right – whoever Rob was, he was handsome. One photo showed him wearing a smart camel-coloured coat, walking a dog alongside a friend, sharing a joke. She zoomed in on his shoes. Brown desert boots. Not bad. In another picture he was making a toast at a wedding, the top two buttons of his shirt undone, revealing a light patch of chest hair. The other squares he'd carefully curated – showing him drinking a pint at a festival, another standing in front of Sydney Opera House – were having the desired effect on her too. Rob looked fun, as though he had a bit of a zest for life, confident. The kind of person who'd be good for her. He'd travelled, was obviously a music fan, and somehow radiated self-assurance through an app without having said a word.

'Why would he be interested in me?' Jessie questioned Priya, sincerely. 'How do I see my profile?

Priya clicked onto it. She'd somehow managed to build an online persona for Jessie that made her look equally outgoing and fun, through a mixture of photos from their university days, before things with Matthew had turned really nasty. It was sad seeing herself like that, sitting so naively on Brighton beach with an ice cream, not knowing what lay ahead.

'What would I say to this guy?' Jessie asked. 'I don't know how to do stuff like this. I'm pretty sure my Twitter picture is still an egg because I've never managed to come up with anything interesting enough to say since I made an account ten years ago.'

At that, their giggles morphed into shoulder-shaking laughter, helped along by the wine.

'I've got so scared of saying the wrong thing that I've taught myself to say nothing instead.'

Priya gave a sympathetic smile, took the phone back, typed out a simple introduction and pressed send.

'There you go,' she cackled. 'I've said it for you.'

Rob replied quickly. Jessie, emboldened by the booze, picked up the phone and looked at it.

'He says he's good and wants to know what I'm up to,' she read aloud, then looked at Priya. 'What *am* I up to?' No, she was determined to respond herself this time. 'Maybe I'll say I've just had a few celebratory drinks as I've got a new job, but am on my way home? It'd be weird to say I'm in the pub with you, wouldn't it?'

Priya spluttered into her wine.

'Yes! You definitely *cannot* say you're on Tinder down the pub.'

Jessie was already hooked on the notification that popped up whenever Rob sent her a message. She'd deliberately slipped in the new job as bait, in the hopes that he'd pick up on it and continue their chat. Her little test to see how interested he was in getting to know her.

Another notification pinged – an email, which prompted a sudden drop in euphoria. She ignored it. As her friendship with Priya had only just got back on track, Jessie was keen not to mention the unwanted messages from earlier either. Instead, she steered the topic of conversation onto Priya's work and put her phone away. She nodded along enthusiastically when Priya began talking about breezing through targets and potentially being up for promotion, but her mind was wandering. By the time last orders had been called, the world was starting to resemble an out-of-focus watercolour and Jessie knew she needed to get to bed. She hugged Priya and promised to let her know if there were any Rob updates, then queued for a taxi home.

After forcing herself to down a glass of water in the kitchen, she crawled up the stairs to bed and threw her phone somewhere down the side of it, swallowed a couple of tablets and settled down under the covers. Then the shouting started and Jessie's eyes opened groggily; she couldn't quite tell if the raised voices were coming from the upstairs neighbours or downstairs in Marcus's room. Maybe it was neither and the wine mixed with medication was playing tricks on her. She listened hard for noises other than her heart pounding, then fell asleep before managing to figure it out.

CHAPTER SEVEN

A tentative knock at the door, followed by the sound of her name being called, dragged Jessie out of a restless sleep. Her tongue was dry. She'd been dreaming of drinking ice-cold water.

'Are you up? Mind if I come in?'

It was Lauren. Jessie cleared her throat and mumbled, 'Sure, I'm a bit of a state though.'

Her bedroom door opened and Lauren ducked down to retrieve two mugs from the landing.

'I've put a bit of sugar in yours to get your energy up,' Lauren said, with a knowing smile. 'And prescribed you a motivational mug.'

Jessie took in the writing on the white china – *You have the same amount of hours in a day as Beyoncé* – and gave a sleepy laugh.

'Amazing, thank you. I hope I didn't disturb you when I came in last night?'

Lauren shook her head and curled her top lip, indicating it was either fine or she hadn't heard. Jessie didn't have the energy to question which, the pulsating in her temples growing stronger by the second. It was difficult to keep her eyes open, but at least she'd managed to change into pyjamas before falling asleep. The heavy brocade curtains, that didn't close fully, revealed a rectangle of white sky outside.

She wanted to look at the time, then remembered all the awful emails from yesterday, which, combined with the thought that Rob probably wouldn't have messaged her back, made her apprehensive about checking her phone all over again. With the alcoholic high from last night well and truly gone, Jessie opened her mouth, suddenly wanting to offload some of her worries onto Lauren. She badly wanted to move them out of her own head and into another place, in an effort to stop the crunching of anxiety taking over her entire day. Instead, she sipped carefully at the tea, trying to focus on feeling grateful for it.

'I'm off work again if you fancy hanging out and having a lazy day,' said Lauren, sitting gently at the end of the bed. 'Maybe we could start a new season of *Real Housewives*? I hear the Orange County ones are proper bitches.'

Lauren smoothed out Jessie's duvet with her free hand.

'Well, what's left of the day anyway, given that it's almost lunchtime.'

She'd managed to sleep for nearly eleven hours and yet Jessie felt drained – she didn't envy Priya who'd had work today as normal. Spending the remainder of the afternoon with Lauren sounded infinitely more appealing than tossing and turning in bed alone.

'That's quite possibly the greatest plan I've ever heard. Let me just have a shower and sort myself out. Give me half an hour?'

The water soothed Jessie as she stood, eyes closed, enjoying the heat running over her wet body. She lathered up some shampoo and, as she washed it out, imagined rinsing away some of her worries too. She sang an old TLC song about chasing waterfalls to herself as she combed the conditioner though – it always came to mind when she was in the shower. Today was a new day and she had lots to look forward to, her new job starting soon for one. When she'd moved into Maver Place she'd vowed to only focus on the positives. But of course, that was easier said than done. She was allowed the odd slip-up, but now she had to get her mental state back on track.

She stepped out of the shower and dried herself off, wringing her hair as best she could over the sink, then wrapped the towel around her chest. Opening the door and looking to her left, Jessie noticed her own bedroom door was ajar. That wasn't right. She'd definitely closed it. A trail of damp footprints appeared on the carpet behind Jessie as she tentatively walked over. She was surprised to find Ian, the letting agent, in her bedroom.

'Ian?' The unease in her voice was palpable.

'Lauren let me in,' he said quickly, holding up his phone. 'I'm just taking pictures of that lock you emailed me about. I did reply but there was no response so … Sorry to catch you at a bad time.'

Jessie had forgotten all about the request she'd sent him.

'Oh, of course. Thanks for coming over so quickly. It'd be great to get that sorted.'

'No trouble. I'll send these to the handyman your landlord uses and have him replace it,' he said, giving her a relieved nod. 'Bad news, though, the landlord wants you to foot some of the bill.'

Jessie pulled the towel tighter around herself, dreading the possibility it might slip in front of Ian, even though he was now intently studying his shiny Oxford shoes, barely daring to look at her.

'Really, why?'

'He said that, as the incoming tenant, you should pay it all because it's your responsibility to liaise with the out-going tenant, but I've managed to bargain him down to half price. I said it's not your fault the one before you did a moonlight flit with the key.'

He delivered the last sentence with pride, hoping Jessie would understand that he was one of the good guys. His industry didn't have the best reputation when it came to morals, after all, but Ian liked to think of himself as an exception to the rule. Very rarely did he bend the truth to make a property seem more appealing to a potential renter or buyer, beyond abbreviating 'the city centre is a half an hour walk from here' to 'it's just five minutes down the road'. Besides, who was to say whether he meant by foot or car?

Jessie's nose wrinkled. She'd never even met Magda, the woman who had occupied her bedroom previously, so it seemed unfair that she was expected to pay out. But Lauren said she'd changed her number, so unless she messaged every 'Magda' living in Brighton on Facebook there was no way she'd ever be able to get the key back.

'That really doesn't seem fair.'

Ian drew his eyes up from his feet to meet Jessie's. She looked different with wet hair and her fringe pushed back like that. Different in a good way.

'I agree, but I'm afraid I can't do much more about it. Anyway, let me get out of your way.'

He gave her his best professional smile and muttered 'Excuse me' as he brushed past her in the doorway, ready to get on to his next appointment across town.

Pulling on her jeans, Jessie thought back to the other thing that Ian had said, about Magda fleeing in the middle of the night. The way he'd slipped it into conversation was almost casual, so perhaps it really had just been meant it as a joke. But she wanted to know. Jessie decided to see how the afternoon with Lauren panned out and maybe ask her about Magda again later on, although last time had proven awkward.

After drying her hair, Jessie steeled her nerves and got down on all fours to retrieve her phone from under the bed. With the screen still facing the floor, she gingerly pulled it along the carpet before turning it over and squinting. Her mouth gaped at the Tinder notification on her home screen. *Know it's short notice but how about drinks this evening? x.*

She stared hard at the 'x' rounding off the sentence. A virtual kiss. Rob's message had only been sent twenty minutes ago. Best to wait a while before replying, so as not to look too eager – things were going to be different from now on when it came to relationships. There'd be no more running after men – time to let them do the running for a change.

Jessie deliberately slowed the process of styling her hair, then applying make-up, but the numbers on the clock had barely changed. Maybe, instead of waiting, it was better not to play games? Start as you mean to go on and all that. She composed a quick response: *Hey, you too. I was just going to have a quiet one with my housemate but I'm up for a couple. Let me know when and where x.* Her thumb dithered over the send button, before hitting it defiantly. It was done now. A flutter of nerves and excitement stirred within her. If this actually happened, it would be her first new date in years. Her first time navigating the playing field as a proper adult, throwing herself into the messy back and forth of texting, agonising waits in between and, hopefully, slow kissing at the end of the night. She tossed her phone back onto the bed, conscious that she'd be checking it too often if she kept it with her, and headed downstairs.

Lauren lay across one of the sofas, propping her head up with her hand, flicking through the TV channels aimlessly before settling on a music video. Three rappers, sitting around a nightclub table heaving with overflowing drinks, were gesturing animatedly at the camera, the fisheye lens making it look as though their fingers and gold jewellery could burst through the screen at any moment.

'Wanna know something crazy?' she asked, sensing that Jessie had entered the room.

'Go on then.'

Lauren gave a coy snort of laughter.

'I made out with one of those guys once, the one on the left. It was at a house party when they were just getting big. His name is B Rock. How shit is that?'

Jessie looked at the screen again. The man was attractive, but he looked intimidating, someone she'd never dare approach herself. He had a gold tooth that flashed whenever he snarled for a close-up.

'I think I'd be nervous around someone like that. Besides, it looks like he already has a lot of female attention.'

They both stared at B Rock, who was now having his face caressed by multiple women in bikini tops. Another, a waitress, bent forward with a tray of drinks and gave him a wink.

'He wishes! I was sooo wasted.'

It was important to Lauren that she sounded aloof when regaling this sort of anecdote.

'But yeah, those kinda guys aren't my scene any more.'

Positioning herself on the arm of the sofa, Jessie continued to watch the music video with curiosity. She enjoyed hearing Lauren's stories like this; they were so far away from her own world. It gave her a good feeling that she was friends with someone who'd lived such a colourful life – it almost made her own more so by proxy.

'Yeah, no more proper bad boys for me now. Too much hassle, too much … heartbreak. Time to look for someone nice, who has all their own teeth and oh, I don't know, a job that's legal.'

It was nice having someone besides Priya to have this sort of conversation with. For years, Jessie had harboured a private daydream of having a flatmate that she could slob about on the sofa with, cracking in-jokes, like she'd seen countless times on the idyllic sitcoms she'd inhaled as a teenager. When she first moved away for university, she used to watch them on her small portable TV all the time. They'd be constantly chattering away in the background as she fell asleep or studied at her desk, helping to ease the anxiety and loneliness of being away from home. Away from her parents and Matthew. Voices to fill the void.

'Me too. Someone on Tinder just asked me if I'm up for a drink later, actually, and I quite like the look of him.'

Lauren's eyes lit up.

'Oh yeah? Go on. Tell me everything.'

Having little to share, Jessie recounted Rob's profile, their minimal messages and the way she'd boldly stepped out of her comfort zone to speak with him. She finished by saying that this was the first time she'd ever done anything like that.

'Ever? Like, literally *ever*?'

Jessie gave an affirmative headshake.

'Pretty much. I was in a relationship for nearly seven years before I moved in here, with someone I met when I was at sixth form. I had a couple of boyfriends at school before that, but only the sort where it's over before their name that you inked on your pencil case had dried.'

Lauren gave a loud exhale and combed her fingers through her bleached blonde hair.

'Seven years, that's heavy. Do you want to talk about it?'

The emails, the degrading names, the lines of bruises on her upper arms that she used to watch fade from purple to yellow all jumped to mind, and Jessie quickly knew that she didn't want Lauren to associate her with any of it. Or to know how stupid she had been. It was a life she was determined to leave behind her. Talking about that relationship now would be like unpicking a slowly healing scab and scratching at the wound underneath with a jagged fingernail, pointless and pain-inducing. She involuntarily winced.

'It's okay. But thank you, seriously,' Jessie said, hoping she sounded breezy and assured.

'I get it,' Lauren smiled. 'We all have things better left in the past, no need to torment ourselves with them unnecessarily.'

While Lauren wanted to know more about her house-mate's relationship, she wasn't ready to begin excavating her own heartbreak in exchange.

'You know what, though? I once read that every cell in your body regenerates after seven years, or something like that. So technically, you're now an entirely new person to who you were when you first met him, whoever he is.'

That was a comforting thought, one that Jessie wanted to keep safe and store away for the future, for the next time she saw a man in a parka jacket walking down the street and her heart began punching at her ribs. Each day she was physically, as well as mentally, turning into some-one Matthew had never met.

'How about a film, before we get stuck into those filthy rich housewives?' Lauren pulled up the movie channels.

They settled on one about two sisters swapping lives for a week. One, a stressed mother of three, the other a carefree socialite. Easy enough viewing on a hangover.

'Excuse me for a second.'

As the credits rolled, Jessie quickly darted upstairs to check for a response from Rob. *8 o'clock at The Mesmerist? It's not far from Pavilion Gardens and the Old Steine bus station.*

She sprinted back downstairs, waving her phone like a trophy. Lauren was back on the music channels, mouth-ing along to a grime track now. Her feet dangled off the edge of the sofa, the burgundy nail polish on her toes sev-eral shades darker than the pillar box red on her fingers.

'It's on for 8 o'clock tonight!'

There was a nagging feeling that she'd already made other plans, though. Jessie thought hard. Dinner with Lauren! Well, they'd spent most of the afternoon together now, so it wasn't as though she would *really* be ditching her to go on the date. Besides, they could still eat together before she left. Best not to go out on an empty stomach anyway.

'Don't you think it's a bit quick to be meeting up with him, if you only started speaking yesterday? You don't want to seem too eager,' Lauren asked airily.

That thought hadn't occurred; instead Jessie had been entirely focused on how handsome Rob looked in his photos and fantasising over how brilliantly their date could go. His profile said he had a Irish accent, which appealed to her too. Maybe he could be The One – how great a story would that be, if she ended up marrying her first and only Tinder date?

'It is fast, you're right,' said Jessie. 'But probably better not to have time to talk myself out of it. Plus we're meeting in a really public place, so I'm sure it will be fine.'

'Fair enough. Call me if he's ugly in real life and I'll come save you. Want me to make us a stir fry before you go?'

It was almost as if Lauren could read her mind.

'Actually, no debate, I'm making it. You can't go out hungry or you'll be trashed after the first glass of wine, très un-chic.'

She popped her eyebrows up in mock horror. Thinking back to the lasagne that Lauren had made her as a welcome meal, Jessie felt guilty that she hadn't properly repaid her flatmate's kindness yet. Putting a bagel in the toaster or making an instant coffee hardly required the same level of effort. She'd been so busy catching up with old friends and nesting.

'Do you mind? I'll cook for us another time soon, I promise. I've only got an hour to get ready now, today has just flown.'

The clock on the wall said it was close to half past six.

'How was your chat with Marcus last night, by the way?' Jessie asked, hovering by the door.

'All fine. He said he was sorry and look …' Lauren nodded her head towards the sink. 'He even did the washing-up earlier and, if you turn your attentions to the fridge, you'll see that I've devised a cunning bin-shaming system.'

Jessie looked at the piece of paper held up with a magnet. It was a table to record when each bin in the flat had last been emptied and by whom, entitled 'Have you bin good or bad?'.

'Love it, very inventive.'

Lauren winked, then shooed her away and began to pull an assortment of vegetables out of the fridge, lining them up with military precision on a chopping board. She grabbed a wok and placed it on the stove, letting the gas whoosh into action beneath it then pouring in a slug of sesame oil, waiting to hear it spit back.

No sooner had Jessie sent a picture to Priya of the two dresses she was debating, than a bone-shattering scream shot through the flat. She stopped still for a moment then ran to the source of the noise. The magnolia wall above the stove tiles had a spray of crimson decorating it in a perfect diagonal line. A kitchen knife lay in the middle of the checked floor, discarded diced onions and whole peppers on the counter. Lauren's face had turned pale and although she'd wrapped the bottom of her thin white vest top around her left hand, blood was pooling through it at a quick rate. The pan on the hob continued to crackle.

'Oh God, Lauren! What happened? Is it bad?'

Jessie felt woozy looking at the growing stain on Lauren's top. The wound needed compression, fast. She searched around in the cupboard under the sink for a clean tea towel, pulling out an old Greek holiday souvenir one.

'It feels pretty deep, but I can't look. It's freaking me out,' her flatmate said weakly. 'I shouldn't have tried to get all Gordon Ramsay on it by doing fancy chopping.'

As tenderly as she could manage, Jessie helped Lauren wrap the towel around her wound and apply pressure to it, while making soothing sounds and stroking her back. Lauren winced and closed her eyes, the minutes feeling endless. Jessie returned to the cupboard under the sink, took out a floor wipe and began to clean up the splatters.

'Maybe try raising your arm up to stop the blood flow?'

'I feel sick.'

How serious did a cut need to be for stitches? Jessie's medical knowledge didn't cover hacked index fingers, so she quickly pulled up the NHS website which said to visit the accident and emergency department as soon as possible if the bleeding didn't stop after ten minutes of applying pressure.

She relayed the information to Lauren. They kept count for a further five minutes and all the while Jessie hoped that Sofie or Marcus would return home and either know what to do, or take over so she could continue getting ready to meet Rob. When it became clear that neither was going to happen, Lauren looked up at her with watery eyes.

'I'm so sorry, I'm making you late, Jessie. You need to get going,' she said half-heartedly. 'Go on, I'll see you tomorrow.'

Jessie was torn.

'It's not right to leave you on your own, Lauren. I think you might need to go to A&E.'

Lauren shook her head vigorously.

'It'll be okay in a minute. You need to get ready for your date.'

Jessie glanced at the time.

'Let me call someone, one of your friends or Sofie?' Jessie tried again, still dithering.

'No.' Lauren's steely eyes met Jessie's. 'I'm sure it's going to stop bleeding in a minute and I'll be fine.'

Another drop of blood hit the floor.

'Lauren, you need to go to the hospital. I think you'll need stitches,' Jessie said, concerned.

Lauren grimaced.

'I hate hospitals, they make me so anxious. All that waiting around and doctors not explaining things properly.'

Jessie knew what she was getting at and switched off the stove.

'Poor thing, it's okay; don't worry, I'll come with you. I'll order a taxi.'

She could message Rob on the way. It was more important to be there for Lauren. In the grand scheme of things, she'd only been speaking to Rob for a day, but that didn't help to soften the pit of disappointment opening in her stomach. Jessie looked back at the blood on the floor and tried not to gag.

CHAPTER EIGHT

With the majority of the weekend still free before she started work, Jessie vowed to spend it turning the flat into somewhere that felt more like a proper home. Sitting in the emergency waiting room with Lauren, her mind had drifted back to her previous flat in Chesterbury, which she'd shared with Matthew. It really had been a beautiful space, with smooth blonde wooden flooring throughout – consistent and modern, unlike Maver Place – with a big bay window that flooded the lounge with light, no matter the weather. The new place, in contrast, seemed to struggle to allow any natural light in, relying on artificial orange-tinged bulbs instead. She hated that none of the furniture, from the cheap steel bed she slept in (which creaked whenever she rolled over in the night) to the curtains she opened each morning, was really hers, either. It didn't matter how many times she polished the surfaces, they still felt covered in invisible fingerprints too. More seriously, the sooner the lock was fixed the better, because she still found herself feeling tense whenever Henry was in the flat after their last encounter, hoping he didn't try and corner her again for a 'chat'.

She was also uneasy around Marcus. She'd lived in Maver Place for weeks now and they'd only spoken twice. Or three times, if you were to include the day his eyes had appeared in the mirror behind her. She couldn't work him out. Lauren seemed not to mind his skulking but it was beginning to bother Jessie. Why was he always bolted up in his bedroom? It was strange that he kept himself so hidden away but then at night bashed about, keeping her awake. If the company of other people made him so uncomfortable, why didn't he just look for a studio apartment and live alone? If she had to guess, she'd wager that Lauren was the reason he stayed. She'd seen the way he looked at her when he thought nobody else was watching.

Jessie wandered into the kitchen in search of food, having not eaten since last night's dinner was abruptly cancelled by Lauren slicing her finger. It had needed three stitches in the end. Her blood was still dashed up the wall, a darker shade now that it had dried. In the light of day Jessie could see it had also hit the side of one of the white wall units. Something they'd missed in all the commotion. She wondered if Marcus or Sofie had walked in and seen it, made their breakfast as usual and walked back out, continuing on with their day, not bothering to clean it. Sofie probably hadn't even slept here last night and Marcus would most likely have been oblivious to the mess. Nobody had messaged the group chat mentioning it.

With a shudder, she picked up a bottle of bleach spray and a damp sponge from the washing-up bowl. She cleaned the cabinet first, watching the blood, with the addition of water, dilute and run down in pale red streaks. The wall would be a harder stain to tackle. Jessie looked around the kitchen, at where the black-and-white tiled floor stopped halfway as it met the lounge area's thin brown carpet, and realised the carpet was covered in stains too. Not blood, though. Dirt that had been trodden in next to the sofas, a faint wine spill that someone had pushed the coffee table over in an effort to conceal. The harder she looked, the more unappealing the flat became; splashes of yellow adorned the ceiling in both sections of the room, possibly indicating some kind of leak. It wasn't a complete lost cause, but it was crying out for some niceties and attention. She scrubbed at the bloody wall again, leaving a large damp circle, then paused to listen for any stirrings from her other flatmates. Nothing. She washed her hands, threw the cleaning sponge into the washing machine and placed two slices of thick wholemeal into the toaster. Back to business as usual.

Using her free hand, the one not holding a slice of buttered toast, Jessie wrote one of her favoured to-do lists on the back of an envelope addressed to 'The Homeowner'. It had been lying abandoned with a pile of leaflets on the dining table since she moved in. First up was to buy new bedding, something to brighten up her bedroom, then curtains, so she could finally take down the dark damask drapes currently occupying the window. They were made of scratchy imitation silk that she hated having to touch and didn't quite meet in the middle. Maybe a vase of flowers to perk up the kitchen would be a welcome touch too, something to show the others that she wanted to make small improvements and perhaps encourage them to do the same. She could get them for Lauren as a sort of get-well present. As she scribbled *plants for bedroom – cactus?* her phone buzzed with a notification from Rob, who'd luckily been understanding about her cancelling at such short notice. He was suggesting they try again that evening, same time and place. *I'll be there!* she replied, leaning in to the stir of internal butterflies. They indicated a good sort of nervousness, one she wasn't as used to, the type twinned with excitement not dread. She then checked her inbox, for the first time since Friday.

At first, Jessie was relieved to see she only had a couple of new messages to deal with, one being from Pamela, until she reread the sender's name on the other. Matthew Eades. She read it twice. It was him. Trying to make contact using his work email address, one that she'd forgotten to block. Her vision wobbled, as though her eyes were unable to look directly at those two words. Too afraid. There could be no convincing herself that this was spam. What could he possibly have to say? Her father had made it quite clear she never wanted to speak to him again, when he'd turned up drunk in the middle of the night at her parents' house, shouting through the letter box. It had been excruciating, listening, crouched at the top of the stairs, as he'd called her all the names under the sun, each insult raining down like a punch in the gut, threatening to kill her and swearing blindly that he'd find her, wherever she went. Her father had phoned the police, but Matthew had fled by the time they'd arrived. The officers had been sympathetic, but told her there was nothing they could do unless there was a serious incident.

Matthew had deliberately left the subject line empty, allowing her mind to go into overdrive attempting to fill in the blanks. The doorbell blasted, making her jump. It was an especially shrill sound that echoed around the flat like an air-raid siren. She took a deep breath and counted from ten to zero. It rang again: whoever was on the other side of the door was becoming impatient. She put the phone down and crept into the hallway. Her skin prickled as she peered round at the frosted pane of glass and she kept her back close to the wall, seeing a silhouette beyond it. She could just about make out that it belonged to a burly man wearing a coat with a fur hood. A khaki-coloured parka with a fur hood? Around his height too. Her muscles seized. Matthew had found her. Just like he'd promised. *No matter where you go, I'll hunt you down.* She'd disobeyed that warning and now she'd have to suffer the consequences. He was mere metres away.

'Fuck,' she whispered, closing her eyes.

There was no back door to escape from, the shared garden only accessible by walking out of the building and through a wooden gate down the side of the house. Jessie's heart hammered as she tried to think of what to do next. The man outside pushed himself close to the glass, a hand cupping either side of his face as he peered in. He'd seen her moving.

'Hello?' the voice was gruff.

The blood swooshed loudly in her ears making it difficult to hear properly. A fist banged against the glass. *How* could he have tracked her down? She ran through all the people back home who could've let her new address slip and drew a blank; not even her closest friends knew her street name or flat number. She'd been so careful to limit the number of people she'd told about her move back to Brighton and had kept social media posts deliberately vague, never tagging or checking in her locations. Marcus's bedroom door swung open and he shuffled out wearing boxer shorts and a Star Wars T-shirt. His hair stuck out at funny angles. Clearly, he'd just woken up. He shot Jessie a confused look as he went to pull down the latch and open the front door, to let the stranger inside.

'No,' she rasped softly, still Velcroed to the wall. 'Marcus, don't.'

The wooden chair rail which ran the length of it was digging into her back but she barely registered the pain, looking in horror as the door opened and the owner of the dark shadow moved inside. A bubble of air lodged itself in her throat.

'I'm here to fix a broken lock?' he grunted, presenting his toolkit like an officer's badge.

A handyman! Jessie couldn't move. The adrenaline that had swiftly flooded her veins was still in full effect. When it came to fight or flight, it turned out she'd managed neither and, instead, had remained frozen.

'Not mine,' Marcus said monotonously, giving Jessie another bewildered stare. 'Yours, maybe?'

Yes, hers. Her bedroom lock needed replacing. That was all. This man had come to help her, not hurt her.

'Second door on the right, just past the bathroom,' she heard herself say, pointing at the stairs.

The man nodded and made his way in the direction of her finger. Jessie listened to each footstep pounding and getting quieter as he neared her bedroom, then the bag of tools hit the ground. He began whistling.

'Are you okay? You're trembling,' Marcus said, moving back to the doorway of his dark bedroom.

His legs were very thin, almost hairless. They reminded Jessie of a bird she'd once rescued as a child and nursed back to health in a shoebox. Behind him, she could just about make out a messy desk littered with strawberry yoghurt pots – the same brand as the ones she bought – and, above it, a Bullet For My Valentine poster. Marcus obviously didn't clean up much in there either.

'The doorbell just made me jump,' she replied, wiping her forehead with the back of her hand. 'That's all.'

'Have you seen Lauren?' he asked, deadpan.

Jessie swallowed, willing her brain to stop screaming and start thinking normally.

'Not this morning. She cut her finger badly last night making dinner and we ended up in A&E until late. She's probably sleeping in.'

Marcus looked at Jessie wearily, then nodded and turned way without another word.

A few moments later, she heard the sound of a guitar being tuned. Not feeling able to go back to her own room whilst the repairs were being carried out, Jessie grabbed her coat off the peg, checking her purse was still in the pocket, and headed into town, desperate to leave the flat. Now that she'd allowed some of her internal fears out into the atmosphere, it was as though she couldn't help gulping them back in with every breath. Trapped in a vicious scaremongering loop of her own doing, she needed fresh air.

In the flat, Marcus sat on his swivel desk chair, strumming at the same set of miserable chords, never quite able to find a melody that captured his longing, or how lonely he felt in the flat without *her* there to talk to. He looked around at his sanctuary, at all the photos up on the walls. He especially loved that shot of her, his perfect girl, over by the bed. It showed her with her head thrown back in laughter. He missed kissing the tip of that perfectly turned-up nose, wishing with every fibre of his being that he could go back in time, to the way it used to be.

*

Hours later and feeling much calmer, Jessie returned to the flat laden with carrier bags. In an effort to distract herself from Matthew's unread email, she'd ended up spending far more than planned, then deleting the email on the bus home, hoping that ignorance was bliss.

'I'm back!' she called out, heading towards her room to unload the bags.

Sofie and Lauren shouted a response from the lounge. Guitar sounds came from behind Marcus's closed door. A full house, for the first time in weeks. Jessie liked the busyness of it; it felt as though some of the earlier skeletons had been tidied away for the night, overpowered by human life.

She stripped off her white duvet cover, ready to replace it with a Cath Kidston duck-egg blue one from TK Maxx. She'd wanted a calming, delicate colour, suddenly finding the white too stark. Next, she placed a newly bought cactus on the windowsill, no bigger than the size of her palm, beside a bowl of bracelets. The new lock had been fitted to her door and a key left on the dresser, which she quickly slipped onto the keyring that also contained her flat keys and ones to her parents' place. She'd not quite managed to find the 'right' set of curtains to replace the oppressive dark ones, but the lighter coloured quilt already lifted the mood of the room. Things were coming together. Catching the time on her alarm clock, Jessie realised she needed to start getting ready for the evening. The rest of the home improvements would have to wait until the morning – she didn't have long until she was supposed to meet Rob at the bar.

Soon after Jessie had left for her date, shouting a cheery goodbye on her way out, the doorbell rang for the second time that day. Lauren, who was watching a slasher movie with Sofie, heaved herself up from the sofa to answer it. Her left index finger still throbbed from the cut, so she'd settled on an easy night in front of the TV and self-medicating with wine, rather than hitting the town.

'Ian? Hi?'

His navy BMW, a source of pride and joy, was parked the perfect distance from the kerb.

'Mind if I come in? The landlord's asked me to check that the handyman did an all right job on Jessie's bedroom lock.'

He rubbed his arms to signal it was cold outside. Surely Jessie would just email Happy Homes if she'd had any problems? Then again, Lauren knew how tight her landlord was, the type always looking to save a quick buck. He was probably hoping the handyman had done a rushed job so he could avoid having to pay out. Still, it was getting late, nearing 8 o'clock.

'Nothing better to be doing on a Saturday night?' Lauren asked, only half-joking but stepping aside to let him in all the same.

'Sadly not, actually,' Ian chuckled. 'Won't be a minute, just need to take a few photos. May I?'

'You're missing the best part,' Sofie called from the lounge. 'He's on his way to stab her!'

'Coming!' Lauren called back, before turning her attention to Ian again. 'You know which one is Jessie's room.'

Lauren didn't head back to the lounge right away, instead choosing to watch Ian mount the stairs. She wasn't keen on the thought of him being alone in Jessie's bedroom. He seemed to be finding lots of excuses to pop by lately and they were getting flimsier every time. Unbelievable, almost, and far too frequent for her liking.

CHAPTER NINE

A mile across town, in a buzzy pub, Jessie dipped a straw into her second gin and tonic. She was still blushing from the kiss on the cheek Rob had given her on their way inside. He looked every bit as handsome in real life as he did online. Although she'd be the first to admit she was no expert on dating, she had a good feeling about him. Two drinks quickly turned to four, as they sat cosied up in a corner of The Mesmerist, comparing their favourite books, films and food, and swapping stories about their childhoods. Everything she'd imagined Rob to be like from his Tinder profile seemed to hold up. He'd even worn the same camel-coloured coat as in some of his pictures. She stroked the sleeve, feeling braver with every sip, and told him how much she liked it.

'A decent coat can do a lot for a man who's not got much else going for him,' he replied, making her laugh.

Really though, Rob knew he was attractive. He carried himself with ease and she was surprised at how effortless it was to be herself around him.

'Sadly, there is one rather large confession that I need to get off my chest,' he suddenly said in a serious tone, using it as an excuse to take hold of her hand. 'The dog on my profile isn't actually mine, he belongs to a mate.'

'Well, I think I'll be leaving then,' Jessie shot back, in an equally sincere tone. 'That's the only reason I came tonight, as I thought you might bring him along too.'

After telling her about his travels around the world – he'd been everywhere from Argentina to Vietnam – and learning to cook with the locals, Rob promised he'd whip up an authentic bowl of pho for Jessie the next time they met. It was an invitation she accepted gladly. As they clinked their glasses in confirmation, he gave her a look that made her bite her bottom lip. It was nearing closing time.

'I'll walk you to the bus stop,' Rob offered, helping her carry their empty glasses over to the bar.

He leant in and gave her a lingering kiss, then they headed to the exit. Jessie floated onto the bus and tried to busy herself looking in her bag for headphones, knowing that Rob was still watching her through the window.

On her way to work the following day, Jessie noticed she was still smiling. The date couldn't have gone better. She sat on the top deck of the bus and listened to branches whack the windows when it rounded a corner and checked her watch frequently, despite knowing she'd left plenty of time to get to her new office. The first day nerves had kicked in when she'd not been able to find her lucky charm bracelet earlier that morning, the one she always kept in her bowl of jewellery on the windowsill. It had a small gold 'J' on it and was the one piece she'd worn during each of her GCSE exams (and any others thereafter), a present from her parents, meant to spur her on throughout revision. She'd have to search for it again properly after work.

After walking up the steep hill and reaching the reception area five minutes early, Jessie found Pamela waiting to greet her and conduct a grand tour of Tulip Court.

'Tea, coffee, milk and all those essentials are just over here by the fridge, where you can keep your lunch,' she said, pointing in the relevant directions. 'Down the corridor we have the filing room where, unfortunately, you'll be spending a fair bit of time. We've a lot of paperwork that needs getting in order.'

Jessie tried to take in the warren of doors and identical-looking metal cabinets as they went, along with the names that were reeled off to her whenever they passed an occupied desk. The smell of printer ink and instant coffee hung in the air.

'Up over there, that's the area the doctors work in when they're not with a patient.'

All the walls were the same tone of not-quite-white. Not dissimilar to her flat.

'And here's where you'll sit, opposite Juliette.'

A pink, plump woman in her forties looked up at the sound of her name and gave Jessie a lopsided grin. She had kind eyes, looking small and earnest thanks to her wire-framed glasses. Judging by the photographs on her desk, Juliette was a cat person, the type who referred to them as 'moggies', and who hugged them just a little too tightly. Jessie put her belongings under her own desk and switched on what turned out to be an asthmatic computer, which wheezed loudly as it tried to load the welcome screen. Her main duties, so far as she could gather, would be to assist the mental health outreach team by drawing up staff rotas, taking notes in meetings, getting patient files in order and completing any other admin that came her way. There was a database with all past and present patient details on it that she needed to be trained up on and which her contract stated she was not to abuse under any terms. Confidentiality was key, said Pamela, tapping the side of her nose. Keeping secrets was a job that Jessie had grown very adept at, thanks to Matthew, so really, that part of the role couldn't have been easier.

At lunchtime she took a short walk around the area surrounding her new office and quickly discovered that Woodingdean consisted of little more than hills, a post office and a Co-op. Deflated, she trudged back to eat a cheese salad at her desk, then got stuck into more paperwork, pausing occasionally to answer Juliette's questions about *Strictly Come Dancing*. She'd never seen the programme but had read enough on the *Daily Mail*'s showbiz section to be able to bluff her way through brief conversations about it. What felt like only a short while later, Pamela stood up and made her way over to the coat peg.

'You've survived day one, my love. Well done!' she said, wrapping a chunky knit scarf around her neck. 'Any exciting plans for later?'

'Not tonight, just a quiet one,' Jessie replied, surprised at how quickly the day had gone.

She wondered if this was the sort of place where people went into proper detail about their leisure time or kept it top line only.

'I'm looking forward to getting an early night and being fresh for tomorrow.'

Pamela looked slightly disappointed – perhaps she had been hoping for some gossip.

'Enjoy it. Have a fabulous evening both, see you in the morning.'

Not long after, Juliette waved her goodbyes too. Jessie locked away the files she'd been working on into the secure cabinets – another rule of importance pressed into her – and placed the key inside the Tupperware box on a shelf in the stationery cupboard, then locked that too. Nothing could be left at risk of prying eyes. On the walk to the bus stop, she checked her phone and saw four missed calls from an unknown number. Probably a telemarketer trying their luck. Nothing from Rob as yet.

Back at the flat, Jessie headed straight to the kitchen for a cup of tea. Her eye was immediately caught by another bright yellow square of paper stuck in the fridge – this time on Lauren's carton of oat milk, tucked inside the door. *Stop drinking my milk please – get your own!! X* The double exclamation marks were accompanied by a firm underlining of the words 'my' and 'your' but the 'X' softened the warning. Jessie reached for her own pint of semi-skimmed, spared by whoever it was that had targeted Lauren's, and gave a small chuckle. This was how it was supposed to be. Flat-sharing banality at its finest; it was all she'd wanted while living with Matthew.

Mug in hand, she wandered upstairs to her bedroom, realising with slight dismay that she hadn't locked her door that morning. Shaking her head she put down her mug on the dressing table. Then she froze. Her laptop, which had been there when she'd left for work earlier that day, was now propped up against her pillow. She'd never have left it like that, she was sure of it. Her eyes darted around the room, scouring it for any other objects that might be out of place, but nothing struck her, then she opened the laptop and checked her homepage. That all looked normal too. The laptop having been moved though, that was too weird to ignore. She pulled up the group chat.

Hey, everyone, hope you've had a good day. Just wondering if anyone has been in my room to use my MacBook? No worries if you have, but could you just ask first next time?

She didn't want to come off as aggressive or distrustful, if on the off-chance she'd got it wrong. Lauren was the first to reply.

Not me babe!

Quickly followed by a blunt one word answer from Marcus.

No.

She saw the message hadn't been delivered to Sofie yet, but she was rarely in the flat anyway. So it must have been Marcus; surely it was him. Then again, she'd had a few drinks last night and had been distracted looking for her bracelet this morning, gearing up for her first day. Maybe she'd thrown it on her bed to clear some space while doing her make-up? It was plausible.

Sofie's reply buzzed through.

I've been out all day, doll, not me either! That's odd.

Now she looked weird. As Jessie thought about how to reply without sounding accusatory, a phone call from a private number flashed up. She let it ring out. If she didn't answer, she could carry on pretending it was a telemarketer. What could she say back in the group chat? After a few seconds, the unknown caller reappeared. It rang out, then called again. What if it was Pamela and she'd forgotten to do something at work? This time, Jessie took a deep inhale and answered. Whoever was on the other line was breathing heavily. The hairs on her neck stood up.

'Hello? Hello, who's there?'

The call ended. Jessie tossed her phone on the floor, not caring if it smashed. She pushed her palms into her eyes. Why couldn't he just leave her alone? She picked it up, hands unsteady as she searched for Priya's number, needing to hear a soothing voice. The flat creaked around her as the electronic purr of the call rang on.

'I think he's just called me, he must know where I am.'

The words escaped Jessie's mouth before Priya had barely picked up.

'He can't know, Jess, please calm down. Take a few deep breaths. What makes you think he knows?'

She'd expected Priya to understand instantly, not to question her. Jessie explained the emails, both the spam ones from 'Truth Teller' and the message from his work account, then the heavy breathing down the line. Her knees jerked as she waited for her friend to take it all on board and repackage what she'd said into something more manageable. Something less terrifying. A scenario where Matthew was entirely absent. Priya took a moment before answering.

'Even if this is him calling – and I'm not saying it is – he still doesn't have your address or anything like that, okay? You are safe. The call could have been an automated survey or kids pranking you; his email could have been an apology, the others a virus. I hate to say this, but you sound completely paranoid, Jess.'

That thought had never occurred to her before. An apology didn't seem Matthew's style. She couldn't remember him ever having apologised for leaving her wrists red raw or for forcing her arm up against the bedroom radiator until it sprang weepy blisters. She had to be paranoid, to remain vigilant, fearing if she dropped her guard for one second that's when he'd appear. Thinking this way helped her to feel safe. If she was suffering already, even by her own doing, then maybe the universe would deem that enough and keep him far away. Or maybe she needed to have more therapy.

'Is the deleted message from him still in your trash folder? Shall I read it for you? It's better to know what you're up against. *If* you're up against anything.'

'I'll message you my login details.'

Jessie fired off her password then waited, typing a quick reply to the group chat as a distraction.

Sorry, just me being silly – thought something had moved in my room then remembered I'd done it. LOL!

She answered on the first ring when Priya called her back, to say that Matthew's message contained just four words.

'Jess, it says "We need to talk".'

CHAPTER TEN

As soon as Priya told her what Matthew's email said, Jessie went into panic mode. That well-known sensation of her chest tightening crept in, as the tops of her arms and legs turned numb. Her tongue welded itself to the roof of her mouth.

'There's no point in working yourself up over what may or may not happen in the future,' Priya said softly over the phone, attempting to placate her. 'I think it's best you keep yourself busy for the rest of the night.'

Jessie promised to try, but knew it wouldn't be easy. She stared at her palms until they stopped vibrating, then decided to search once more for her missing bracelet – anything to stop her worrying about the message.

She rifled through the carrier bag she was using as a makeshift bin, finding nothing, then wondered if it could have fallen down and become trapped behind her dressing-table drawers. Upon pulling the bottom one out as far as it could go, a glint of gold, pushed into the furthest right-hand corner, caught her eye. This must be it, she thought triumphantly, reaching her hand into the dark space to retrieve the bracelet she'd lost. As soon as her fingertips met the cold metal, her certainty wavered. It felt unfamiliar. The chain was too thin and there was something attached to it. She uncurled her hand to discover not a bracelet, but an oval-shaped locket with an ornate floral design on it. Turning the jewellery over, she found a large looped letter 'M' engraved on the smooth back. The piece was heavy and probably quite old.

It took Jessie a few seconds to flick the clasp open with her fingernail. Inside was a curl of dark hair tied with thread, preserved behind a sheet of glass. On the opposite window was photograph of a stern-looking woman in a high-necked dress whose gaze was focused somewhere beyond the camera. A sepia image. She looked closer, trying to deduce from her clothing whether or not she'd been wealthy, wondering if the person had lived a happy life. She realised quickly it must belong to Magda, the former tenant, who'd been in this room before her. Maybe Ian would have her details buried within a stack of paperwork somewhere from when she first signed on to live at Maver Place.

Jessie remembered the letting agent's weird comment about Magda having moved out in the middle of the night. A small sense of unease about the flat, that she'd tried to ignore, felt a little more palpable. People didn't run away from a place unless something was seriously wrong – Jessie, more than most, could vouch for that first-hand. She had been so terrified of leaving Matthew that she'd waited until he was on a job out of town before hurriedly packing her suitcase and peering anxiously through the letter box, waiting for a taxi to ferry her to safety at her parents' house. Had Magda felt like that too? Desperate and fearful because of … Marcus, maybe? But his loud music couldn't be the only reason. He must have done something more than that. But what? If he had been the one to drive Magda away, then maybe he did move the MacBook after all. She hated the idea of him being in her room while she was out, running his bony fingers all over her things. Perhaps Ian was only joking, she eventually reasoned. Her mind was just in overdrive after Matthew's email. Not everybody was a threat. She looked at the locket she was now gripping. It still needed to be returned to its rightful owner. She put the drawers back into their correct slots and placed the necklace safely in the top one, next to her collection of near identical dusky pink lipsticks.

In doing so, a vision of the junk cupboard in the hall-way downstairs came to mind. It housed the boiler, as well as bags filled with old Halloween decorations, an assortment of tools and various bits of paperwork that nobody wanted to throw away in case they were impor-tant, but which hadn't belonged to anybody in a long time. Fragments of previously rented lives, all shoved together and forgotten, in one place.

She headed downstairs, yanked the door open, and began looking for something – unsure as to exactly what. A clue. Another signifier of Magda's existence which would tell her more about the woman who had once lived in her bedroom and perhaps help return the necklace to her. The handle was sticky. It annoyed Jessie that nobody had bothered to clear this cupboard out, instead choosing to just add to it by shoving in more junk mail. She grabbed a pile of envelopes and rifled through them, taking in the various names they were addressed to. One with a Specsavers logo for a Miss E. Holliday, several to the homeowner. A magazine about motorcycles, calling for the attention of a Mr Carlos Ramos. Then, finally, she struck gold with a plain white rectangle bearing the name Ms Magda Nowak. It was difficult for Jessie to pinpoint exactly why she felt so determined to go out of her way to return the jewellery to a woman she'd never met. Obviously it was the right thing to do, but it was more than that. Besides the fact it was clearly an heirloom she felt an affinity with Magda, not just from sharing a room but because maybe – if Ian hadn't been joking – they'd been in similar situations. Jessie knew if she'd accidentally left anything behind when leaving in a hurry, she would have been so grateful for its safe return. She opened the letter. It was a reminder to make a dental appointment, dated October 2018, just a few weeks before Jessie had moved in. Slipping it in her pocket and walking back to the stairs, she hurried past Marcus's bedroom door, fearful of bumping into him.

Back upstairs, door locked, Jessie sat cross-legged on the bed and opened her laptop, resting it on a cushion.

She logged into Facebook and slowly typed the words 'Magda Nowak Brighton' into the search bar. A profile came up as a match. Whoever it belonged to had tight security settings, with nothing on their account visible to anyone who hadn't been accepted as a friend. Not even a profile photo on display. There was no option for Jessie to send a friend request, meaning the only chance she had of making contact was to message and hope Magda would still get a notification for it. She drafted a few short sentences introducing herself, explaining she'd not long moved into Maver Place and had just discovered a locket, along with a brief description of the item and her mobile number.

The front door slammed shut and fast-paced footsteps approached her room. They stopped outside her door, then faded in the opposite direction. Somebody had just gone into Sofie's bedroom. Maybe she could shine a bit of light on why Magda had left so suddenly and was now untraceable. Maybe Marcus was part of the reason Sofie herself stayed out of the flat so often? Jessie mustered up the courage to knock and ask.

'Come in! Hey, Jessie, how's it going? Oh wow, I love your hair. Have you done something different to it today?'

Unsure as to where she ought to position herself, Jessie stayed hovering in the doorway, attempting to lean on it so as not to look too formal. Sofie, meanwhile, was still bent over her laundry basket.

'Thank you, no, just the usual. How are you?'

Once the pleasantries had been exchanged, Sofie looked at Jessie expectantly.

'I just wanted to ask you something about Magda, the girl who had my room before me.'

That wasn't what she'd been anticipating. Sofie's arched eyebrows wiggled up her forehead slightly. She threw a T-shirt back into the hamper and shut the lid, all ears.

'Go for it.'

'Ian from Happy Homes made a weird joke about her fleeing in the dead of night,' Jessie said, contemplating how best to word the question. 'Is that really true?'

She decided against asking about Marcus just yet, preferring to take it one step at a time. Sofie's features smoothed back to normal, then her mouth spread into a tight smile.

'It's true, yeah. She did a moonlight flit to avoid paying the last load of rent and bills, which sucks as none of us are exactly made of money. I had to borrow a bit from Henry to cover my share.'

It was a perfectly reasonable explanation. One that had never occurred to Jessie. It would also explain why Magda had changed her number and seemed to be flying under the radar on social media. Yet she still couldn't shake the feeling that Marcus had played a part somehow, or that there was more to it. Why hadn't Lauren just been honest and said it was money-related in the first place?

'Why would she do that? Sorry, it's just ... weren't you guys all friends? It seems weird she'd screw you over.'

Sofie nodded, undoing her messy bun and letting her hair fall to her shoulders before immediately retying it in the same style. The army print crop top and chunky, vintage cable-knit cardigan she had on today were especially flattering. Jessie knew if she wore anything like that she'd feel self-conscious of her soft stomach the entire day, convinced that people were judging her.

'We all got on well enough, sure. We sometimes went running together, actually, but it was Lauren she was closest too.' Sofie looked thoughtful. 'She was upset when Magda left, in fact she got really down about it and would just sort of cut the conversation if you tried to bring it up. I think she was embarrassed that somebody *she'd* invited to move in had stitched us all up like that.

'And Marcus?'

'Well, he kind of just does his own thing, doesn't he? I barely see him. Though I know I'm hardly ever here.'

Jessie hummed a sound of agreement; that much was true. Her digging hadn't come up with any concrete answers, but at least it didn't sound as though Marcus had done anything overtly terrible after all. Actually, it now seemed that maybe Magda wasn't faultless. She could understand why Lauren would be incensed by her behaviour, particularly if she had thought she and Magda were good friends. But why would she lie about it, try to make it seem as if Marcus was to blame? Something didn't add up. She stayed chatting about how her first day in the new office had gone, before letting Sofie get back to sorting her laundry. Following Priya's advice, Jessie spent the rest of the evening watching a film in her room, attempting to distract herself from stressing about the bizarre phone call and email. The message she'd sent to Magda remained unread.

CHAPTER ELEVEN

The temperature outside had dropped so low that Jessie could see her breath, as she shivered waiting for the bus to work. She'd lived at Maver Place for over two months now and the festive season had well and truly arrived. As she hung her coat up on a peg in the office, a Christmas song played merrily on the radio. A few weeks ago, on the first day of December, Juliette had insisted they tune in to a station dedicated entirely to festive songs and had started sporting naffer novelty jumpers than usual. Today's number featured a gigantic snowman in a Santa hat on the front. But Jessie wasn't feeling particularly festive this year – every time she thought about heading home to stay with her family and catch up with old friends, all she could picture was Matthew ringing the doorbell in the middle of the night again, or cornering her in the local pub. Just knowing they'd soon be in the same town was enough to make concentrating on work a struggle. Those feelings of paranoia, a sense that something terrible was edging closer towards her, were only increasing. Whenever she waited to cross the road, Jessie found herself flinching at passing cars. Upon Priya's suggestion, she'd finally registered with a GP surgery in Brighton, but couldn't get an appointment to discuss her medication until next year. There was still no response to her message to Magda, but even more worryingly, the withheld number had continued to call. It had become a daily occurrence. She had no way of blocking the calls so the best she could do was refuse to answer. He was goading her and it was working.

She planned to swing by Churchill Square mall on her way home to look for a Secret Santa gift for Sofie and hoped that a spot of Christmas shopping might lift her spirits a little. The women of the flat, spearheaded by a message from Lauren, had decided to do a present exchange with the rule being nobody could spend more than £10. They'd gathered in the kitchen conspiratorially and picked a piece of folded paper from a saucepan, then stifled giggles when Marcus had walked in and stared at them despondently. Jessie had felt a pang of guilt about that, but stayed silent and turned her back on him, putting the saucepan back in the cupboard. It was reassuring that Sofie and Lauren seemed to find Marcus as odd as she did. It wasn't ideal living with him, but it was tolerable, at least, especially now that both the girls felt like genuine friends to her.

Jessie had settled on buying Sofie a nice candle from Urban Outfitters, a vegan one, of course. Something hard to get wrong and less of a cop-out than her original plan – the least pensioner-smelling bath and body set she could find within budget. Apart from a gift card, it really was the most dull of ideas. Besides, Sofie's tray in the bathroom caddy they shared was already packed with Lush scrubs and home-made bottles of coconut conditioner. Marcus's entire toiletries range consisted of a toothbrush, his own toothpaste which he kept separately from theirs and a plain bar of soap, no frills whatsoever, which was Jessie's idea of a nightmare. She could happily spend hours trawling Superdrug or Boots, sniffing at all the products promising they'd transform her into someone happier and more beautiful.

The working day passed at an average speed: Jessie spent most of it registering new patients onto the internal database and updating the list of missed and kept appointments, breaking to eat a jacket potato in the staffroom at lunch, checking again to see if there was a response from Magda. When home time rolled around, she was glad to be finished with staring at a screen for the day and gave her colleagues a cheery wave goodbye.

Luckily, despite it being rush hour, the bus into town didn't take too long and she used the journey as an opportunity to message Rob, who was heading up a building project out of town for a couple of weeks. He'd sent her a photo of himself wearing a hard hat and suit, which she'd appreciated. It proved he was still thinking about her, even when he was away working. Hopefully they'd be able to meet up again before she left Brighton for the holidays.

Upon reaching the city centre, Jessie saw that the Clock Tower had its annual canopy of twinkling Christmas lights switched on. If you stood underneath them and looked up, it appeared as though the sky were packed with hundreds of silvery white stars, just a few metres above your head, almost within touching distance. It was one of her favourite things about the city at this time of year. She took a moment to appreciate it and remember how far she'd come since she'd first lived here. Although Matthew still lurked in the recesses of her mind, tiptoeing around her thoughts uninvited, she'd moved away and was making it work on her own. As strung out as she felt at the thought of potentially bumping into him over Christmas, she could at least be proud of that.

Jessie got the sense that someone was watching her. Out of the corner of her eye she noticed a young woman around her own age sitting on the steps of the Clock Tower with a group of other homeless people, staring unblinkingly in her direction. Her pale face sagged with exhaustion and was curtained by long dark hair upon which sat a black beanie. Jessie turned to look back and smile self-consciously. She never quite knew what to do when approached by homeless people – she rarely carried cash on her, which she felt made for an uncomfortable exchange. This woman, though, if she'd been in cleaner clothes and just walking down the street, could easily have been a friend of hers. Her expression was so pained that maintaining eye contact felt like leaving your hand on an increasingly hot stove. She had an aura of complete and utter defeat, those eyes offering only a small glimpse into her world. Jessie's heart went out to her. If she didn't have the support of her family, who knows where she could've ended up after running away from Matthew? A few seconds later, the homeless woman broke her gaze and went back to forlornly lighting a half-smoked cigarette that she'd scavenged from the pavement.

The traffic lights switched to red and Jessie made her way over to the shopping centre, telling herself she'd visit an ATM machine and offer a note to the woman if she was still there later on. She drifted into the familiar warmth of Topshop and flicked idly through the sale rail, not really looking for anything in particular. Lots of sequin dresses. Maybe she'd come back for that blue one if work announced there'd be a last-minute Christmas party. At the moment the plan was just to have a few drinks in the office, nothing exciting or worth buying a new outfit for. The centre was busy this evening – half of the city seemed to be out doing their shopping. She wandered around the homeware section of Urban Outfitters, aimlessly picking up scatter cushions, reading the price tags, then putting them back. Next to a shelf of photo frames was a tray of candles for just under a tenner each. Exactly what she'd been looking for. The label said they were all cruelty free and the smell coming from the sandalwood one was easily the nicest. She headed to the till, sure that Sofie would be appreciative, but it felt bittersweet tapping her card on the reader, still thinking about the homeless woman she'd seen earlier.

By the time she headed back to the Clock Tower, the woman had gone.

Back at the flat, Jessie put the candle in a gift bag and hid it inside her wardrobe, ready for Friday night when she, Lauren and Sofie planned to exchange gifts. She was looking forward to it, especially as hanging out with them both at the same didn't seem to happen all too often. It was funny how easy it was to live with people and yet barely see them. In the mornings she hardly ever bumped into anybody on her way to the bathroom or in the kitchen, as she sat at the table eating her usual slices of toast.

She flopped onto her bed and flipped open her laptop to book train tickets home to Chesterbury that weekend, then pulled the covers around herself. Her usual trick of envisioning herself on a beach, in an effort to placate the hamster wheel of anxious thoughts constantly rotating in her mind, wasn't working. All Jessie could think about was the woman she'd seen earlier, freezing on the steps while surrounded by joyous, dancing lights. She thought about her eyes that spent the day scanning a sea of hurried people and felt more thankful for her flat than ever: no matter how ropey it was in some parts or how scared she was that Matthew might find her in it, she'd never feel as afraid as that woman looking for a place to rest in the dead of winter.

Across the landing, Lauren was sat on the floor of her bedroom, wrapping a gift she'd selected too. She took great care to cut the sheet of gold paper, ensuring it was a perfect square for the crushed velvet box that was an easy shape to wrap. She then tied a gold and white ribbon around the paper, scoring it with the edge of a scissor blade. It sprang back satisfactorily, perfectly coiled. It was exactly how a present for somebody special should look.

A few days later, the thought of a takeaway and chilled glass of white wine was the only thing getting Jessie through Friday afternoon, on her last working day of the year. Juliette and Pamela's warbled efforts at singing along to the radio were beginning to grate on her, so much so that when Slade came on for the second time that afternoon she made an excuse to visit the filing room at the end of the corridor, just to get a break. The high-pitched chorus was more than a challenge for her colleagues – as endearing and lovely as they both were, Jessie was starting to feel like the odd one out, unable to join in with the majority of the conversations that took place in their nook of the office. She didn't have a bathroom that was being renovated or watch any soap operas and the strain of knowing Matthew would soon be within walking distance made discussions about which supermarkets produce the best mince pies seem trivial. Despite her quietness, Pamela and Juliette still dropped sincerely written cards onto her desk, thanking Jessie for her help over the last couple of months and wishing her a restful Christmas.

When it neared 5pm, Pamela brought out a home-made yule log which Juliette made a big fuss over, calling her a 'culinary genius'. Jessie made a half-hearted joke about secretly entering her onto the next season of *The Great British Bake Off*, which seemed to go down well, then helped to share out slices among the wider team of doctors, receptionists and support workers, who had all popped in to pull a cracker and swap season's greetings. Most of them, Jessie knew, having compiled the rota, barely had any time off. She'd used the tiny amount of annual leave she'd accrued to get out of being in the office on Christmas Eve, a short straw drawn by Juliette this year.

After clearing away the last of the confidential documents on her desk and being handed a lukewarm glass of fizz, Jessie felt the first sprinklings of Christmas cheer slowly stir within her. With every sip, her shoulders loosened.

'Cheese puffs?' Juliette waved a bowl of crisps under her nose.

Jessie took a handful to be polite.

'Gosh, almost the end of another year! It doesn't feel real, does it?' said Pamela, her mouth hanging open in exaggerated disbelief.

She topped Jessie's plastic champagne flute up, then refilled her own.

'Are you seeing anybody special while you're at home, my love?'

Jessie laughed and decided to indulge her boss with a snippet of information about her life outside of Tulip Court.

'Just the girls from school, who I don't get to see very often. There is someone that I've been seeing in Brighton, actually, but it's very early days. So we're not swapping presents.'

She could sense that Juliette was listening in too, as she'd slowed her conversation with Dr Statham right down.

'Nothing serious! Well, what's he like? A proper gentleman for a lovely young lady like you, I hope?'

'He's very nice, Pamela, I promise. Anyway, I've got dinner plans with my flatmates so need to be making a move. See you all on the other side!'

She hugged both Pamela and Juliette goodbye, something she'd never done before and genuinely meant it when she said she was looking forward to seeing them in the new year, then waved at Cheryl on reception on her way to the exit. Outside, it was starting to rain. She checked her phone before walking into it, wishing she'd brought an umbrella, and saw that Lauren, thoughtful as ever, had texted to ask what she wanted from the local Chinese.

As soon as Jessie pushed the front door open, she was instantly hit by the smell of food. She hadn't realised how hungry she'd been until that moment. Sofie and Lauren's chattering from the kitchen paused to greet her.

'I'm just going to get changed quickly, one second!'

She slung her bag over the bannister post at the bottom of the stairs and dashed up to her bedroom, to slip into some comfy jeans and collect Sofie's present. Walking back into the kitchen with it hidden behind her back, Jessie found Sofie and Lauren both sitting at the table wearing paper crowns, with the brown takeaway bags before them waiting to be opened.

'Are we going to do the big swap before or after food?' she asked, arm still twisted behind her.

'Let's do it now!' Lauren clapped her hands together in anticipation.

She'd been waiting all day for this moment. Sofie shrugged, as neutral as ever.

'Yeah, no time like the present for presents.'

They all laughed at the bad joke and Jessie revealed Sofie's gift bag from behind her back.

'In that case, here we are!' She passed it to her. 'I hope it's okay. If not I've got the receipt and you can swap it.'

She bent down to hug Sofie, then took a seat next to Lauren, who turned to face her and slid a gold box across the table. It had been wrapped with military precision. Sofie ducked under the table and picked up a squashy looking parcel, with a printed snowflake design on it.

'For you, Lauren. Shall we all open on the count of 3 … 2 … 1?'

Jessie was relieved they weren't opening their gifts one by one – it was always a process that made her feel distinctly uncomfortable. Even as a child, she'd hated having the unwelcome attention on her, along with the pressure to react in the 'right' way. She readied herself to thank Lauren, who she knew was still watching her and waiting, in an appropriate way – whether she liked the gift or not. At least she could honestly praise the wrapping.

She read the tag addressed to 'My little sister of the flat!' and slid her finger under a loose section of paper, revealing a jewellery box. Inside was a gold bracelet, not dissimilar to the one she'd lost during the move, with a small heart-shaped charm attached to it. There was an engraved J on it too. Jessie looked up and shook her head. It was clearly worth far more than the allotted £10 limit they'd agreed on and a lot more effort had gone into it than her after-work dash to the mall.

'Oh, Lauren! This is stunning. It's – it's so beautiful but really, you shouldn't have.'

Sofie peered over the table.

'Let's see?'

Awkwardly, Jessie turned the open jewellery box to face Sofie.

'That's really gorgeous. How lucky are you?' she said, wide-eyed. 'And how lucky am I? Thank you for the candle, Jess. It smells amazing.'

Sofie put the gift bag down and went to get plates out of the cupboard, ready for the food.

'Lauren, this must have cost a lot more than a tenner,' Jessie said in a low voice.

'Seriously, don't think of it like that.' Lauren smiled serenely, loosely waving a hand. 'Money isn't important and I know how gutted you were about losing your other one. Besides, it's vintage, not Dolce and Gabbana.'

Jessie closed the lid and bit her lower lip. It was an incredibly kind and generous thing of Lauren to do and she almost found herself welling up.

'Thank you so much. Really, it means a lot.'

She leant over to hug Lauren, who squeezed her back.

'My turn!' Lauren exclaimed, as Sofie put a plate down for each of them. 'Slipper socks, thanks, Sofes.'

'Well, we all know how cold it gets when the boiler plays up.'

Sofie winked and reached for a box of vegetable chow mein, then passed it to Jessie.

'You have to show me how you do your hair like that,' she said, looking at her wistfully. 'And I love your outfit too; where's that top from?'

Jessie blushed and stroked her hair bashfully. It had gone wavy after being caught in the drizzle.

'I was going to say the same thing,' Lauren laughed. 'Did you curl it this morning?'

As they settled into an easy chatter, Marcus appeared at the doorway, glanced in nervously, then quickly turned away.

'Marcus, wait!' Lauren called. 'There's plenty going spare if you'd like some?'

Sofie murmured in agreement through a mouthful. Jessie stayed silent.

Marcus shook his head. 'I'm on my way to a gig. I have a spare ticket and just wanted to see if you fancied it – it's my mate's band, Dark Destruction. You remember, we saw them once with ...'

He looked down at the floor as he spoke, as though wishing the ground would swallow him whole. Lauren's face gave nothing away.

'Oh I'm sorry, they were never really my thing. Plus, I said I'd hang with these two tonight. Enjoy, though.'

Before Lauren had even finished her sentence, Marcus had gone.

'I didn't realise metal was your scene, Loz. Or that you'd ever hung out with Marcus?' Sofie laughed. 'That would be even stranger than being into heavy metal.'

'Oh, I just went once to be polite. I felt sorry for him.'

Strange indeed.

CHAPTER TWELVE

It seemed to Jessie that her hometown was permanently frozen in time. No matter how long she left it for, the cobbled lanes, faceless housing estates and sturdy castle remained unchanged. The streets were still littered with the shadows of ex-boyfriends and school bullies that she'd rather avoid, but the chance to see Nicole, her best friend from school, was enough to lure her out of the warmth of her parents' house for a Christmas Eve drink after a few days of hibernation.

She exchanged smiles with the doormen posted in the cold outside the Grey Dog pub – the first place she'd ever tried tequila, on her eighteenth birthday – who nodded her inside. The familiar refrain of Mariah Carey's 'All I Want for Christmas' could just about be heard over the excited whoops and chatter. The bar was heaving, Jessie instinctively scanning it for khaki parka jackets like Matthew's, could only fully exhale after confirming to herself that he wasn't there. She spotted an old friend of his in the corner, deep in conversation with a woman she didn't recognise – she presumed a new girlfriend he'd brought home for Christmas. He was too engrossed to notice her and she was pretty sure he and Matthew weren't in touch any more, so felt safe enough to slip past him into a smaller back room of the bar, a few steps up beyond the bustling crowd. Nicole waved and pointed to an empty chair. After high-pitched greetings and hugs, Jessie dutifully wiggled herself onto the seat. Her friends had already bought a bottle of wine and had a glass waiting for her. Jessie tried to crack a whip in her mind to scare away the negative thoughts; she wanted to allow herself to sink into the magic of the season. The wine would help with that, she decided, playing with the new charm bracelet linked around her wrist, still half-looking around the room.

'Happy Christmas Eve, ladies!' said Nicole, raising a glass in the air.

Jessie lifted her own in response and clinked it against one held by Nicole's younger sister, Demi-Leigh. As the group branched off into smaller bubbles of conversation, Nicole turned to her in hushed tones.

'I've been worried about you. It's like you've just vanished off the face of the earth recently. How are you?'

Before Jessie could open her mouth to spin a line about how she was fine and apologise for not keeping in touch, Nicole interjected again.

'And I mean that, how are you *really*? Don't bullshit me.'

The familiarity of having her oldest friend so close by was akin to being wrapped in a soft blanket. Jessie could feel her lips twitching, wanting to talk and tell her all about how she'd finally managed to escape Matthew's ever-suffocating grip. But the truth was too embarrassing. Really, she hadn't mustered up the courage to leave by herself. He'd come home drunk, after a week of barely coming home at all, and when she'd plucked up the nerve to ask where he'd been, his response was a short three words.

'With someone else.'

He'd finally admitted what she'd long suspected. Jessie cried, asking who and why. He laughed. Then spat. The large globule sat on her cheek and hurt more than any of the times he'd dug his nails into her upper arms.

'I'm bored of all of this,' he snarled, waving a hand around the living room that she'd made sure was pristine for whenever he decided to return. 'So fucking bored of you. It's been, what, seven years? We were kids when we met, you can't expect me to only be with one woman my whole life.'

That much was true. Whenever she'd lain awake next to him, questioning whether their relationship was worth fighting for, she would think back to those early days when she had just turned sixteen and was sitting on a wall outside her sixth form college with Nicole, and Matthew – a few years older and therefore immediately cool by default – had first approached her. He'd bounded over, exuding self-assurance, and said he'd seen Jessie around town. He asked if she fancied getting food sometime, while running his thumb across the edge of his jaw. That contrast of confidence and vulnerability drew her in, and when he made both her and Nicole laugh by doing an impression of one of their tutors, she was a goner.

They had their first date a few days later in a nondescript Italian chain restaurant. He ordered a carbonara, she went for the pesto spaghetti. Afterwards he'd dropped her home, parking around the corner of her parents' house so that she wouldn't have to answer any questions about who the owner of the red Fiat was. Matthew's car became their lifeline out of the suburbs, a ticket to freedom, taking them to other nearby towns for day trips. It made Jessie feel so much older than she really was. She felt in control, desired and sure that she knew what love was. She was drowning in it. Love couldn't be anything else *but* this. Matthew quickly became all-consuming. Lyrics in songs she'd heard countless times before took on new meanings. She closed her eyes and listened as she sat in the passenger seat. Finally, she got it.

But after they'd been together for a year, had met one another's families, Matthew began to hold her hand a little too tightly. When she wanted to spend more time with her friends, he'd give her the silent treatment, claiming that she obviously didn't love him, sending her head into a wild spin.

'I've never loved anybody as much as I love you! Stop it,' she'd recite each time.

Eventually it became easier to stay at home with him, sitting in the dark, in his cramped single bed, staring blankly at the luminous television screen. If Matthew's fantasy football team ever lost a match, or if she fell asleep, he'd jab an elbow sharply into her chest and throw the controller on the floor, muttering that it was her fault for distracting him. The jabs soon morphed into new forms of torture: one minute he'd be kissing the soft insides of her thighs, the next he'd have her flesh gripped between his teeth, biting down on it, hard, until she yelped. Jessie found herself staring at the ceiling fan in his bedroom, counting each rotation it made as he panted in her ear, wishing that her mind would further disconnect from her body. Yet, at the same time, she was terrified Matthew would stop wanting it, stop wanting her. She'd do anything to please him, including turn a blind eye to his phone lighting up in the night with messages from unsaved numbers.

On the day of celebrating her exam results at Nicole's house party, she'd drunk too quickly and felt lightheaded. She wandered upstairs to a bedroom to take a breather. It didn't take long for Matthew to find her. He pulled Jessie up from the bed and she clung onto the jacket he was wearing, giggling. A button came loose. The red mist descended. He shoved her, then when she turned to leave, aimed a glass beer bottle directly at her head, only narrowly missing her. The following morning, he was back on her parents' doorstep bright and early, begging for forgiveness as she stood, embarrassed, wearing threadbare pink-striped pyjamas, in the doorway.

'I've never been physical with a woman like that before, Jess. I'm so sorry, it won't happen again. I'm disgusted with myself.'

She had to believe him because this man was her future. It was her own fault. She had got too drunk, hadn't been entertaining enough or behaving right. Matthew had grown up with a difficult childhood – his mother left when he was a toddler, saddling him with an alcoholic father – and Jessie had hoped that, if she could practise enough patience, eventually his temper would settle back down. He'd go back to worshipping her like he did in the beginning, rewarding her for remaining loyally by his side. Leaving this relationship, this love, was not an option.

But that party wasn't the last time Matthew had laid a finger on her. Looking back now, she realised it wasn't the first time either. After a long and sticky summer of arguments, the majority of which stemmed from his anger over her heading off to university, she almost dropped out of her course in Brighton before it had even started. The only way she managed to placate Matthew enough to let her go was to swear she'd visit him every weekend and move back to Chesterbury, to live with him, the second she handed in her final essay.

And so when Matthew returned home, on what would be the final night she slept in their shared home, even after everything that he'd put her through, he was the one to end it. Although he often shouted about breaking up when he was drunk, something about this particular time, about his callousness and lack of effort to lie about all the other women she'd suspected he'd been sleeping with since the start of their relationship, served as the final blow. She'd sobbed, snot running down her chin and he looked over in repulsion.

'I'm going to bed.'

When she didn't immediately follow, he began calling for her.

'I said, we're going to bed.'

Taking a deep inhale, Jessie swore that this would be the last time she'd let him use her body like this. No matter how much Matthew apologised in the morning, as was their usual routine, this time there'd be no second chances. She'd wait until he was at work, then slip quietly out his life and begin breathing again.

Jessie still hadn't responded to Nicole's worried questions.

'Really, I'm so much better now we've split up. You should come and stay with me in Brighton sometime, meet my new flatmates.'

Nicole squinted and she shook her head.

'Jessie, we all heard that he showed up at your mum and dad's house in the middle of the night and the police had to be called.'

Jessie looked around the cramped room of the pub. Did everybody in here know what had happened? Could they all tell that she was still half-numb with fear, replaying the sound of his laugh over and over like a scratched CD stuck on loop in her mind? That she jumped whenever a man with messy brown hair, a khaki jacket or a gold chain necklace walked past her in the street. She was sure they were staring. Demi-Leigh was certainly peering over her glasses in Jessie's direction.

'I know you're coming from a good place, but I'd rather not talk about Matthew tonight,' she said, trying to sound firm. 'I'm here to have a good time.'

Nicole raised her hands apologetically.

'Totally fair. I just want you to know that I'm here, should you need me.'

The subject was swiftly changed and, as the night wore on, Jessie found herself partially able to forget about Matthew and really focus on spending time with her friends. She hadn't felt this free in Chesterbury in years. The novelty of it was disarming.

'Let's get some shots in!' she suggested, after they'd drained another bottle of wine.

'Okay, but this *has* to be my last drink,' Nicole laughed. 'I can't be hungover on Christmas Day again, my mum was furious with me last year.'

Demi-Leigh followed them over to the bar.

'To be fair, you did almost fall asleep on your dinner,' she snickered. 'I'm just going to call a taxi and we can drop you off on our way, Jessie.'

Demi-Leigh headed to the door, phone in hand. It'd be quieter outside, easier to make the call. A few minutes later, she reappeared.

'I've managed to flag one down. It's waiting, so let's go!'

Jessie clipped her seatbelt in and rested her head against the window. Another challenge had been conquered. She'd had a successful night out in her hometown. Something that would seem so run-of-the-mill to most other people was a big milestone for her.

As she opened the porch door to her parents' house and waved goodbye to Demi-Leigh and Nicole, Jessie noticed something red on the tiled floor. It was a rectangular envelope with her name scrawled on it in familiar handwriting. Her stomach lurched. An invisible hand placed itself around her neck, choking away the breath. She opened the envelope and pulled out the card. Cramped blocks of text filled both sides of it. The first sentence read 'I still love you', the next 'but I know people have to pay for their mistakes'. Jessie leant against the door frame. He'd been here. Her legs felt close to buckling. She was queasy. The headlights of a car, a red Fiat, snapped on across the street.

CHAPTER THIRTEEN

Jessie saw the lights and ran into the house, slamming the front door behind her, and up the stairs. Her whole body shook. She raced to the bathroom at the front of the house which faced the street and peered out. The car was no longer there. He'd gone. She imagined Matthew laughing as he pulled away from the kerb, knowing he still had the desired effect on her. Humiliation surged. She stayed looking out the bathroom window, her mind swirling, heart pounding, until eventually the sky began to lighten. When the birds started singing, Jessie made her way back downstairs for a glass of water, then curled up into a ball on her dad's armchair which had the best view of the front door. She wanted to give herself as much warning time as possible if he came back. Should she call the police again? Fat load of good that had done before. A blanket had been thrown over the back of the armchair. She drew it tightly around herself, then drifted off into a fitful sleep. A few hours later, her dad gently shook her awake.

'Merry Christmas, poppet,' he said, handing her a fried egg sandwich. 'Good night, was it?'

She blinked a few times, then remembered the card stuffed into her handbag, the erratic handwriting, the revving sound of Matthew's engine. She dreaded to think what he might do next.

'If only you knew the half,' she replied quietly.

She hadn't even bothered taking her coat off. But at least a hangover was a plausible alibi as to why she didn't feel like eating or talking much that day.

'We'll need to set off for Grandma's house soon,' her dad said. He ruffled her hair and returned to the kitchen, whistling as he went.

Grandma's. Matthew had never been there. She'd be safe until Boxing Day at least, then she could head straight back to Brighton. It might even be nice having some time alone in the flat until the others returned in the new year. Head space. A solitary tear rolled down her cheek.

Sofie was the second to arrive back at the flat after Jessie, the day before New Year's Eve.

'Hello, stranger! I didn't expect anybody else to be in,' she said, switching the kettle on and slinging her coat on the table.

Jessie looked up from her spot on the sofa. She'd barely moved from it in days, and when she had it was only to walk down the road in search of more family-sized bags of Doritos.

'Did you have a nice Christmas?' Sofie asked, launching herself onto the opposite sofa. 'How come you're back so early?'

Jessie lowered the volume on the TV.

'Lovely Christmas, thanks. Oh, I'm on call for work tomorrow,' she lied.

'On New Year's Eve? That's a rough deal,' Sofie commiserated.

A woman on the television gasped as Santa's sleigh landed in her front garden.

'Yeah, I've never been big on New Year's anyway. What about you?' Jessie asked, eager to change the subject.

The kettle rattled on the counter.

'Henry's parents always throw a big party. Figured I'd come back today and give myself time to prepare.' She laughed. 'Both physically and mentally.'

Jessie laughed too. She could only imagine the type of people Henry's family might be. If they were anything like him, it'd be all swagger and self-indulgent stories.

'Tea?'

'I'd love one, thanks.'

Would it be rude to pry more about the party? Visions of coiffed, Gatsby-esque attendees drifting through marbled corridors sprang to mind. So very different to Sofie and her boundless enthusiasm for whatever the latest wellness craze or political cause was.

Jessie couldn't help herself. 'What sort of shindig is it tomorrow, then?'

'Well, it's quite fun really, although I know I've probably made it sound awful. There's a big fireworks display, champagne fountains, that sort of thing.' Sofie paused, pulling a face. 'Obviously, all of Henry's family are super posh and find it really "interesting" that I'm a vegan and come from a single-parent family, but Henry and I usually just sneak off to his room with some booze after midnight and play cards. I think he sometimes finds them difficult too.'

Jessie imagined Sofie would stick out like a sore thumb in that sort of crowd.

'Must be a good place for people-watching at least?'

'The best! Last year one of his uncles called my tattoos "jolly amusing". You should come along, if you fancy it? Henry's mum would love you, actually.'

It was sweet of her to offer, but Jessie didn't feel much like drinking or celebrating. When her anxiety levels were at a crescendo she found it difficult holding a conversation with friends, never mind strangers. She constantly misheard things, often thinking somebody had called her name when they hadn't. She'd not switched her phone on since it ran out of battery on Christmas Day, either.

'That's really kind of you, but I said I'd be on call for New Year's Day too, so better not risk it.'

'Shame. I hope you get paid extra for that?'

Jessie felt bad, thinking about poor Juliette and Pamela who really would be stuck in the office.

'Mind if I hang out here with you tonight?' Sofie asked, reaching over to the bag of Doritos on the coffee table, checking that they were dairy-free. 'We could stream a movie or something.'

Now that she'd made the suggestion of company, Jessie realised how much nicer it would be than sitting around on her own, fretting, moping and picking at her nails. Sofie was so kind and easy-going, she didn't need to put on a front around her.

'Perhaps you can help me pull together an outfit too? You're so naturally chic, you remind me of one of those *Made In Chelsea* girls or something.'

The following morning, Sofie left the flat early. She'd booked a hair appointment before the party and wanted a total restyle, a change to bring in the new year. Cutting her hair had always been a therapeutic process. She loved watching the dead ends fall to the salon floor, imagining any negative thoughts – about what she was doing with her life, whether or not her relationship was really working – shedding with them. When the stylist spun her back around to face the mirror, she gasped at her reflection. It had been a long time since Sofie had framed her face with a blunt fringe. The previous home dye pastel colours were gone, replaced with a sturdy all-over deep chocolate brown and swirls of caramel highlights carefully placed throughout. It looked just like the picture on Jessie's Instagram that she'd shown the stylist.

Sofie hoped that Henry would be pleased, as it was an offhand comment of his that had inspired her. Something about how well put together Jessie was and how she had such a 'classic' style. The more she thought about it, the more Sofie agreed. Jessie was so beautiful, and although she was sure Henry never meant to sting at her feelings, underneath her carefree hippy façade, she still had a nagging worry that her boyfriend wanted her to be like the privately educated women his mother was constantly introducing him to. Women like lovely Jessie. She tipped the hairdresser, rebooked for six weeks' time and headed to Henry's parents' place in the country. For once, she felt quietly confident about spending time with them. They were about to meet Sofie Version 2.0.

Back at the flat, Jessie sat on her bed. She could feel herself edging closer towards a darker, angrier place. Her festive break hadn't been remotely peaceful. It enraged her that her own mum still couldn't see how controlling Matthew had been throughout the entirety of their relationship. She'd even asked how he was over Christmas dinner at Grandma's, making no mention of his 'drunken episode', which almost prompted Jessie to throw a plate on the floor. It was easier to just stay quiet and say, 'He's fine.' In her mum's defence, it had taken Jessie herself years to realise all of the mind games she'd been subjected to so how could anybody on the outside be expected to understand? Matthew was such a charmer around her friends and family, and she'd been the one to play down his drunken banging on the front door and shouted threats through the letter box as a one-off.

Fireworks burst and hollered outside. Jessie wished Lauren or Priya were there, or that she'd taken up Sofie's invitation and gone to the party. She grabbed her laptop from the bedside table and opened Facebook, then began scrolling aimlessly through her newsfeed which was full of shiny, smiling faces, photos of friends from university posing in glittery outfits, wishing all of their loved ones a happy and healthy year ahead. Still no word from Magda. Priya had checked in at The Mash Tun, and uploaded a selfie with her girlfriend, Zoe, who Jessie knew and liked well enough. She looked around her bedroom. The anger in her belly strengthened. This isn't how she wanted to start a new year. She heaved herself off the bed, grabbed a coat and ran out into the night.

CHAPTER FOURTEEN

Sofie returned to the flat around lunchtime, just as Jessie was making pasta in the kitchen – the first proper food she'd cooked herself in days. She was glad she'd forced herself out for a couple of drinks with Priya, who'd shrieked with delight upon seeing her walk into the pub, and Zoe. It had helped snap her out of her funk a bit.

'What do you think, then? New year, new me and all that jazz!'

Sofie swished her head around like a Pantene advert, pouting at Jessie.

'Wow, you look so different!' she replied. 'It really suits you, Sofe.'

'Honestly?'

Sofie was pleased that Jessie had voiced her approval and nodded enthusiastically, her opinion being the one she most respected out of all the flatmates. A saccharine, fruity smell suddenly invaded her nostrils. Lauren walked into the room, a vape pen in hand.

'Honeys, I'm home!'

She looked at Sofie and did a double take.

'Oh my God, you've changed your hair!'

Again, Sofie preened and twirled, pretending to walk down an invisible catwalk.

'And you've quit smoking?' she replied.

Lauren held the pen up to the room.

'New Year's resolution, I'm trying to ditch the fags. Seeing if this helps.'

As Sofie busied herself with unpacking a Sainsbury's bag of cut-price veg, she didn't notice Lauren nudging Jessie and whispering.

'I didn't realise you were both hanging out in the flat,' Lauren said softly. 'I'd have come back too if I'd have known.'

'I've been here since Boxing Day, but Sofie only got back the day before yesterday,' Jessie replied. 'It's so great to see you.'

She hugged Lauren and hoped that Lauren hadn't messaged her while she'd been ignoring her phone. It was time to get it charged and reconnect with the world.

'Take two guesses as to where she got the inspiration for this new look from?'

At first, Jessie didn't quite understand. Sofie looked nice. Her new hairstyle suited her, surprisingly so, considering what a contrast it was to her previous choice of grown out candy floss pink.

She studied Sofie as she made her way around the kitchen, pulling out a saucepan from the top cupboard and filling it with water. Her movements seemed more restricted than before, somehow, as though each one was being carefully considered. Her usual incessant humming had vanished. The penny dropped.

It was the first time Jessie had seen Sofie wearing anything with long sleeves too, covering up the delicate swirls of cherry blossom she had inked all along her right arm. The navy polo neck she had on in place of her trademark crop tops, come rain or shine, wasn't entirely dissimilar to one she wore to work herself. Lauren widened her eyes.

'It's only you she's spent much time with lately,' Lauren whispered. 'I don't want to freak you out, but I think she came back early hoping to catch you alone. I think she's jealous that we're friends too.'

Jessie stayed silent. That couldn't be true. It made no sense. Sofie said she came back to get ready for the party. Besides, why would anybody want to look like boring old Jessica Campbell?

'I guess it's flattering? If it is deliberate, but I'm sure it's just a coincidence. Sofie's probably run out of other colours to dye her hair by this point.'

She'd only just pulled herself together, so the last thing Jessie wanted was to be caught in the middle of a flatmate tug of war. She watched Sofie put on a slick of dusty pink lipstick, similar to one she often wore.

Don't be silly, she told herself, *we're all friends.* Jessie smiled, rising to her feet. 'Guys, I'm knackered after last night. I'm going to have a lie down.'

Lauren looked worried.

'I've not annoyed you, have I?' she asked, her voice still low. 'I messaged you over the Christmas break but didn't hear anything back.'

Jessie shook her head.

'God no, so sorry about that. My phone's been playing up, so I've not bothered charging it. Thought I'd have a bit of a digital detox,' she replied earnestly, knowing she'd definitely have jumped to the same conclusion if it had been the other way round.

'Sounds like a blessing in disguise.' Lauren looked relieved. 'I think *I* need one of those. Let's catch up later then?'

'Definitely.'

Upstairs, Jessie examined her own fringe and caramel highlights in the bathroom mirror. Plenty of people had blunt fringes, it wasn't like she was the first woman on the planet to have ever had their hair cut this way. If Sofie had deliberately gone for a look similar to hers, well then, it was a compliment. Wasn't it? Maybe it meant she wasn't so dull after all. Nobody had ever wanted to copy *her* before. Back in her bedroom, Jessie searched through the boxes of clothes tucked away under her bed, just to check that her own navy polo top was still there as it ought to be. It wasn't. Her heartbeat quickened; being stolen from by a housemate she liked but didn't really know all that well, was less flattering. She'd never go into Sofie's room and take something of hers without permission; it wasn't that sort of friendship. Jessie tried to think whether their piles of washing could have been cross-contaminated before they'd both headed home for Christmas. They often shared drying racks, so perhaps it was an innocent mistake on Sofie's behalf? It was perfectly plausible. But somehow, she didn't think it was that.

She put her phone on charge, tepidly waiting for it to buzz back to life and silently hoping that there'd be nothing from Matthew. There was, of course, an email from his work account. This time containing a video as an attachment. She didn't need to click the play button to know what it was. From the pixelated thumbnail she recognised her own naked body. It was a video she'd never wanted to be in and that he'd sworn blindly he'd erased from his phone, before scowling at her for "ruining the fun".

I know you're in Brighton.

Jessie froze. Despite all of the precautions she'd taken, she'd failed. Her mouth fell open. She tried hard to think how he could have discovered her whereabouts. Someone must have slipped up. Nicole? Demi-Leigh? Then the thought of her family seeing the video hit. An image of her poor dad's face looking deeply ashamed. Why hadn't she tried harder to check that Matthew really had deleted the clip of her, weak and unwilling? He knew all of her friends from school too and could send it to any one of them. He could put it on Twitter, where men from around the world could ogle her and women could vilify her in the comments. Pamela and Juliette might see it, then she'd be fired. That's what he was trying to say. It was the last weapon in his arsenal, the ultimate trump card when it came to backing her into a corner, and he'd unexpectedly played it with a vengeance on an icy New Year's Day. It was back to being the rodent in Matthew's game of cat and mouse, where the rules were she must co-operate with whatever he wanted. He would never change. He thrived on making her feel as though her hands were bound with an invisible rope, that he alone had the power to untie. If only she'd blocked his work email address too, she'd never have been plunged into this state of panic. She placed her head in her hands. Now all she could do was sit and wait for his next move.

The following day, Ian sat in his car and waited for the time to signal exactly 6 o'clock before lowering the radio and dialling Jessie's number.

She picked up almost immediately. 'Ian, how are you?'

He drummed his fingers on the dashboard.

'Sorry for the short notice but your landlord has asked if I can swing by and check the boiler, what with the temperatures seriously dropping this week and it playing up last winter.'

It was already pitch-black and, despite having the heating switched on inside his second-hand BMW, Ian could see his breath spiral into the air as he spoke. The row of takeaways he'd parked outside penetrated the gloom with their buzzing signs and the scent of fried chicken wafted in despite the closed windows.

'No problem, if that's what the landlord wants,' Jessie replied. It sounded busy wherever she was. 'I'm out at the moment but one of the others should be in if I'm not back in time. Failing that, you've got keys in the office, haven't you?'

He was disappointed to hear that she wasn't at home.

'We do. I'll be over in about half an hour.'

The tenants at 4 Maver Place had been Ian's responsibility ever since he started working for Happy Homes. He'd seen plenty of faces come and go in that particular property – some lasted just a couple of months before he had to go through the rigmarole of paperwork required for incoming tenants. In that time, he'd only managed to score one promotion, taking him from a property manager to a senior property manager. This new title actually meant nothing really changed in terms of his day-to-day duties but he'd enjoyed updating his email signature and receiving a much-coveted handshake from the company director all the same. It had finally given his mother something to put in the Christmas newsletter that year too, a document blasted out to all extended members of the Palmer family, which his name was usually omitted from, given that his life (especially compared to his siblings) was rather bland. Other than the occasional five-a-side match or a college friend's stag do, Ian spent his spare time in front of his plasma screen watching *Top Gear* reruns.

He never minded popping by to help the girls whenever they emailed their various complaints about damp patches, mould or a leaky washing machine. It was company policy that a member of staff ought to inspect any of the properties on Happy Homes's books before sending a handyman in to help, just as a matter of formality (and as a means of hopefully keeping costs down). Marcus, however, Ian was unsure about. His beady eyes reminded him of a sewer rat, constantly pinballing around the room.

The short drive across town was relatively easy and Ian was pleased to find a parking spot right outside the flat. He couldn't see any sign of life inside, but gave his cursory knock and bell-ring all the same. As he was about to retrieve the keys from his pocket, which he'd grabbed from the office on his way out, Sofie opened the door.

'Jessie messaged to say you'd be popping round.'

She stepped aside, letting Ian pass down the hallway, before closing the door.

'Isn't it a bit late for you to still be at work?'

Her new haircut made her look different, as did that buttoned-up shirt. She looked more like Jessie. As Sofie reached up to re-tie her hair, she revealed the small gold hoop protruding from her navel. She was still the same underneath these new clothes, then. Ian tried not to stare at her stomach, but told himself it was only human to be intrigued by bare flesh – it was an innate, animal instinct to want to drink in the smooth skin of a woman. Sofie had probably started dressing that way for a reason, to encourage smart men like him to notice her. That made him feel less guilty about the stirring in his trousers.

'It's on my way home, so it's no trouble,' replied Ian cheerily, pulling his knee-length coat closer to his body. 'The boiler is in that little storage room on the ground floor, isn't it?'

Sofie nodded and pointed to the cream door opposite Marcus's bedroom.

'Go for it; I'll be in my room if you need anything.'

Ian slid the bolt across and entered the little room-cum-cupboard on the ground floor that went largely ignored. When the flat first came on the market the landlord had been keen to turn it into an extra bedroom, regardless of the fact that a futon would barely fit inside. Ian felt for the light switch and blinked when the bulb sprang into life. The space was full of junk; shelves of cardboard boxes and binbags lined the walls either side of him, and at the end of the room was the rotund boiler. Cobwebbed copper pipes emerged from behind it and ran all along the edges of the skirting boards. They'd be hot to the touch. He stood still in the middle of the room and got his phone out, checking the Sky Sports app for match updates. Even if the landlord *had* asked if someone from Happy Homes could check that the boiler was working efficiently, Ian wouldn't really know how to tell either way. Maintenance wasn't his forte.

Still, he went through the motions of checking around the barrel-shaped object and couldn't see anything obviously amiss. Then, after hearing the soft thump of music from upstairs, he let himself back out into the hallway. He was disappointed that Jessie wasn't around. Perhaps, seeing as he was already here, he ought to check that the radiators in both her and Lauren's bedrooms were running okay too? He could always say he was acting upon the landlord's instructions again. That was the beauty of it: none of them ever having met the landlord.

There was no strip of light poking out from underneath Marcus's door, so it was just Sofie he'd need to avoid. Padding gently up the stairs, Ian made his way into Jessie's bedroom and knocked, before trying the handle. It wouldn't budge. Good thing he'd also brought a spare key for that too. Opening the door, the smell of Jessie's jasmine perfume hit his nostrils as soon as he stepped over the threshold. It was feminine and comforting, exactly how he'd like a girlfriend to smell. She'd make a good partner, he just knew it; she was friendly and unaware of how pretty she was. Plus, he'd noticed her full cleavage that day she'd leant forward in his office to sign the contract and had been unable to stop thinking about it since. Ian took in the magazines stacked on Jessie's busy dressing table, which the radiator was situated behind. Listening to the internal voice that told him to further push himself uninvited into her world, Ian crouched down so that if anybody unexpectedly came into the room it would appear he merely was checking the valves. It was then that he spotted the ball of black lace curled up by a foot of the wardrobe. The opportunity was too irresistible to ignore. She'd never notice them missing. He slid the knickers into his pocket and smirked, feeling a flutter in his stomach. Finally, a piece of Jessie that he could keep all for himself. Back downstairs, he bumped into Lauren in the hall. It was almost as though she'd been waiting for him.

'I was just using the bathroom.'

'No problem,' she said, the faintest trace of suspicion in her tone. 'Are you off now?'

'Yes, all sorted,' Ian replied, with a breezy smile.

Lauren folded her arms and looked at him, her eyes giving nothing away.

'You've been around a lot lately. Has Jessie got you at her beck and call or something?'

Ian pushed the stolen underwear further into his pocket and gave an awkward laugh.

'Not Jessie, no, just your landlord,' he said, heading towards the front door. 'Sorry to have disturbed your evening, I'll try to give more notice next time.'

Half an hour later, a few miles across town, Ian buzzed himself into his rented flat overlooking Brighton Marina. He headed to the fridge and pulled out a chicken tikka ready meal and stabbed a fork through the plastic film lid. He enjoyed the cracking sound that accompanied each jab, then turned the heat dial on the microwave all the way to maximum power. Five minutes. That should be enough time, he thought, slumping into his favourite armchair and loosening his belt. The buckle clinked as he pushed it to one side and hurriedly unzipped the crotch of his trousers. He slipped his right hand beneath the waistband of his boxers and brought the black lace knickers up to his face.

CHAPTER FIFTEEN

Jessie awoke to a text from Rob asking if she was free the following evening. It had been a couple of weeks since she'd met with him last, despite constantly exchanging messages ever since, so she was relieved he was still interested. Matthew, meanwhile, would be waking up in their flat alone – or maybe not alone – but still trapped in their tiny hometown, whereas she'd flown away for good. But what good was flying when he'd just hunt her down? When he could be waiting for her at the bottom of any street. She'd barely slept since receiving that video, nor had she dared speak to anybody about it. The cold snapped at her cheeks on the way to the office. All the trees lining the car park outside the entrance were skeletal and bare, the gravel crunched underfoot as she punched in the same door code as last year. Cheryl was sitting beaming behind the reception desk as usual, her hair twirled into a neat chignon like an air hostess. Everything looked both different and the same. That stale coffee smell would certainly take some reacclimatising to.

'Did you have a lovely Christmas, sweetheart?' Pamela trilled, as Jessie automatically hung her coat on the last peg next to Juliette's.

She was so tired she could barely manage more than a 'Fine, thanks'.

Jessie tuned out as Pamela began going into detail about how her grandchildren had been delighted with the toy kitchen set she'd bought them – and had then spent most of the day playing in the box it came in instead. Jessie made cutesy noises at the right moments, but her gaze was focused on the top patient file stacked on Juliette's desk. She recognised the name on the front. Henry Goldsmith-Blume. It had to be Sofie's Henry – his surname was too unusual for it to be a coincidence.

Jessie knew they had all kinds of clients come through the doors here at Tulip Court, the majority of whom were completely harmless, people suffering with an array of disorders from deep depression to severe OCD. It would be wrong to look him up on the system, to sneak the blue paper folder off her colleague's desk and pry into the medical history of a patient who believed they were being treated with confidentiality. There were laminated posters all around the building, preaching the importance of privacy and not breaking trust. If she felt in serious danger that would be one thing, but Henry didn't seem to be a serious threat, just a bit boisterous and full of himself. Wasn't he? As if reading her mind, Juliette picked up the folder, humming to herself, and began adding paperwork into it. Given that it was on a pale yellow sheet of paper,

Jessie knew it was the summary of an appointment. A recent one.

'Drink, love?' asked Pamela, cutting through her thoughts.

Maybe that would be a good idea, something to help her regain focus and get back into working mode.

'I'd love a coffee, thanks. Are you sure I can't go for you?'

'Don't be silly, I need a quick word with Cheryl anyway.'

Jessie took her seat opposite Juliette and studied her face carefully, analysing it for any tiny mark of distress resulting from something she may have just read in Henry's file. Nothing. She seemed perfectly normal. A sea of calm. Jessie reminded herself that after her therapy sessions for anxiety she would've had her own folder somewhere too, back in an equivalent office in Chesterbury. She fiddled with the radio volume, upping it ever so slightly.

'Is this okay, Juliette? Not disturbing you?' she asked, letting a familiar pop song fill the room.

Anything to drown out the constant angst pounding in her head.

'Not at all.'

Juliette gave one of her sweet, dopey smiles and put the file into her drawer, then reached for another. As if suddenly remembering why she was sitting behind the desk, Jessie booted up her computer and began to write a to-do list for the day. She checked her emails. Nothing exciting. A few frazzled doctors asking about booking in their annual leave, a round robin from the area manager wishing everybody a great start back. The patient database logo sat temptingly in her toolbar, but she ignored it. Pamela came back with a latte from the machine in reception and placed it next to her, the scent of her Chanel No 5 lingering for a while afterwards. Before long the lunchtime news and weather report came on, then eventually the *Drivetime* playlist and a new presenter took over the airwaves, signalling it was almost time to head home. Another cycle completed.

It was difficult to make out what colour the parked cars were on either side of the street, given that they were all bathed in amber from the streetlights, but none of them were Fiats, thank God. Reaching the flat, it took Jessie a few seconds to realise that something was amiss. It was only when she went to put her key in the front door that she noticed it was already open. Not wide open, but a good few inches and, inside, the flat was dark. She dithered in the doorway, not daring to go in. It could have been a simple error on one of her flatmate's parts. Sofie was notoriously ditzy, after all. Or maybe Marcus was actually in his room, having walked in with his headphones on and not twigged that the door hadn't slammed shut behind him. But the welcome mat was at an angle too, when usually it was perfectly straight. Jessie pulled Lauren's number up on the screen, willing her to answer with every ring.

'This is the Vodafone voicemail service for oh, seven, four—'

She hung up and tried Sofie instead. It was almost 5.45 pm, meaning she'd be in the café a while longer yet. Jessie moved closer to the door and tried to see if anything had moved from the hallway. At the very end of it, she thought she could see smashed glass on the kitchen floor. Her skin began to crawl.

'Hello?'

Her voice echoed down the corridor.

'Is anybody in?'

Priya was still in New York visiting Zoe's parents, not due to return to Brighton for another week, and it didn't feel appropriate to call Rob – they still barely knew one another and she didn't want to come off as a damsel in distress or incapable. What could she say? 'Hello, I think my flat has been broken into, it could be my psychotic ex-boyfriend or maybe not, actually, I might just be making a fuss over nothing and Sofie's forgotten to shut the door.' Marcus was her last resort. He picked up almost immediately.

'Hey, it's Jessie. Sorry to call you randomly, you're not in the flat, are you?'

She heard herself garbling, the words all fighting to leave her mouth at the same time. Marcus leant against the cash register, his brows knitted together. She sounded panicked. He was instantly concerned.

'I'm at the shop, but almost finished. What's happened? Is it Lauren?'

She could hear people talking and heavy rock music playing in the background.

'No, she's fine. Well, I've not spoken to her but I'm sure she is. I've just got home and it looks as though there's been a break-in. The front door was left open and I can see smashed glass in the kitchen.'

Jessie's mind took an itinerary of everything in her bedroom which could have been stolen. Her door was locked, but if Matthew, or whoever it was that had broken in, had come with tools, she didn't think it would take much to crack it open. Her laptop, Magda's necklace, which was still in the top drawer of her dressing table, her charm bracelet from Lauren … They could all be gone.

'Shit! Shit, my guitars. Okay, stay calm and go and wait somewhere nearby until I can get there.'

To her surprise, Jessie suddenly felt grateful that Marcus had picked up. For somebody usually so mute, he sounded in control.

'Maybe you should phone the letting agency as well; if there's any damage they'll need to sort that. They don't close until 7 o'clock. I'll call the police when I get back after we've looked to see what's missing, if anything.'

Jessie felt braver with his voice at the other end of the line.

'If you stay on the phone I'll switch the light on and look?'

'Don't risk it, Jessie. Just shut the door if you can and wait in The Hare and Hounds. See you soon.'

She followed his instructions and harshly yanked the door shut, pushing back into it afterwards to double-check.

Life was relentless at the moment. This was just the icing on a very bleak cake.

At the pub, Jessie ordered a gin and tonic and sipped it greedily, desperate for the alcohol's calming effects to kick in. She headed to a wooden booth and searched her emails for the Happy Homes main office number, then hit the call option, as Marcus had advised her to do.

'Happy Homes, Craig speaking.'

He sounded very young. Not ideal for what she wanted to discuss.

'I'm a resident from Maver Place. Can I speak with Ian, please?'

She stirred the straw around in her glass, hoping it might encourage some of the ice to melt, and took another quiet sip.

'He's off ill, I'm afraid.'

'Do you think he'll be back in tomorrow?'

Craig made a noise that suggested not.

'Nah, he's pretty bad. I didn't even think you could go to hospital with food poisoning, but apparently they've kept him in overnight. So yeah, basically I dunno when he's coming back.'

He must have eaten something seriously bad, Jessie thought. It sounded dodgy. But maybe he was just skiving.

'Are you able to help at all? We've had a break-in at the flat.'

'Probably not, to be honest. I'm just an intern.'

She could tell that Craig was chewing gum as he spoke.

'If you call again tomorrow morning, everyone else will be back in. They'll know what to do.'

After thanking him for his help (although she didn't know why), Jessie hung up. A stained paper menu lay on the table in front of her but she wasn't hungry, her stomach still knotted at the thought of an intruder being in the flat.

A man with a swept-back fringe approached her table, carrying a pint of lager. His black jacket was unzipped.

'You okay?' Marcus asked quietly, fixing his eyes over her shoulder. Jessie nodded.

'I went to the flat on my way here, nothing looks damaged or missing.'

It was strange, sitting alone with him. She could tell that he was uncomfortable with the situation too and wondered if the barman presumed they were a couple. Or maybe it looked as though they'd never even met before. She doubted anybody would ever guess they were flatmates.

'But someone had broken in?'

'Well, there was a glass smashed on the floor in the kitchen but there is a window open. The lock hasn't been forced. It's weird.'

On that last word, Marcus's eyes met Jessie's, as if silently trying to tell her something.

'So maybe one of us just didn't shut the door properly on their way out? Maybe the wind knocked the glass off the side or something?'

Marcus nodded, his entire slender body moving too as he did so.

'Yeah, could be that. We all need to be more careful.'

They finished the rest of their drinks without saying much else. She messaged the group chat telling the girls what had happened and they all pledged to be more vigilant in future. Back at the flat, Marcus paused before entering his room.

'Glad you're all right.'

CHAPTER SIXTEEN

After their second date, Rob offered to walk Jessie back to Maver Place. She was relieved, still jumpy at the thought of Matthew potentially roaming the streets looking for her, and keen for the evening not to end. Their chemistry, as also evidenced by their constant texting, was well and truly out in full force. Rob had yet to follow through on his promise to cook though, which had become somewhat of a running joke between them that night at dinner.

'I *promise*, as soon as my housemate is next away I'll have you over,' was his catchphrase. 'He's just a bit in your face and doesn't quite grasp the concept of privacy, so I know he'd be lurking around the kitchen the whole time, trying to embarrass me. Quite off-putting when I'd be trying to impress you.'

Jessie understood, but it made her all the more curious to see inside Rob's home. She wanted to nosy around his bookshelf, to see how clean he kept his bathroom and judge his bed sheets. To be away from Maver Place. It was a Friday night, meaning neither of them had to think about getting up for work the next day and the evening stretched out with endless possibilities. They'd split a bottle of red wine over tapas, which Rob had refused to let her go halves on, and which helped Jessie to relax somewhat, and decided to pick up another bottle on their way to the flat. The man in her local newsagents, who Jessie was now on small-talk terms with, gave them a knowing look as he served them. He put the shiraz into a blue carrier bag and nodded to her.

'Have a good evening, lady.'

She linked her arm through Rob's as they left the shop, listening to his story about the architecture office he worked in, but not retaining much of it. Something about a colleague who was caught cutting corners on a job? Her concentration was elsewhere. Anticipation and desire made her eyes shine bright under the streetlights. Rob noticed, tucked a stray hair behind her ear and kissed her until her knees felt weak. The first man since Matthew. Whatever happened next was going to be significant. She desperately tried to remember if she'd left her room a mess and thought about texting Lauren to ask if she could hide any clothes scattered on the floor under the bed, knowing she'd find it funny. A better scenario, though, would be to discover that they had the flat all to themselves. Christ, it was time to buy some sexier underwear.

As they approached the flat at Maver Place, there were no obvious signs of life inside. Maybe everyone was out after all. Jessie felt along the hallway wall for the switch, then flicked it on, illuminating the corridor. Seeing things afresh, through Rob's eyes, she noticed how scuffed all the paintwork was. Things she'd become blind to about the flat, having lived there for a few months now, suddenly became disgustingly obvious. The cobwebs gathering in the corners – had they seriously been there the whole time? And had the bulb always hummed so loudly as it warmed up? Given that Rob was a foot taller than her, he'd definitely have noticed both.

'I'll grab some glasses and we can chill in my room?' Jessie suggested, eager to distract him from looking too hard.

She hung her bag over the end of the bannister, walked into the kitchen and quickly swiped two wine glasses that were face down on the drying rack. Rob was waiting at the bottom of the stairs.

'It's a sweet place you've got here.'

Before Jessie could reply, he took her face in his palms and lightly brushed his lips against hers.

They'd fallen asleep, tangled together in sweaty sheets in the early hours of the morning and Jessie awoke around eight o'clock, barely stirring at first, enjoying the feel of the cotton cover against her bare skin. It took a moment to remember the previous night in all its glory – the way Rob's weight had felt so necessary on top of her, his heavy breath in her ear, how he'd whispered her name. She stretched out a hand to the left side of the bed but found no warm flesh waiting to greet her. When she opened her eyes, she was alone. Presuming Rob was in the bathroom, she quickly jumped up and inspected her face in the mirror. She licked the side of her index finger and tidied some of the mascara smeared under her eyes from the day before, then remembered there was an open pack of gum in one of the dressing table drawers. Quickly, glancing back at the door, she bit into a piece and chewed furiously, before spitting it into the bin – important not to look as if she was trying too hard – and scurrying back into bed. Things felt different today. They'd slept together, and she couldn't wait to tell Priya, Lauren and Sofie all about it. Not only was it another milestone checked in moving on from Matthew, but she'd finally have some gossip to bring to the table when talk turned to relationships. That said, Sofie rarely divulged much about Henry, seeing as they all knew him. Priya and Zoe had been together for years too, but Jessie loved hearing Lauren's stories of her one-night stands and past romances. They made her a bit envious that she'd never been able to see sex as a one-time thing herself.

She couldn't tell how much time had passed before the niggle of doubt began to worm its way in. What if Rob wasn't just freshening up and it had it all been a vivid dream? Or worse, he'd woken up, taken one look at her and run? A condom wrapper on the floor confirmed he was real at least. Jessie reached under the bed for a pair of joggers, heaved herself up, then rummaged in her drawer for a vest top. Birds outside were tweeting intently at one another, discussing something she didn't quite yet know about. The bathroom door was ajar, showing it was empty inside, the mirror still fogged with condensation. Her heart sank a little further. Then lifted. It would be bizarre for Rob to have showered before ditching her. She clawed back another minute to pretend that he might be downstairs making them both coffee. Faint sounds of Marcus's usual miserable music met her ears; this morning it was The Smiths' classic 'Girlfriend in a Coma'.

As soon as Jessie reached the kitchen, any hope that Rob might have feelings for her instantly evaporated. Even though the fridge door was already busy with postcards and bill reminders, four cheerful magnetic letters stood out immediately.

They'd been arranged to spell out the word 'SLUT'.

Jessie's feet sprang roots, anchoring her to the floor, and a hard lump formed in the middle of her throat. It made no sense. They hadn't rushed into anything, they'd been speaking for months now, and she genuinely thought Rob had respect for her. He'd even said so right before starting to unbutton her blouse.

'You stupid idiot,' Jessie whispered to herself.

She dug her nails into the palms of her hand, trying to inflict some minor self-punishment. *Not again, not again, not again.* Back in the hallway she checked the pocket in her bag where she usually kept her phone. It was empty.

CHAPTER SEVENTEEN

Jessie unhooked the strap of her bag from the bannister and emptied it out onto the kitchen table. Purse, keys, medication, hair grips and lipstick, but no phone. She went back into the hallway and checked the pockets of the jacket she'd been wearing last night, but they were empty too. Her purse was missing a £20 note. She badly wanted to call Priya, who should've landed back at Gatwick around the same time that she and Rob had started tearing each other's clothes off. Her face felt hot at the memory. For him to leave like that was one thing, but to steal from her in the process was a different level of cruel.

'Bastard,' she muttered to herself, slumping down in her chair.

Trusting someone after Matthew had been a cumbersome task, one that she'd deliberately treated with caution. But her desire to be loved had, combined with wine and loneliness, created a potent cocktail that outweighed all the fear she felt about letting someone new in. What a fool. Jessie tried to retrace last night's steps and came to the same conclusion: her phone had definitely been in her bag when they'd reached the flat. She hadn't taken it out in the restaurant and had last glanced at it somewhere between the shop and the front door. As she sat staring at the fridge, Jessie didn't notice Lauren walk into the room until she waved a hand in front of her face, jerking her out of deep thought.

'All right, space cadet? Anyone home?'

Lauren studied Jessie's face. She looked drained and upset.

'What's wrong? How was last night?'

Lauren took a seat at the table and leant forward with obvious concern. At first, Jessie didn't know how to answer. Talking about it would make it even more real. Once somebody else knew, there could be no pretending that there was a nicer explanation for Rob vanishing along with her stuff, other than the fact she'd been royally played. She pointed to the insult left on the fridge.

'That pretty much sums it up. Rob came back here for the first time last night.'

Jessie watched Lauren's face change from confusion to anger as she read the magnets.

'And now I can't find my phone, it's not in my bag.'

'You're joking? Do you think he's taken it? We have to go to the police then! What a nasty ...' Lauren trailed off. 'Honestly, sometimes I just hate all men. *All* of them. Slut is such a stupid word; I mean, it takes two people to have sex. Why do we have to shoulder all the stigma for it?'

They fell silent.

'Let me call it for you, just in case? You never know, I'm always losing things when I've had a few. Marcus once found my keys in the fridge.'

Lauren pulled her own phone out of the back pocket of her black, slim-fitting jeans.

'It's switched off.'

The sound of Jessie's automated voicemail filled the kitchen, until Lauren hung up.

'It's been a really difficult few months and this is the last thing I needed,' Jessie said, her voice catching. 'Have you ever had someone get inside your head so much that, even when you know they're bad for you, you continue to let them in?'

The words came tumbling out before she'd even had a chance to formulate them properly in her own mind. A sickly cloud of vape smoke left Lauren's lips, smelling of imitation strawberry chews and burnt sugar.

'Yes,' she said quietly. 'A guy called Zach.'

Lauren spoke slowly and looked thoughtful.

'Even though it's been years since we were together, saying his name still makes me feel on edge. He's been harder to quit than any cigarettes, I still find myself looking at his Instagram when I'm having a bad day. Nothing like rubbing salt in your own wounds.'

She laughed at her own half-attempt at a joke and sucked at the pen again. It crackled as the liquid inside hit the hot coil and turned to mist.

'If I hadn't met him, I …' She trailed off. 'I'd be a different person.'

In a way, and without knowing the details, Jessie understood. It was a foreign concept that Lauren could ever have come off worse from a relationship, given how charismatic and self-assured she seemed.

'It's all a learning curve, I guess,' Jessie sighed, trying to convince herself in the process.

She'd thrown herself back into the dating pool too quickly and learnt a lesson. Instead of trying to meet someone new to make herself feel less alone or lost, it was time to make a conscious effort to enjoy her own company for a while, cultivate deeper friendships. She'd place her trust in friends only. In people like Lauren, Nicole and Priya, who all had her best interests at heart.

'How about a girl's night out?' suggested Lauren. 'We can really let our hair down. You've lived here for ages now and we still haven't managed a proper night on the tiles.'

It sounded the perfect tonic to an otherwise miserable morning. Jessie's head was softly pounding from the wine she'd sipped until the early hours of the morning, but it wasn't bad enough to put her off drinking again. She had a new dress from ASOS that she needed an excuse to wear too.

'Let's do it. I'll text Sofie and …' she started, before remembering. 'Never mind.'

Lauren shot her a sympathetic smile.

'I'll do the organising. Look, I feel awful leaving you but I have to pop down to the studio for a couple of hours. Are you going to be okay on your own?'

The thought of running a deep bath and sinking under the warm water suddenly felt like the only thing in the world that would soothe Jessie. She wanted any trace of Rob's touch washed off her and down the plughole.

'Of course. Sorry for being such a downer,' she said, plastering a grin on and deciding she'd use the bubble bath her grandma had given her for Christmas.

'Not at all. We're friends, best friends, you're like a little sister to me. You know I'd do anything I could to cheer you up.'

Lauren stood up and stretched her arms out. It took Jessie a second to work out what she was doing, then she rose from her seat too and hugged Lauren back, hard, feeling lucky to know her.

Once she heard the front door slam shut, Jessie walked upstairs, grumbled as she fished a clump of hair out of the plughole and turned on the taps. She listened as the water thundered down into the empty tub. It was depressing how adrift she felt without her phone. Wandering back into her room as the bath continued to run, she logged in to Facebook to send a message to Priya, explaining why she couldn't be contacted, then pulled up the message she'd sent to Magda about the locket, to see whether or not she'd read it yet. She mustn't check her inbox all that often because it remained unseen.

Had Magda been happy while living here? Was she also kept awake at night, by a combination of her own thoughts and unexplained noises? She still had no real idea as to why Magda had left. Jessie closed the laptop and went back to the bathroom, taking care to slide the lock fully across. She'd never forgotten that morning when Marcus had appeared behind her in the mirror. Even though the way he'd responded during the burglary scare had revealed a different side to him, a more human one, she was still wary around him, although she could empathise with him about how difficult it must be to feel so socially awkward and uncomfortable in your own skin. It also couldn't be easy living with Lauren and having a crush on her, when she so clearly didn't reciprocate those feelings.

The sky outside was sludge grey, which Jessie took as further permission to wallow in a state of pensive thought and subdued unhappiness. It was always easier to feel melancholy when the weather outside was dreary, somehow less guilt accompanied it. She combed conditioner through her hair and hugged her knees to her chest, waiting for the minutes to pass. The air was thick and a few degrees too warm to breathe comfortably, akin to sitting in a sauna. The bathroom window only opened a crack, barely wide enough to fit a fist through. Jessie ran the cold tap a little and bent forward to drink some of the water, to cool her throat, and resumed her hunched over position. This always happened when she took a bath. The idea of it was so much more appealing than the reality. Boredom set in quickly. An unexpected tear fell from her right eye.

Sofie was glad when her shift at the café came to an end. A night out with Lauren and Jessie, the chance to let her newly styled hair down, was exactly what she needed after a long day. She wiped down the last set of tables, mopped the kitchen floor with a disinfectant that stung her nostrils and said goodnight to the other manager on duty, who'd offered to stay late and cash up.

'Night, Kate!' he called, not looking up from his calculator.

Sofie rolled her eyes. Her colleagues had spent the day joking that she'd morphed into 'Kate Middleton with tattoos'. Not that you could see them any more. She had continued wearing long-sleeved roll-necks and today she'd added a new floral tea dress over the top. No more jewellery that jangled as she walked either, that was all gone, and she was making an effort to enunciate her words in the same way Henry and Jessie did. She'd been trying hard to win over his mother since the start of their relationship, and if it was to go the distance, Sofie knew how important it was to get her seal of approval. Henry wasn't perfect – he could be loud and a bit boorish – but when it was just the two of them, he was softer. He listened to her opinions, asked sensitive questions and made her laugh harder than anyone else. She loved him, and apart from her dead-end café job, their relationship was all she had. Sofie would do anything to make it work. Anything.

Henry's mother, Mrs Goldsmith-Blume, on the other hand, was a sickly and quick-tempered woman who spent most of her days lying on a Chesterfield sofa in what they all referred to as the 'big sitting room'. She'd made it very clear on numerous occasions that she thought her son could do better than 'a pink-haired waitress'. Their family set-up was a complex one. Mr Goldsmith-Blume was often away on long business trips, which seemed to aggravate Mrs Goldsmith-Blume's already fraught mood. It was plainly obvious that he was having an affair and had minimal regard for his ailing wife.

Sofie tried her best to be understanding of the unusual dynamics and kept a low profile whenever they stayed at the family's countryside manor, where Henry's bedroom was bigger than the entire kitchen-living room at Maver Place, and the place smelled of old wood and fresh laundry. Henry continually tried to mediate any awkward interactions between Sofie and his mother over the breakfast table in the mornings, cracking one of his cack-handed jokes to break the tension, but she often left feeling as though she'd said or done the wrong thing. She was glad to have the option to retreat back to her own flat sometimes too. Maver Place wasn't perfect, but she liked her cosy room, and now that Jessie had moved in she had someone to study. Someone whose looks, manners and movements were *exactly* what Henry's mother would approve of. She was sure of it.

After opening the front door, Sofie darted straight up the stairs and into her bedroom. She pulled a blue lace dress out of her wardrobe and zipped it up. She smoothed it down and admired her reflection in the mirror. It was an exact replica of one she'd seen in Jessie's wardrobe, that day she'd left her room unlocked. Sofie had learnt to be more careful after that, having almost been caught snooping when she forgot to put Jessie's laptop back on the dressing table. It was fascinating, living in such close quarters with the exact person she'd always dreamed of becoming.

CHAPTER EIGHTEEN

'He sounds nuts, Jess. A lucky escape in any case.'

Sofie had been brought up to speed on Rob's hit-and-run.

'Did this Rob guy really not give any sort of indication that he might have a screw loose before this?'

She couldn't believe that somebody could steal from a person they'd been dating, especially not Jessie of all people.

'Nope, nothing at all,' Jessie replied, pouring a glass of Prosecco and passing it to her. 'Which is pretty scary when you think about it. I guess you never really know if someone has a bad side until you're on it. Especially when you meet them on an app.'

The three of them sat quietly, contemplating. Lauren stared at Sofie's dress.

'It's definitely easier for people to pretend they're someone else,' agreed Sofie. 'I think we're quite similar you and me, Jessie. We're both very trusting.'

Lauren could feel the atmosphere threatening to wane. They needed music. She pointed the remote at the TV and searched through the radio channels, settling on one playing an Ariana Grande remix. Something upbeat and poppy.

'Where's Henry tonight then?' Lauren asked, not really interested in the answer.

'Another stag do. There seems to be one every week; it's like all the guys from the rugby club proposed to their girlfriends at the same time last summer.' Sofie kept her tone deliberately neutral. 'Except him, of course. So what's everyone else wearing tonight? What do you usually go for on a night out, Jessie?'

Jessie described a dress hanging in her wardrobe that she'd bought months ago and had been desperate to wear ever since: she'd been waiting for the right opportunity. It was a fitted lace number in navy, that finished well above the knee and had three-quarter-length sleeves. She planned to team it with chunky black wedge sandals and bare legs, despite it being cold outside.

'It's quite similar to what you have on now, actually,' she realised, properly taking in Sofie's outfit for the first time. 'Maybe I should go for something else.'

'Oh no! Please don't change on my account,' Sofie implored, shaking her head. 'We'll have different shoes and make-up on anyway.'

'You're welcome to borrow something of mine, Jessie,' Lauren offered.

Jessie mentally rifled through her wardrobe. She didn't really have any other clubbing-appropriate clothes and she doubted she'd be able to pull off any of Lauren's.

Maybe it would be okay to stick with her original plan and just make sure her hair was styled differently to Sofie's. Although now that she had a fringe too, that'd be easier said than done.

After topping up their drinks, the girls retreated upstairs to their separate bedrooms to get ready. It was actually sort of freeing, not having a phone, Jessie decided, now that she was getting used to it. Perhaps it'd be better to never replace it and just remain uncontactable to the outside world. As she teased her hair into curls, something different to Sofie's poker-straight do, she could hear Lauren rapping along to the tinny noises coming from her laptop in her room across the landing.

Lauren had left her door slightly open, which was rare – they tended to naturally drift into Jessie's room or hang out in the communal spaces of the flat. Her curiosity bubbled up. She put the curling tong down and took the few steps over to Lauren's room, then pushed her head round the gap. Lauren was jumping up and down, wriggling herself into a pair of tight PVC trousers. Her top half was kept simple, with a silver, sequined vest. As always, she looked like the type of woman the lead singer of a band would pick out of a crowd and take back to his hotel room – if that sort of thing actually happened in real life.

Lauren's room matched her nonchalant, cool aesthetic too – her bed consisted of a mattress laid across wooden crates, with orange-tinged fairy lights twinkling under-neath. At first glance, it almost looked as though the bed were on fire. The white wall next to it was covered in photos from disposable cameras, most of which seemed to have Lauren herself in. A pink and red hand-painted canvas, showing a distorted woman crying, was drying on an easel in the corner. Jessie found it unnerving; not only the bright colours depicting a scene so distressing, but there was something about the woman in the paint-ing that seemed familiar. She couldn't quite put her fin-ger on why. Still, she wasn't exactly an art critic and Lauren was obviously very talented.

'You look nice, Lauren.'

Jessie didn't have more than a half a minute to study the room before Lauren pulled on her trademark red leather jacket and made her way over to the door.

'Thanks, so do you! Shall we head down to the kitchen and get the party started?'

Lauren switched the main light off, leaving her bed glowing like a spaceship in the dark.

'I'll be down in a minute, just need to finish my eye-liner,' Jessie replied, watching as Lauren took a key out of her purse and locked her bedroom door.

Jessie stared in the direction of Lauren's room for a few more seconds, then headed back to her own. Lauren had mentioned previously that she saw her bedroom as being like her own little at-home studio, her sanc-tuary. It was funny that she obviously didn't want any-body to see her work until it was finished either – when clearly she had more talent than anybody Jessie had ever met. She sometimes sold her paintings through Instagram, whereas Jessie could barely manage a stick man.

She heard Sofie call from the bottom of the stairs, 'The taxi will be here in a minute!' and then ask Lauren, 'I don't own any heels yet; will these pumps be okay to wear?'

Jessie threw a make-up bag into her satchel, locked her bedroom door and hurried down to the kitchen, where Lauren was lining up three egg cups on the table. She poured a small measure of vodka into each. Sofie hovered nearby, looking smaller than ever, next to Lauren in her clumpy platforms. Jessie wondered for a moment if she ought to say something about how similar their outfits were – near identical, in fact – but thought better of it. Imitation is supposedly the most sincere form of flattery. Wasn't that what they said? This must just be how it felt being a leader not a follower. There was no harm in Sofie trying to dress a little more mainstream, surely?

'One for the road,' Lauren said, with a devilish glint in her eye. 'Let's all cheers on the count of three!'

They winced as the liquid slipped down their throats, waiting for the split-second burn to fade into a pleasant warmth in their chests. Jessie was glad to feel the hit of it. Tonight would be about two things only: drinking and dancing.

Aware that the cab was arriving imminently, she headed back to the hallway to grab her coat, the same one she'd worn for the majority of the winter. Jessie pulled it on in a rush and noticed it felt heavier on one side, as though something was weighing down one of the pockets. Putting her hands inside both, her fingers met something hard and rubbery. A phone case. Her phone! It had been in there the whole time.

'No way,' she muttered to herself. 'I definitely checked.'

The device had completely run out of battery; Jessie held down the "on" switch but nothing happened. She walked back into the kitchen, holding it up to show Lauren and Sofie, then plugged it into the communal charger next to the microwave, shaking her head.

'You found it!' exclaimed Sofie. 'Where? How?'

'In my coat pocket. But I checked in there, I'm sure of it.'

'Calls for another shot if you ask me,' said Lauren, quickly unscrewing the bottle of own-brand vodka once more.

Jessie thought back to earlier that morning, which already felt like so long ago. She remembered the way she'd emptied the contents of her bag and patted down all of her coats hanging on the hallway pegs, even the ones she hadn't worn the night before. It didn't make any sense. Lauren thrust an egg cup into her hand.

'Drink up. Perfect excuse to celebrate!'

When a car horn sounded from outside, they all tipped their heads back and downed the second load of shots, then cackled as they made their way down the steps to the waiting car. Jessie left her sense of mistrust in the hallway.

Lauren had managed to get them all free entry to a club not far from the seafront. It was a 90s themed night and the baseline of a Tupac song could be heard rumbling from inside as the doormen nodded them in.

'The promoter is an old friend who fancies me,' Lauren had shrugged. 'No biggie.'

Once inside, it seemed that every few minutes Lauren would bump into someone she 'used to know' or 'used to hang around with'.

'Let's head to the bar,' Sofie whispered to Jessie, grabbing her arm, leaving Lauren chatting to a man holding a fistful of flyers.

'Have you seen Zach around lately? Is he here?' Jessie heard Lauren ask, in a hopeful voice.

The bass thumped so hard that the floor, ceiling and walls were vibrating.

'Are you guys, like, supposed to be twins or something?' a thin drunk woman in her late teens snickered, stumbling into them.

Jessie laughed nervously, unsure of how to react, and kept moving through the bundle of pulsating limbs. Neither she nor Sofie came to clubs like this very often – Sofie felt more at home on a silent retreat and Jessie was more at home, *actually* at home, sitting in the flat.

Reaching the bar, Sofie ordered three vodka, lime and sodas, then dug around in the bum bag she had clipped around her waist for some cash. As she heaved herself over the bar, to better hear the man serving them, Jessie turned to survey the crowd. The vodka had left everybody blurred around the edges. They all looked so happy, as though they had nothing better to think about than what song might be played next. She longed to be like that, carefree like Lauren and Sofie, and felt a fraud in comparison – the events of the past day, the last few months even, had left her exhausted. She could see Lauren dancing, not caring that she was alone, her red-jacketed arms waving in the air wildly, head thrown back in raucous laughter, sequined vest catching the light as she moved.

'Here's your drink!' Sofie shouted, handing it to Lauren, who mouthed a 'thank you' back.

Jessie only knew half of the tracks that came on, whereas Lauren seemed to be word perfect, putting her hands over her abs and grinding her hips as she sang along, apparently oblivious to all the men staring in her direction. They remained in their trio for what felt like hours, only breaking apart occasionally to go to the bar.

'I need the loo. Anyone else coming?' Lauren said, when the rhythm switched to something with a slower pace.

'Me!' Sofie replied, raising her hand in the air, as though she were back at school.

Jessie shook her head.

'I'll get the next round in, meet you back here after.'

Jessie felt more confident striding over to the bar this time. She was having fun, dancing with friends, drinking her worries away for the evening. Despite her head spinning and her constant need to scan the crowd for Matthew, she was passing for normal.

'Three vodka cokes, please.' Her words were slurred, but the barman understood all the same.

He pulled out three plastic cups and Jessie watched as he filled them to the brim with ice. She leant against the bar and screwed her eyes up, noticing the bleached blonde hair and red leather jacket standing next to her, facing the opposite direction.

'Lauren? I thought you went to the bathroom?'

Lauren didn't turn around. The music was loud, so Jessie shouted again.

'Hey, Lauren! I thought you went to the bathroom?' She jabbed heavy-handedly at a shoulder.

The head whipped around. Those dark eyebrows and red lipstick were eerily similar to Lauren's, but it wasn't her. This woman had a rounder face, which lacked the textbook symmetry of Lauren's and her perfect dainty nose. Taking a second look, she was also slightly taller. Jessie blinked with confusion, then laughed. It wasn't just her who had a double in the club tonight.

'I'm so sorry, I thought you were my housemate. I must be drunker than I thought but you really look like her,' she prattled. 'Don't worry though, Lauren – that's her name – is really pretty. So it's not a bad thing!'

'Did you just call me Lauren?' the stranger asked. She had an accent that Jessie's soaked brain struggled to pinpoint.

She opened her mouth to apologise again, but was cut off.

'Do you mean Lauren McCormack?' The woman sounded alarmed and her eyes shot over Jessie's head, searching the throng behind her.

'That's right, Lauren McCormack. You know her?'

The woman's eyes widened.

'Did you say you're *living* with her?'

Jessie realised the barman was still waiting to be paid and handed over her debit card. He returned it to her in the card machine. She struggled to jab her pin code in, her coordination running on a time delay.

'I am, yeah.' Jessie shook her head when the barman asked if she'd like a receipt. 'Are you a friend of hers?'

A woman with hair twisted into intricate braids moved closer and looked just as puzzled as Jessie.

'Are you okay, Magda?'

Magda? Was this Magda the former tenant, who used to live in her room? The same Magda who'd run away, leaving the rest of the flatmates, Jessie's friends, saddled with her share of the rent and bills? No wonder she looked panicked. Jessie felt anger churn within, no doubt fuelled by the drinks.

'They've told me about you. You're the one who screwed them all over,' she said accusingly, clutching one of the drinks to her chest.

She prepared to collect the others and disappear back into the crowd. But as much as Jessie disagreed with Magda's choices, she still felt she ought to mention the locket she'd found in the dressing table. She didn't know her side of story, after all. Before she had a chance to,

Magda moved her head closer to Jessie's ear and whispered, in a low voice, something that sounded like a warning.

'Whatever they've said it's not true! It's not how they made it out to be. You need to leave.' She looked over her shoulder again.

It was hard to make out her exact words over the music and Jessie squinted as she tried to listen, not entirely sure she'd heard correctly.

'I messaged you on Facebook about a necklace I found, but you never replied. It's gold with an "M" on it. Is it yours?'

Magda's friend made it clear she was getting frustrated at being left out of the discussion by huffing and folding her arms. It only added to Jessie's already mounting annoyance.

'I should get back to my friend, but can you meet me for coffee next week and bring it? Wednesday evening. I'll reply to you on Facebook with details.'

Something about the terror on Magda's face, that seemed to stretch beyond the thought of a potentially awkward run-in with her former flatmate, made Jessie agree. As soon as she had, Magda grabbed her bewildered friend's arm and ran for the exit.

CHAPTER NINETEEN

An elbow struck Jessie's stomach. The shots had suddenly taken a hold of her in the worst way. She placed the plastic cups back on the bar and looked for the toilet sign. The queue snaking out of the restroom meant she'd never make it in time. The music was too loud and she couldn't follow the melody any more, so she made her way to the exit, in need of air. Outside, she sat on the kerb a few metres away from the club, not able to stand the smell of the smoking area, and hoped the nausea would pass in a few minutes. When it didn't, she knew it was time to leave. The thought of going back in and having to shove through the crowd to find Sofie and Lauren was unbearable; hopefully, they would soon realise she'd made her way home and wouldn't be too worried. She couldn't call or message them until she had made it back to her phone.

Jessie's fingers were so cold it almost felt as if they were burning. The lights of the city danced madly before her and waves crashed in the distance. She focused on putting one foot in front of the other, regretting having left her coat in the cloakroom.

All of the quirky boutiques and restaurants down The Lanes were cloaked in darkness, but some of the bars still had the last few stragglers standing around outside, smoking and jeering at one another. As she neared the narrow passageway past The Font, a former chapel-turned-pub, Jessie prayed silently that nobody would say anything to her. She wanted to remain invisible and slip through the street unnoticed, to get back as quickly as possible, but in the dim light and in her inebriated state, the cobbled alleyways felt tighter than ever. It was as though she was on a gameshow where the walls were slowly closing in. More than once she glanced back over her shoulder, certain she could hear footsteps trailing slightly behind her own, but saw only her shadow. Her brain must be playing tricks again, the usual daily paranoia amplified by all that vodka. Jessie's arms were rough with goosebumps and she rubbed at them furiously; then, realising she had already passed the chocolate shop with the gigantic cakes on display in the window once before, she stopped still. The alcohol had turned the streets she knew so well into a maze and, without noticing, she'd been walking around in circles. Feeling small and uncertain, she slumped against a wall and slid slowly down, her bag falling from her shoulder and onto the ground. The simple task of getting back to Maver Place felt overwhelming. If she told a passer-by that she'd lost her flat, would they find it funny?

'You all right, love?' a pair of scuffed Nike trainers asked.

Jessie didn't look up; instead she focused on a piece of chewing gum stuck to the ground and tried not to cry, willing the man to continue walking. He hesitated for a second, then followed the call of his friend in the distance, leaving her alone. She suddenly became aware that the part of the alleyway she'd come to a halt in smelled strongly of urine and the nausea kicked in all over again.

Heaving herself off the floor, Jessie wobbled and tried to grip at the brick wall, tearing a fingernail in the process. Just put one foot in front of the other, then another. That was all she had to do, she told herself. She reached the entrance to the warren of side streets leading out onto North Road, a main road with the Clock Tower at one end and the Pavilion Gardens at the other. Light raindrops quickly turned to a harder downpour, causing a group of women across the street to shriek and huddle under one shared umbrella. They were splitting a polystyrene tray of chips and Jessie licked her lips. The thought of chips absorbing some of the booze and leaving a salty tingle on her tongue was so tempting she briefly considered crossing over to buy some too. That smell of vinegar was enticing, but the shop was so packed, she couldn't stand the wait. Instead, she wobbled past the women determinedly, heading towards the misty gardens of the Royal Pavilion.

It was a building she'd always been fascinated by, with its Indian-inspired domed roofs looking in some ways so out of place in the middle of a British city, yet still perfectly in keeping. It would take around half an hour to get home from here. The neatly manicured lawns, which during the summer would have chattering groups sprawled across them, sharing ciders and playing guitars, were all deserted. Jessie moved through silently, wondering for a brief moment if she should put her headphones in, then remembered her phone was still charging at home. Her limbs were becoming heavier, eyes drooping more with every step. Would it be so bad to stop and rest? Just for a few minutes. She barely registered the rain soaking through her dress as she stood in the centre of the pathway, trying to work out her next move. The world spun madly, as though she were being pushed on a park merry-go-round, one that she desperately wanted to jump off of but was somehow superglued onto. Vomit sat at the very back of her throat, filling her mouth with saliva, threatening to burst forward at any moment. She tried clumsily putting her fingers in her mouth and jabbing at her tonsils to try and coax it out of her system – anything to give her heaving stomach some relief. There were those footsteps again and this time she was sure of it. Jessie withdrew her fingers, laced with spit, and looked over her shoulder once more, straining her eyes to see where the noise was coming from. Fear clawed away in her chest and something was telling her to run, but instead she was stuck in treacle, sinking in quicksand, her insides screaming, begging her feet to move ...

It took a few seconds, or maybe even a minute, for Jessie to realise that her head had been slammed into the wet ground repeatedly. That a heavy foot had kicked at and crushed her lower spine, then sped off into the distance. One eye blinked open and saw the pavement. Why did her mouth taste of metal? There was a warm and sticky feeling in her right ear. Had she been hit so hard that the fluid protecting her skull had actually begun to leak? She made a small moaning sound and tried to move the fingers of her left hand closer to investigate. Raising them into the glare of a streetlight felt like lifting a hefty kettlebell and she saw that they were stained dark with the blood running down her palm and wrist, that was soon washed away by the rain. Her vision vibrated as she watched. The gardens were now moving in slow motion. Dark red blood, dark green leaves, dark grey pavement. Orange streetlight. White-hot pain. The rain had left her bones filled with ice and her body no longer belonged to her. It wouldn't co-operate or move when she told it to. Jessie tried with the last of her strength to turn her head and see if there were any passers-by who could help, but found she was only able to shift it a few centimetres. Just enough to confirm that the gardens were empty.

'Help,' she tried, voice croaking, closing her eyes again. 'Please.'

Even if there had been anybody around to hear, her voice was so minuscule that it came out as a whisper and was immediately lost to the wind. Her teeth chattered as the flower beds came in and out of focus. Where was her bag? Slowly, Jessie tried to push herself up onto all fours and look around the path. No phone. No money for a taxi. No keys to get in. It was nearing the middle of

January, the time of year when snow showers hit the south coast and buses came to a standstill. She slumped back down and curled into the foetal position, then screeched and sobbed, like an injured animal waiting to die, her muscles convulsing under the spray of icy rain. Jessie had foolishly thought that Matthew sending that video, plain evidence of the power imbalance in their relationship and the way he used to force himself on her, was rock bottom – but it was nothing compared to this. Nothing at all. How would she feel safe again? How could she ever leave the flat? If she made it back to the flat. The black screen, the inside of her eyelids, fell again.

CHAPTER TWENTY

Lauren and Sofie stood by the water cooler not knowing what to say. It was gone midday.

'I just can't fathom it. Who would do something like that?'

It was Sofie who eventually broke the silence in hushed tones, repeating the same refrain they'd already wheeled out countless times. The hours in the waiting room were crawling by.

'I'm so glad those girls found her,' she continued, shaking her head in disbelief, glancing at Jessie's bag lying on a chair next to them, the strap torn and half the contents missing. 'I wish we'd left the club sooner, instead of spending so long searching for one another in there.'

Thinking back to the crowd of people gathered around Jessie's limp body made Sofie shiver. A group of strangers on their way home had found her lying across the path at an odd angle, a dark pool around her head, and immediately phoned an ambulance.

'Imagine if we hadn't walked that way too,' nodded Lauren. 'We'd still be sitting in the flat, wondering where she was.'

She looked tearful and her face was blotchy.

'*Why* would anybody ever want to hurt her?' Sofie repeated.

Neither of them wanted to answer that, not daring to acknowledge how much worse things could have been. Paramedics had taken Jessie to the Royal Sussex to run precautionary tests and keep her under observation. Lauren was grateful they were taking things so seriously. Her feet were pulsing in her platform shoes so she leant forward to unbuckle them and sat back down. Sofie took a seat beside her and rested her head on Lauren's shoulder. Eventually, they both fell into a light doze until a nurse holding a clipboard came over and woke them with a gentle shake.

'We've cleaned and stitched Jessica's facial wounds and have the results back from her CT scan, which shows she has a linear fracture on the back of her skull,' the nurse explained, tilting her head to one side. 'What that means is the break is in a straight line and that she's a very lucky girl not to have suffered a depressed fracture, which would require surgery, given the level of force she was subjected to. The police have been informed, of course.'

Lauren looked up at her aghast.

'We're currently waiting for the consultant to prescribe antibiotics to prevent any infection and then, as Miss Campbell is proving neurologically sound, I expect she'll be able to leave later on this afternoon. Are you able to arrange her transport home?'

They nodded that they would.

'Someone will also need to keep a close eye on her over the next few days, given that she'll be suffering from a heavy concussion, along with bruising. It goes without saying that your poor friend has been through a hell of a time and is very shaken. She may well experience post-traumatic stress disorder and might want to think about counselling when she's ready.'

The nurse removed a couple of leaflets in primary colours, bearing the words 'Concussion' and 'PTSD', from her clipboard.

'Are we able to see her?' Lauren asked in a wobbly voice, clutching the pamphlets tightly.

'Not at the moment, but I'd be happy to call you once the doctor has discharged her?'

'We'll wait,' Lauren said, arms crossed over her chest. 'I'll wait here for as long as she needs me to.'

Once the consultant had prescribed painkillers and antibiotics, Lauren and Sofie gently helped Jessie into the taxi waiting by the hospital entrance. The journey back to the flat felt as though it stretched out for days, but in reality was only around fifteen minutes. Jessie sat very still and stared out the window for the duration of it, her head burning, swirling, thunder-clapping, her face swollen. She was desperate to take off her lacy dress, shower and cocoon underneath her duvet, to have a place to cry in peace. She saw young families wrapped in thick scarves pushing prams down the street. She lightly brushed her fingertips against the stitches on her forehead, mostly hidden by her fringe. The driver kept glancing nervously in the overheard mirror, worried that one of the three drained-looking women wearing party clothes and pained expressions at 3pm in the back of his car might be sick. Sofie was the only one who thanked him as they pulled up outside Maver Place.

'Do you need a hand with the stairs, Jess?' Lauren asked, as she ran around the cab to open Jessie's door.

'No, it's fine.'

'You go ahead and get comfortable, we'll bring you up tea and water,' Sofie added, walking into the kitchen to switch the kettle on.

Jessie shrugged, then began dragging her heavy limbs up the stairs to her bedroom. Pushing down on the door handle had no effect.

'It's locked,' she said flatly.

Nobody replied. Jessie had no idea how loudly she was speaking, as the hammering in her head made it feel as though she were underwater. She could be whispering or shouting.

'Lauren, I can't get in my room,' she called, leaning over the bannister this time. 'It's locked.'

The sound of the kettle drowned out Jessie's timid voice. She sighed deeply and slowly thudded back downstairs to the kitchen and repeated the problem; this time they both understood. Sofie looked at Jessie's distorted, purple face and felt her own bottom lip start to quiver.

'Shit, I'm so sorry I hadn't even thought of that,' said Lauren. 'We could build a nest on the sofa for you?'

'Henry is on his way over, I can see if he'll break the door down?' Sofie suggested feebly. 'He might be a while though.'

'I just want to be in my own bed,' Jessie replied with a deep sigh, sinking into the sofa. 'Is Marcus in? Maybe he could try.'

She caught sight of her reflection in the mirror above the television. Her eyelashes were split into clumps around her puffy eyes and mascara had crumbled down her bruised cheeks. She used the back of her hand to wipe it away, then stared at the black smudge on her skin for a while. It was like dirt. Her coloured wounds contrasted oddly against her pale face.

'Of course. I'll go and see if he's awake. He's pretty strong for such a skinny guy.' Lauren knew her chatter sounded inane. 'Probably from lugging those massive guitar cases around all the time.'

Moments later she returned with Marcus. He was wearing the Star Wars T-shirt again and tartan pyjama bottoms. Seeing Jessie, his own face blanched, then contorted into a concerned grimace.

'I think we should call a locksmith,' he said, nervously glancing from Jessie to Lauren. 'If I try and break the door down, the landlord will definitely charge you for the damage. You'd be better off spending the money on getting it done professionally.'

It was a good point. Even in her lowest hour and as desperate as she was to get into her bedroom, Jessie knew her bank balance couldn't take the hit.

'Why don't you have a shower and we'll call someone now. I'll try Ian at the letting agents too,' Sofie added, pulling herself together and screwing her sensible head on. 'You never know, maybe they'll have a spare key. Help yourself to a towel and any clothes from my room, Jessie.'

Sofie took herself into the hallway to make the phone calls and Jessie went upstairs for a second time. The sound of running water soon started up.

'Tell me again, what happened?' Marcus asked Lauren, who shivered as she was still wearing the silver crop top under her red leather jacket, leaving her chest and stomach exposed.

'We had all split up in the club. I found Sofie again but neither of us could find Jessie, so after looking everywhere, we figured that she must have gone home and decided to leave too, taking a shortcut through The Lanes,' she said, clutching at a mug of tea for warmth. 'Some of Zach's lot were out as well and had got us free entry. I told them if Jessie reappeared that they should let her use one of their phones to call me and we'd come straight back for her. We were probably too drunk to notice but she must have been really wasted, Marcus.'

Hearing the name Zach, Marcus's mouth disappeared into a thin line.

'Why were you speaking to them? You know Zach's reputation. Everyone in Brighton knows his whole crowd is messed up,' Marcus spat.

Lauren thought for a few seconds before answering.

'I know, I know – it's as pathetic as it sounds, but they're the only link I have left to him and I wanted to … I wanted to know how he is.'

'Who cares how he is? Fuck Zach!' Marcus hissed. 'You're so stupid for even speaking to them, Lauren.'

Marcus slammed a fist against the kitchen counter.

'I bet they've got something to do with this. They're a bunch of addicts. Why would you ever – and I mean *ever* – want to be anywhere near someone who ploughs through gear the way they do? I've seen them around town, Zach included, off their heads in the middle of the day. It's pitiful.'

Panic danced in Lauren's eyes, her mouth hanging open wordlessly. Her chest felt tight. The mug was starting to scald her fingers.

'They can't have been involved! You're paranoid. When we left the club … I'm sure they were all still there. She was found on the ground in the Pavilion Gardens, which she'd short-cutted through, Marcus. You know that area is dodgy at night, she'd have been an easy target. Whoever it was stole her wallet too.'

A tension hung in the air between them, the image of Jessie, vulnerable and hurt, at the forefront of both of their minds. Sofie walked back into the kitchen, holding her phone, oblivious.

'Ian's not there. He's left the company, apparently.'

'That seems sudden,' Lauren said. 'And he was always popping over, so you'd think he'd have at least emailed to say goodbye.'

'Yeah, I guess it is odd,' Sofie replied. 'But at least whoever it was I spoke to said they've got a spare set of keys in the office and someone called Craig is going to drop them over in the next hour.'

Marcus muttered something about that being good news and stormed off in the direction of his bedroom. Sofie couldn't say for sure, but it sounded as though he kicked a wall in the hallway, en route.

'I feel so guilty ...' Lauren's voice cracked as she spoke. 'We should never have let her go to the bar alone, Sofe. She was so drunk, wasn't she?'

Sofie nodded in agreement, guilt also bubbling away in her core.

'What kind of world is it where someone as lovely as Jessie can't walk home alone, without getting hurt? We have to look after her from now on, Lauren. We shouldn't have split up and all we can do is be thankful things weren't worse.'

Lauren pulled herself up to perch on the edge of the sink, her mood unreadable. She looked as though she were in a sort of trance for a couple of minutes, before spotting Jessie in the doorway. She darted over to the sofa and plumped the cushions.

'The letting agents are bringing a key over in the next hour,' she explained, helping Jessie to lie down. 'Would you like the radio on?'

'No,' Jessie whispered hoarsely. 'No, I don't want any noise.'

The door rang and Sofie went to answer it. Jessie winced.

Moments later, Henry walked into the kitchen, swivelling his car keys. Seeing Jessie lying forlornly on the sofa, his eyes widened.

'Christ, whoever did that must be a right nasty piece of work.'

'Jessie, maybe you'll be more comfortable in my room until the key arrives?' Sofie started. 'Henry, can you give her a hand? I'll make us all some herbal tea and bring it straight up.'

Henry stuck his thick forearm out in front of Jessie, who used it to steady herself. She felt dizzy again, from moving too quickly. As he gripped her shoulder, she flinched. His touch stirred up the husk of a memory, which quickly evaporated again. Lauren followed behind.

'One step at a time, babe,' she said softly.

A few cups of tea later, Craig rang the doorbell and handed over an envelope containing the spare key. Lauren unlocked Jessie's bedroom for her, then watched as she crawled under the duvet. Although she was shattered, Jessie couldn't sleep right away. She tried her usual trick of taking a few sertraline tablets, then tiptoed downstairs, desperate to avoid bumping into any of her flatmates, to swipe her phone off the top of the microwave where it had been left charging. It was hot from being plugged in for too long.

Back in the safety of her bedroom, she thought about calling Priya but didn't feel strong enough to relive what had happened again, in any detail, so soon. Instead she sent a text.

I was mugged last night, was pretty drunk so don't remember much. Been checked out and am back home now. Are you around later? Would love some company, I feel so broken.

Next, she logged on to Facebook. A red notification told her she had a new message: a message from Magda Nowak, sent in the early hours of the morning, not long after she'd disappeared from the club. With everything else that had happened, Jessie had clean forgotten about bumping into her. The message was simply an apology for the delay in replying to Jessie's own effort at making contact and asked her to meet at the Starbucks on Western Road this coming Wednesday at 6.30pm. Magda had signed off with the words 'Take care'. Jessie struggled to remember their conversation. The music had been so jarring and the concussion was screwing with her brain, but the look of fear in Magda's eyes was still crystal clear.

CHAPTER TWENTY-ONE

Another full day passed before Jessie emerged from her bedroom early on Sunday evening. At some point her nightmares, where the incident replayed itself on loop, became difficult to separate from reality and she'd taken another dose of anti-anxiety medication, along with some mild sleeping tablets left over from a plane journey to lull herself back to sleep. That feeling of being watched and followed was so hard to shake. Underneath the over-sized T-shirt she'd been sleeping in, her back felt clammy. Her legs had started to itch from being in bed for too many hours and while her brain still felt slow, some energy had been restored to her body at least. It was time to get up and face the world. She sat at her dresser and looked at the blood crusted into her hair. One of her eyes had a purple bruise underneath and her knees were covered in plenty more. Her palms wept where the skin had been torn away by the rough ground. Jessie checked her phone and was dismayed to see that Priya hadn't responded. Probably had enough of putting me back together, she thought, probably thinks it's my own fault for getting too drunk and wandering off. But it wasn't like Priya not to get back to her, especially after something like this.

I'm scared it might have been something to do with Matthew. Do you think it could have been him? Should I tell the police? All I've said to them so far is that I can't remember anything and don't want to pursue the case she texted again, in a last ditch attempt for a response.

Jessie pulled on her tracksuit bottoms and another baggy T-shirt, then brushed her teeth in the bathroom. The extractor fan groaned overhead. More than anything, she wanted things to feel normal again. She wanted her biggest concern to be that Lauren was forever leaving pencil shavings on the table or that Marcus's music kept her awake, echoing up through the floorboards. But really, nothing was normal any more – she'd been attacked and left abandoned in the rain. Her heart rate quickened, reliving it. Yet the thought of following up again with the police, who'd taken a basic statement from her at the hospital, wasn't appealing either. "Grievous bodily harm" was how they'd referred to it. She didn't want to have to sit in a stark interview room and give a detailed description of everything she'd drunk that night, how she'd downed so many shots she could barely remember her own name. They'd only tell her that she shouldn't have put herself at risk, surely. Jessie also knew she hadn't seen or heard anything that might help the police identify whoever it was who had snuck up on her from behind, struck her hard and grabbed her bag. Snatches of images came to mind then disappeared again before she could properly take hold of them and investigate. It was best, she decided, to file the assault away in a box at the back of her mind, something that she'd got used to doing during and after the trauma of Matthew: the flash of pleasure in his eyes when she had sobbed on their living room floor, the sex she had stopped wanting to be a part of years ago – all of that had been pushed as deep down as possible, along with the searing embarrassment she felt for having stayed so long. It had taken a long time and a lot of therapy to realise that, just because Matthew had never punched her square in the mouth, what he'd done to her still counted as abuse. She missed her counsellor back in Chesterbury, who undoubtedly would have something reassuring to say. It was definitely time to find a new one in Brighton.

When she reached the living room, Jessie was glad to see Lauren spread out on the sofa in her usual position. On the round table was something new. A large translucent bowl containing pebbles, brightly coloured mock coral and four fish. Hearing her walk in, Lauren sat up.

'How are you feeling? We've all been really worried,' she asked with a pained expression.

Two of the goldfish were swimming proudly near the surface of the water, which vibrated slightly from the filter pump. Another was hidden inside the silk leaves of an imitation plant and the fourth was merely floating at the bottom of the tank, millimetres away from the gravel, looking lost. The soothing motion of the swimming left Jessie captivated.

'I've been better. I owe a huge thanks to you and Sofie for waiting there at the hospital and getting me home,' she replied, taking a glass out of the cabinet and filling it with orange juice.

It even hurt to lift the carton.

'I wouldn't leave you, of course not. I'm glad you're up and about,' Lauren pointed at the bowl. 'I thought they'd be a nice little addition to the family. They're supposedly very calming to have around. Given that there's one for each of us, Sofie said we should name them after ourselves, but I'm not sure. What do you reckon?'

The fish that had been lurking in the plant swam out, revealing black freckles on its tail.

'She said that one looks like Marcus and has been calling it Marcus Junior slash MJ all day,' she continued, laughing then regretting it.

It felt too soon to laugh about anything.

'He does a bit. I suppose that makes me the one with the bewildered look on its face, sinking at the bottom.'

As if suddenly aware it had an audience, the fish began whirling around in circles, showing off flashes of silver mixed into its orange scales. It was the smallest in the tank by far.

'Oh, Jess. Do you want to talk about it? Have you thought about talking to the police any more about what happened?'

Lauren stared at her intently, waiting for an answer.

'No. I'm not going to do that,' Jessie replied firmly. 'They said at the hospital that they're scouring for CCTV footage and have asked me to give a more detailed statement, but I told them I don't want to. In all honestly, I just want to forget about it and move on. I'm not even going to tell my parents. They'll only worry.'

Lauren wasn't sure how to react, so instead just stood up and walked over to Jessie, hovering awkwardly in front of her. Lauren looked tired, her white-blonde hair was scraped up into a harsh bun, ageing her. For the first time Jessie wasn't envious of her face. The tough-girl mask had slipped and the raw, human version of Lauren was poking out – in a way it was reassuring, that even she had been rocked by the attack. It made Jessie feel less alone.

'Did you manage to get a glimpse of the scumbag that did it?'

'Nothing. Another reason why trying to prosecute would be pointless.'

A red container of fish flakes had been put on the windowsill next to the spider plant. Lauren unscrewed the lid of the food, pinching some between her hands, and scattered it above the bowl; together they watched as the fish all rose to the top, their greedy mouths opening like small tunnels.

'They're meant to be good for anxiety and depression, you know,' Lauren eventually said. 'Fish, I mean. That's apparently why they often have them at doctors surgeries.'

Her comments were met with silence. Jessie's mood was extremely low, especially now that Priya was giving her the cold shoulder too.

'How about we order a curry?

'I can't, Lauren, I don't have any money. I need to sort out some emergency cash until I get my new bank card.'

'Don't worry, I'll get this. My treat,' Lauren tried again.

Realising she hadn't eaten in almost two full days, despite the girls having left yoghurts and sandwiches on her bedside table, along with bottles of water she'd merely sipped at, Jessie nodded.

'Thank you, that's really nice of you. Will you be around all night? We could start a new Netflix series together – I just want to stare at a screen and distract myself.'

'I'll be around whenever you need me to be, babe,' Lauren replied, squeezing her arm.

The following morning Jessie was torn between calling in sick and forcing herself to head into the office as normal. After a long internal debate, she decided to allow herself a few more days of rest – the concussion still made her feel slightly drunk and her hands hadn't stopped shaking – and left a voicemail on Pamela's mobile saying she'd been struck down by a virus, but that, hopefully, she'd be back in a few days. Old habits seemed to die hard when it came to admitting what she'd been through. Jessie needed more time before she was ready to sit next to a stranger on the bus or make idle chat with Juliette and Cheryl. She also wanted to think about whether or not meeting with Magda was a good idea. Lying in bed for hours on end, her mind had explored every avenue as to why the attack might have happened. There was a very strong possibility that it was simply coincidental she'd been mugged the same night as meeting the former Maver Place resident with a bad reputation, but a definite worry still lingered that maybe it wasn't. Would meeting Magda on Wednesday to return the locket be walking right into the arms of trouble? She wished Priya wasn't ignoring her texts, so that she could ask for her advice or maybe even get her to come along too.

Jessie spent the whole of Monday gazing blindly at her laptop in bed, pausing once to put a frozen pizza in the oven, feeling too lethargic and dizzy to cook anything requiring effort. The row of dissolving stitches in her head was beginning to itch, but she was terrified to touch them. More than anything, she was desperate not to have a scar of the incident, which would serve as a permanent reminder that almost nobody could be trusted. She thought of her family back home in Chesterbury and imagined being back in her childhood bedroom, safe from all the turmoil that adulthood seemed to bring with it. Only, in reality, she knew that if she were to buy a train ticket home, she'd spend the entire journey worrying that Matthew might happen to be at the station or worse, waiting outside her house again. What if he was outside the flat right now?

After finishing another season of *Queer Eye*, Jessie tapped in the address for the same housing website she'd found Maver Place on. Instead of searching for Brighton flats, she browsed for cottages in the Scottish countryside, desperate for an image she could squirrel away for the next time she needed a fantasy to soothe her overactive imagination. Something to replace the footsteps she'd heard before hitting the ground. Brighton was supposed to be a fresh start for her, yet had been nothing but a curse since she arrived. Or maybe it was the flat that was the problem, not the city. Right now, running as far away from everything as possible, to somewhere in the Highlands with a small population, none of whom knew her name, and becoming a recluse felt tempting. She could still stay friends with Sofie and Lauren; they could FaceTime or come to visit her whenever they liked. Anything felt better than spending five days a week in an office that smelled of stale coffee and toner, and the majority of her nights in a cramped kitchen on a sagging orange sofa. Instead, she could go for long, meandering walks. She could take in crisp air and work in a bookstore or library, somewhere wholesome and satisfying, where people spoke calmly and quietly.

On Tuesday morning Lauren knocked on the bedroom door, as she'd taken to doing every few hours, and offered Jessie a cup of tea. She declined.

'I'm off to the studio now,' Lauren said, 'but just call if there's anything you need and I can come straight back.'

She placed a paper bag containing five Sainsbury's milk chocolate cookies on Jessie's bedside table and kissed the top of her head.

'You'll get sores if you don't leave this bed soon, doll.'

Her voice was a little higher than usual.

'I know I'm wallowing,' Jessie mumbled. 'I'll be going back to work tomorrow, though.'

'You're *more* than entitled to wallow. Although for what it's worth, I don't think you are.' Lauren patted Jessie's hand as she spoke. 'I know it's been a tough time lately, even before the attack, what with Rob and that horrible ex-boyfriend of yours, but I just want you to know I'm here for you. We've always got each other, haven't we?'

Jessie squeezed her hand back.

'Life may not be perfect or even good right now, but I'm glad to have you as a friend.'

Lauren smiled and closed the door softly on her way out. A few minutes later, Jessie opened her laptop and replied to Magda's message.

Tomorrow at 6.30pm is fine with me. I'll see you then.

After all, they'd be meeting in a public place – even if Magda was behind the attack, she could hardly do anything else in a well-lit coffee shop with other people in close proximity. Jessie's phone buzzed and she snatched it out from under her pillow, hoping it would be Priya, but was disappointed to see it was only Marcus, asking everyone to transfer him £7.58 for the Internet bill. Thinking of Marcus, she pictured him in his red tartan pyjama bottoms. It jogged something in her mind. A memory was fluttering up to the surface and she tried hard to let it push through. Had she seen the flash of something red the night she was attacked? Before she could solidify the thought, it vanished.

CHAPTER TWENTY-TWO

Having spent so many days cooped up indoors, Jessie was grateful when Lauren offered to walk her to the bus stop. It was her first day back at work since the attack and her stomach churned at the thought of leaving the safety of the flat. Large flakes of snow fell over the city as they strode on in silence, feet hitting the ground simultaneously. The snow vanished as soon as it met the road, but had built up on car windows and grassy spots. Jessie's legs ached from lack of use as they trudged up the hill.

'You've got this,' Lauren said, hugging her at the bus stop, before heading off to the studio. 'You're being so brave but call me if you start feeling overwhelmed.'

Jessie forced a smile and waved goodbye. She was apprehensive about returning to work so soon, but knew her mind needed to focus on something other than the attack and Matthew, the man who had crushed her heart until she swore it had almost stopped beating. Crushed heart and crushed skull. Crushed spirit. At this point even laborious paperwork would do as a distraction.

Lauren, and Sofie too, had been so kind, constantly offering to make her drinks and checking in. Even Marcus had sent a WhatsApp message: *I hope you're okay.* Managing to get out of her bedroom felt something akin to a small win. She'd put Magda's locket in an envelope and zipped it safely inside an old black handbag that she was using as a substitute for her broken satchel – meeting her later that evening was the last thing Jessie wanted to do, but her need for answers was overpowering her desire to run straight home. She touched her cheek lightly, conscious of the tattoo cover-up make-up she'd ordered online and layered over her face to hide the damage.

'How are you feeling, love?' Pamela clucked, the second she'd stepped over the threshold. 'There's so much of it going around at the moment; even Dr Statham was off with the lurgy yesterday as well.'

It had never occurred to Jessie before that doctors might also take sick days. Juliette held up a balled tissue.

'I think I'm its next victim.'

She blew her nose loudly on a fresh one, as if feeling the need to provide further evidence under Pamela's watchful eye.

'You're still looking a bit peaky,' Pamela said, switching to her concerned face. 'Are you sure you're all right to be back in the office?'

Jessie bowed her head, hoping they wouldn't notice her bloodshot eyes, and smoothed her fringe over the stitches.

'Oh, definitely, I'm so much better today,' she replied, with as much enthusiasm as she could muster. 'Hopefully this is the worst of it, Juliette, and you'll be on the mend soon too.'

Jessie took her seat and wished she'd applied more blusher and bronzer, to give herself a bit of a glow over the top of the heavy concealer she'd plastered on all the bruises. It had done the job but given her the pallor of a sickly Victorian child in the process. At least Pamela hadn't noticed the marks though; the thought of being fussed over or having to explain how she got them terrified Jessie. What could she say? That she'd gotten so drunk she couldn't remember how to walk home and had left herself vulnerable to an attack? Or that her ex-boyfriend was potentially roaming the city looking for her, and that in her paranoid state she feared he was somehow behind it? Then there was the third option, that Magda might somehow, in some way, be involved. It was all too confusing. Jessie looked out of the window and gave a deep sigh, then loaded up the computer as she had done countless times before. She unlocked her desk and retrieved the case notes she'd been inputting last, finding that the monotony of typing helped to distract her all the way through until lunchtime, then again until the end of the day.

Finishing work almost an hour and a half before she was due to meet Magda meant Jessie had time to kill. She exited the bus not far from the coffee shop that they'd agreed on and headed to a pub opposite for a small glass of red wine. The first drop of alcohol she'd drunk since the attack. She'd briefly considered going teetotal but couldn't fight the lure of it, a glass of crisp Malbec offering to soothe her anxiety. A message appeared from Lauren.

How was today? My shoot should be finishing up around 8, then I can make us dinner? Let me know what you want x

Jessie slid her phone back in her pocket and tried to rehearse in her head what she wanted to say to Magda, but couldn't settle on an opening line. There were too many questions to ask, ranging from how had she found living with Marcus, to why she had really left Maver Place. Then whether or not she knew anything about the attack.

Eventually she came to the conclusion that it'd be better to just wait and see what Magda had to say, having come to learn that people more often than not made an effort to fill silences if she let them. Trying to guess what Magda might want to tell her was pointless, but Jessie already knew if it involved a bad word against Lauren that she wouldn't hear it. Lauren had been such a good friend to her from the moment they met, but especially so since Saturday night, barely leaving Jessie alone for more than hour, apart from when she had to work. She half-wished Lauren were here now or that she could at least call her and say where she was, who she was about to meet. Jessie pulled a small mirror out of her bag and dabbed more concealer under her black eyes and over her bruised chin, wincing as the scabs on her palm cracked slightly from the movement. She drank her wine slowly, trying to make it last as long as possible.

She walked to Starbucks, jumping when anybody in the street brushed too close, and after ordering a latte, took a seat at an empty table by the window. Best to sit somewhere obvious, in case Magda missed her and thought she'd bailed. Luckily, she was still ten minutes early. Jessie liked that. It made her feel as if she'd given herself some control over the situation. In reality, her mouth was dry despite the coffee – and, lately, nothing really seemed within her control.

She stared at the barista, then back out the window, continuing to people watch until her phone flicked from 6.29pm to 6.30pm, her heart slamming against her ribs the entire time. The urge to plunge her nails deep into the itchy stitches on her forehead was strong. Jessie tried to practise slow breathing, the way she'd been taught in therapy but whenever a blonde woman walked past the window, her body tensed in anticipation – should she stand up to greet her? – but none of them were Magda. By quarter to seven, Jessie had finished her latte. She pulled up her Facebook chat with Magda but there were no unread messages. Her legs juddered up and down underneath the table.

'Another?' the barista asked, collecting her empty mug.

Jessie shook her head. The minutes continued to crawl. Where was she?

Hi Magda, I'm in the Starbucks on Western Road sitting by the window. Are you still coming?

The barista shot her surly glances, clearly irritated that she hadn't ordered anything else. By quarter past seven, it was obvious that Magda wasn't coming. She'd been stood up. Jessie pushed her chair back, gritting her teeth at the scraping sound it made, then called herself a taxi, too afraid to walk alone in the dark. She waited in the coffee shop until it arrived, just in case, then buckled her seat-belt feeling a sense of betrayal. Magda had let her down. Although she didn't know her, in her head they'd made a pact and it had been broken. Another rejection to add to an ever-growing list. A total anti-climax.

The flat was empty, so Jessie decided to make the most of having a free kitchen by cooking a chilli; it would be nice to do something to repay Lauren a bit for all her support over the last few days. Giving her hands some-thing to do would help with the anxiety too. Jessie felt restless and wanted another glass of wine to untangle her twisting insides. There was an open bottle of chardonnay in the fridge that she was pretty sure belonged to Lauren, who she very much doubted would mind her taking some. Another passive-aggressive note fluttered to the floor; this time Marcus was warning everyone to stop using his ketchup. Jessie stuck the note back on the bot-tle, rolling her eyes, and poured the wine into a glass, savouring the glugging sound it made. Life, in no uncer-tain terms, was shit. May as well get drunk.

She sipped at the wine and peeled open a can of kidney beans that had been in the cupboard since the day she'd moved in, adding them into a saucepan with some chopped tomatoes. The smell of garlic and onions frying quickly overtook the whole flat and would linger for at least a day, thanks to the poor ventilation. As Jessie put some rice on to boil, her phone sounded with a message. Presuming it was Lauren saying she was on her way home, she left the stove briefly to rummage through her bag on the sofa.

Remember, I know everything about you, from the old r&b songs you sing in the shower to the way you take your coffee. I know you, Jessie, and that means I know you're afraid.

The message had been sent by an unsaved number, but the tone was familiar. Jessie stored it to her phone, stomach dropping, then checked WhatsApp to see if a profile picture came up. Nothing. She didn't need visual confirmation anyway; she knew it was him. Everything fell silent for a moment. Then a creak came, like a foot hitting the bottom of the stairs. Jessie spun around and scanned the room, The hissing of the blue flames continued as the pan of rice on the stove bubbled over with foam. She couldn't see anything; it had been a figment of her imagination.

'Fuck off!' she screamed at the phone, before smashing it face down onto the counter. 'Just leave me alone!'

She switched off the heat in a daze, hands unsteady, no longer hungry. A burnt mess stuck to the base of the pan, the water all but evaporated. She'd spent her entire life trying to do the right thing and *this* was the culmination of her efforts. Paying an extortionate rent to live with three others, one of whom copied her every move, another who near enough ignored her, in a damp and rundown flat, all the while receiving relentless threatening messages. She was single and miserable, with one long-term disastrous relationship behind her, the world's worst one-night stand, and a victim of a brutal assault. Even her best friend, Priya, had had enough, never mind Magda who hadn't even bothered to show up to collect her necklace. Lauren's friendship was the only constant, the one thing she could always rely on. But even she could be a little overbearing at times.

Jessie had never felt so alone, yet devoid of space. This was not at all how she'd envisioned her life would look at twenty-three. Her mum was already married by this age with a mortgage, car and lifelong plan, baby on the way. When she was a teenager and had heard about girls in her town having children at the age of eighteen, the grown-ups whispering about them, she couldn't understand the fuss. Being eighteen sounded *so* old. Until she'd turned that age herself. It was as though any age she mentally underlined as being the one to signify 'adulthood', jumped a little higher as soon as she reached it. Maybe the idea of fleeing to Scotland to live as a semi-recluse wasn't such a bad plan after all. It would just mean seriously saving for the next few months and hoping she could get her full deposit back from Happy Homes. But deep down, Jessie knew that no matter how far she ran from Matthew, her memories would always have to come along too. They were something she'd never be able to escape. Why was her life, and everybody in it, suddenly so ruthless? Unless she was drunk, her nerves were frayed.

Time to block yet another number. Or better still, in the morning have her own number changed, so that Matthew could never get to her again. She should have done that months ago. Jessie picked up her phone and hit the 'block' option, finding that she was then automatically shown a list of other banished contacts. She looked at the list twice. Strangely, alongside Matthew's original number that she'd already barred, was another number ending in '813', which she recognised. She couldn't remember having ever blocked anybody else on this particular phone. Then it hit her. That was Priya's number.

Quickly, she checked the digits she had saved under 'Priya Chandra' in her phonebook and saw they were entirely different. Could it be a glitch? Or had Rob somehow messed with her phone when he'd snuck out in the early hours of the morning? She couldn't understand why he'd do that but not steal it. But who else could have taken it? Jessie helped herself to more of Lauren's wine, unblocked Priya's real number and rang her to explain what had happened. As she hung up, a voice came from the hallway.

'I'm back!' Lauren called. 'Where are you?'

CHAPTER TWENTY-THREE

The following morning, Jessie woke with a cloudy head. Although she'd been asleep for a decent amount of time, a tiredness ran through her body. She was relieved not to bump into Marcus on her way to the shower. Afterwards, she sat on the edge of the bed wrapped in a towel and stared at the wall, wishing she could call in sick again. All she wanted to do was hibernate under the covers and shut out the world, maybe swallow down some more of the medication she was already doubling up on, wash it down with wine. Instead, she put on an old gym playlist and tried to summon the energy to get dressed, throwing on an old pair of high-waisted olive trousers and a white shirt. The pointed black court shoes she'd worn for her interview would go well enough with the outfit. She tied her hair back into a low ponytail and sighed; even using a hairbrush seemed to take extreme effort, but Jessie knew she couldn't let her façade slip. Inside, she was falling apart, a sea of turmoil, but on the surface, the water had to stay looking calm.

On her way to the bus stop, Jessie dropped into the local corner shop to treat herself to an iced coffee for the journey. It was the same shop she and Rob had been to. The front page of the *Argus*, a local paper, caught her eye, its main headline totally arresting: *Brighton Woman Vanishes*. She picked up a copy and scanned the page, taking in the accompanying photo. Her heart skipped a beat. In it, the missing woman was sitting in a café, smiling and looking directly at the camera, the top of a milkshake just seen on the table in front of her. She had bleached blonde hair and dark eyebrows and her face, a face Jessie had seen before, was round, warm and approachable. At first glance the missing woman could be mistaken for Lauren. No, surely, it couldn't be …? Hurriedly, she scanned the page again, searching for a name, desperate for confirmation. The article said the woman was a Polish student midwife, who volunteered at animal shelters and who had last been seen on Monday evening, four days ago, before she'd gone out running along the seafront. Nobody had been able to get hold of her since, which, apparently, was very out of character. Then Jessie's eyes settled on what she'd been searching for. A name. There it was, written in black and white: Magda Nowak. Her blood ran cold. *That's* why Magda hadn't shown up. An appeal from her friend and flatmate had been included too, begging Magda or anybody with information to get in touch. '*She is the type of person who'd do anything for anyone, we're all incredibly worried about her.*' The man behind the counter heard Jessie gasp. He recognised her because she came in often although today she looked different. Her knuckles had turned white.

The police were also calling for anyone with information to come forward. Should she contact them? Maybe it would be helpful for them to know that Magda had a history of running away. Although that might mean having to come clean to the girls about messaging and planning to meet Magda in the first place. It wouldn't look good to confess she'd been sneaking around, trying to meet up with a former flatmate who owed them money. She also still didn't want to answer any of their questions about her own attack. Jessie pushed the thought of contacting the police out of her mind – the last thing she needed on top of everything else was to get tied into another criminal investigation or have any tension in the flat to worry about. She carried the newspaper over to the till.

'Just this, thank you.'

As she put a £2 coin down on the counter, the shop owner noticed Jessie's hand was trembling.

'Awful what's happened, isn't it?' he said, bouncing his eyes from Jessie's face to the newspaper, then back again.

She nodded, unable to find the right words.

'Keep the change.'

He watched her walk out the door, head bent, reading the story again. From his counter, he observed Jessie take up her usual spot on the bus stop bench. She had pulled out her phone and appeared to be speaking urgently to whoever was on the other end.

It had been impossible to concentrate on much else, besides Magda going missing, for most of the day. The news had unsettled Jessie, and even Juliette had picked up on her nervy energy from across their shared desk, sending an email to ask if everything was okay. Jessie appreciated her concern but found it difficult to answer. In the end, she'd fobbed Juliette off by blaming her jitters on having drunk too much coffee to overcompensate for a bad night's sleep. Half true, at least. The second the clock hit five, Jessie sped towards the door and caught the first bus to Priya's – Priya, whom she'd called after seeing the news about Magda. She buzzed at the intercom impatiently.

'I'm so happy to see you,' she said, falling into the hallway the moment Priya opened the door. 'I've really started to freak out about everything, I can't get my thoughts in order properly. First my attack and now this? I kept expecting the police to come bursting into my office today, asking questions I can't answer.'

Priya and Zoe's flat smelled of home cooking; a Jamie Oliver recipe book lay open on the kitchen counter, their cat snoozed under the coffee table.

'Hey, hey, steady now,' Priya soothed, rubbing Jessie's back. 'One thing at a time.'

Priya could tell that Jessie had lost weight since she'd last seen her on New Year's Eve; her collarbone was poking out precariously.

'You look really gaunt, Jess. I'm worried about you. Take a seat, make yourself comfortable,' Priya said, pointing at the sofa. 'Zoe's not in. I'll dish up some dinner and we can talk about everything properly,'

Her home had a kitchen and lounge combo too, like Maver Place, only it was even smaller, meaning there was no room for a dining table. Priya and Zoe either ate their meals sitting on the sofa or curled up in bed. There was no separation between where they ate, slept and wound down.

Priya handed Jessie a plate to balance on her knees and noticed she was eyeing up a bottle of wine on the kitchen counter.

'Fancy a glass?'

'Yes please.'

Jessie gulped a mouthful down immediately. It was becoming a habit now, whenever she felt stressed or afraid, which at the moment was constantly, to reach for a bottle. Anything to soften the sharp edges.

'I just can't believe it. What do you think has happened to Magda? Do you think the police will be able to find her?' Jessie babbled, not paying attention to the wine she was sloshing over the sofa. 'I hope she's okay.'

Priya gently pushed the wineglass upright again.

'Forget Magda for a moment. Are *you* okay? You've been through hell, Jessie, you can't keep everything bottled up. Talk to me.'

After draining the wine in just a few mouthfuls, Jessie banged the glass on the coffee table, startling the cat.

'Please, talk to me,' Priya tried again. 'What are you most upset and worried about?'

Jessie began to bite frantically at the side of her thumbnail.

'What if our attacks are linked, somehow? What if it was Matthew who hurt Magda? Could he somehow have known we were planning to meet?'

It was a suggestion that caught Priya off guard. She stayed silent for a moment, mulling the idea over.

'What makes you say that? He doesn't even know Magda for starters and he has no reason to want to hurt her.'

That much was true, but still, Matthew had managed to unearth that Jessie had moved to Brighton without her being able to figure out how. He'd made it very clear that if she ever left him only bad things would happen. His resurfacing last night only confirmed those threats and that he wasn't going to let her move on without a fight. Matthew was like a worm buried deep inside her brain, wriggling through all of her jumbled thoughts and turning them rotten.

'No, but he knows me. When he sets his mind to terrorising me …' Jessie trailed off. 'Well, he does a pretty good job at that.'

Her thumb was beginning to bleed from all the gnawing. Priya tenderly pulled it away from her friend's mouth. This was a version of Jessie she hadn't seen in a long while. One who was a single pulled thread away from completely unravelling.

'Okay, well, what if Matthew isn't involved but the person who attacked me *has* done something to Magda?' Jessie continued. 'Christ, what if there's a madman going around targeting young women? Only Magda hasn't been so lucky? She's still missing.'

Jessie hugged a cushion to her chest and looked at Priya expectantly, chewing on her bottom lip.

'I wouldn't exactly say you were lucky, Jess, you have a skull fracture, for God's sake. Maybe it's the concussion making you feel like this, you've probably gone back to work far too soon.'

The sound of a neighbour's television blaring through the walls made them both jump.

'For all we know, Jess, this Magda woman could be completely fine. You mentioned before that she's got a history of leaving flats without paying her bills, so maybe she's just getting settled in a new place before reaching out to people, especially if she owes money again,' said Priya, as confidently as she could. 'Everything is going to be fine, don't let yourself get carried away.'

Jessie's eyes danced furiously across the ceiling, as if the answers might be hidden up there somewhere. Neither of them had touched their food.

'This is horribly familiar, you acting like this. It's exactly how you used to get at university,' Priya continued, as delicately as she could. 'You were constantly paranoid that Matthew was watching you or that he was engineering your life from afar, somehow. Don't get me wrong, I know he was awful to you and it's not easy to move on after being in a controlling relationship like that. But he's not here now. He doesn't exist in your life any more, other than in your head.'

Jessie knew the way Matthew operated though. One of his favourite tricks was to leave her second-guessing herself. For years she'd constantly found herself apologising for things she had no business apologising for – like not washing a plate 'correctly' or supposedly looking at men in the street. Living in fear and believing that everything that went wrong was *her* fault, that she was the reason Matthew behaved the way he did, was an ideology so deeply ingrained it had practically been tattooed over every inch of her skin with invisible ink.

'I need to speak to him, Priya,' Jessie announced suddenly. 'I have to know what it is he's trying to do by sending me these messages. Why has he dragged up that video again? And that card over Christmas. Then the attack. What if this Magda woman is in danger because of—'

Priya shushed her softly.

'You know that responding to him is a bad idea. Promise me you'll give it a few more days before making any decisions?' Priya said, looking stern. 'Promise me? Because you're obviously still in shock.'

Jessie shrugged defeatedly, looking dejected.

'If you're going to contact anybody, shouldn't it be the police?' she continued. 'I could come with you, if you want to go and talk an officer in person?'

Jessie wriggled uncomfortably in her seat, her cheeks flushing red.

'It's too late for that, isn't it?' Her voice trembled. 'They'll blame me for not coming in as soon as I saw the paper this morning.'

They looked at one another in silence, before Jessie broke away to pour herself more wine. She needed the numbing agent and the flat was getting gloomier by the minute.

'Is it all right if I crash on your sofa tonight? I don't want to have to head home now it's dark.'

Jessie sucked at her bleeding thumbnail once more. She could barely feel it.

CHAPTER TWENTY-FOUR

By the time Friday came around, Jessie felt an overwhelming sense of relief that it was the end of the working week. Her body jolted forward as the bus groaned its way down the hill to Woodingdean, her eyes sore from staying up late. She'd spent the night switching between staring out of Priya's living room window at the sea below and searching for Magda's name online, hoping there'd be more news. She'd quickly read every report written about her disappearance. The latest update from police was that they'd stepped up the search and had officers all across Sussex on the case. Press outlets beyond Brighton were taking an interest too and the same photo of Magda in a café, which had been splashed across the front page of the *Argus*, had been joined by another which looked as though it had been taken on a night out. Magda had an arm slung casually around the waist of a friend who had been cropped out of the shot. Jessie had lost track of the amount of times she'd tried and failed to find Magda on Instagram, desperate to see more photos of her and get information about her life, which somehow seemed intertwined with her own. She'd even asked Priya to search Matthew's friend list on Facebook to ensure they weren't connected on there, then checked Sofie and Marcus's too. Lauren had deleted her profile years ago, apparently.

On the short walk from the bus stop up to her office, Jessie texted Lauren to ask if she fancied catching up over dinner later that night in the flat, apologising for not making it home the night before. Lauren quickly replied saying she'd be back by seven and would grab a bottle of wine on her way. With Jessie having stayed at Priya's, she still hadn't asked the other Maver Place residents if they'd seen the news about Magda. Nobody had said anything in the group chat and she didn't want to bring it up. The story was starting to garner more public attention and, more than anything, Jessie wished she had seen whoever it was who had hurt her. Who had left her bloodied and afraid on the hard ground. She tried willing herself to remember, but reliving the memory instantly made her head spin and her pulse speed up. Life still looked blurred around the edges, but who knew if that was because of the concussion and the medication – not helped, of course, by her drinking wine – or whether her biggest fear had finally been realised: she'd lost her mind for good.

The day at work dragged slowly. Jessie tried to speed things along by regularly offering to make tea for Pamela and Juliette, and taking several lengthy trips to the bathroom, where she sat on the closed toilet lid and again searched for news online. A fresh quote appeared from a Sergeant Fiona Langley shortly after lunchtime, urging anybody who might have information to come forward. It gave Jessie a stomach ache, thinking about making a call to Sussex Police. Could she be withholding vital clues, without knowing it? When she returned to her desk, having spent her break walking aimlessly to the Co-op and back, Pamela and Juliette were waiting for her.

'Just in time. We thought you'd forgotten about the staff meeting.'

She had. Jessie followed them to a room in the doctors' loft, where a round table of people sat waiting. Pamela took out a notepad and began to jot down scribbles in shorthand, as Dr Statham shuffled a pile of papers and spoke dryly about how further budget cuts would be impacting their day-to-day. It was an effort for Jessie to concentrate. She tried to think of an intelligent question to ask at the end, to show Pamela she was engaged, because with everything else going on, she couldn't handle being in trouble at work too. Juliette and Cheryl looked worried as they listened.

By the time the meeting wrapped, it was almost the end of the day. Jessie schlepped wordlessly back downstairs to her desk with the others, dying to check if there had been any further updates on Magda's disappearance.

'They may ask us to reinterview for our roles,' said Pamela, once they were all safely back inside their area of the office. 'This happened a few years ago too.'

Juliette nervously drummed her fingers on the desk.

'These cuts are relentless,' she sighed. 'The workload gets bigger and the resources just shrink and shrink. Same with the police force.'

Jessie's ears pricked at the word 'police'. Her stomach somersaulted. The police *had* to find Magda and prove that she wasn't hurt. They just had to. She needed to know there wasn't still a monster out there, Matthew or otherwise, stalking the streets. Waiting for her in the shadows. Who had them both marked as targets.

'Mmm, awful,' Jessie mumbled, sensing that Pamela and Juliette were awaiting some kind of response from her.

'Well, let's try and enjoy our weekends as best we can still,' Juliette said resignedly, searching in her bag for car keys and heading towards the door.

Once Pamela had wished her a pleasant evening too, Jessie drew her phone out and typed 'Magda Nowak' into Google for the tenth time that day. Nothing since Sergeant Langley's statement.

Back at Maver Place, Jessie could tell Marcus was home by his thumping music. She kicked off her shoes, adding them to an ever-growing pile in the hallway, then headed into the kitchen to begin cooking dinner for herself and Lauren. As she brushed past the table, she trod on something slippery. Slimy but firm. A teabag that had fallen out when someone was changing the bin? Jessie looked down, then recoiled. In the centre of one of the white checked floor tiles, lay a limp goldfish with silver flecks on its tail, its insides forced out from the pressure of her step. She felt her throat constrict as she stared, revolted by it. She looked around the room, not knowing what else to do. The poor fish couldn't be left there, but the thought of having to scoop it up made her queasy. She retched.

'Hey, Jess, is that you who's just come in?' Sofie's voice came from the hallway.

Jessie whipped round and waited for her to walk into the room, then had a flash of panic that it might look as though she were responsible for the death of the fish. She heard two sets of footsteps and Henry's laugh. They both appeared in the doorway.

'I just found it like this,' Jessie stammered, pointing at the floor. 'How could it have happened?'

The couple looked at the dead thing by Jessie's feet. Registering what it was, Sofie screwed up her face and buried it on Henry's chest, refusing to look again.

'Oh Jesus, that's horrible.'

'It must have jumped out,' Henry said calmly, after a few moments.

He began stroking Sofie's hair, in an effort to comfort her.

'Seriously?'

Jessie looked at the bowl in the centre of the table. It had an open top but was placed about a metre in; the tiny fish would have had to be seriously powerful to reach this far. It couldn't have jumped. Nor could it have landed there as a result of someone accidentally bumping the table. She just knew it had been done deliberately.

'Henry, I really can't see that being the case,' she said, noticing that Sofie was wearing yet another dress similar to one she owned.

'Sure you can,' he smoothly replied, continuing to caress Sofie, who had turned her head slightly so that she could see Jessie with one eye.

They all kept their gaze deliberately away from the floor.

'This happened to my sister's fishes a bunch of times when we were kids,' Henry continued.

'Which one is it, Jessie?' asked Sofie, still not wanting to look herself.

'It was mine, Sofe. The fish meant to represent me!' Jessie could hear her voice getting increasingly higher.

She knew she was starting to sound paranoid, unhinged even.

'And now someone has killed it. Or so it seems.'

Henry almost smirked.

'It's not like it's a dog.'

He walked towards the counter and tore off a few sheets of kitchen roll, then bent down to scoop up the remains of the fish. Jessie remained rooted to the floor as Henry crouched down by her knees then stood back up. There was still a red smear on the floor and gunk covering her foot. That had to go. Now. Jessie took a floor wipe out from under the sink and scrubbed at her sole, while balancing against the table. The other three fish swam on, oblivious to being one short. Her foot still didn't feel clean.

'Who did this?' Jessie asked again, as Henry threw the bundle of paper towels in the bin.

The lid clanged shut.

'Did what?'

Marcus had heard raised voices from his room and had come to investigate. He'd picked up a familiar unsettled feeling ever since Lauren had confessed to talking to Zach's friends on her night out with Jessie and Sofie. He'd primed himself to be on red alert for any more trouble.

'One of the fish went kamikaze and jumped out the bowl,' Henry interjected before Jessie could speak, plonking himself down on the sofa. 'And now the girls are all in a tizzy about it, acting like Freddy Krueger's just burst through the door with a goldfish vendetta.'

Sofie walked over to join him, deliberately avoiding the patch on the floor where the fish had just been, checking the bowl on her way to ensure the others were unharmed.

'Henry, stop it. This isn't funny. Jessie's having a difficult enough time as it is.'

Henry shrugged, but didn't apologise.

'Actually, I looked up about caring for them when Lauren brought them home – apparently they can jump out of their own accord,' said Marcus with an unnecessary cough, 'if they get scared by loud noises or have dirty water.'

'Well, I've made sure the bowl is clean,' Sofie shot back. 'It's you who always has the music blaring.'

'I wasn't being accusatory,' Marcus deadpanned.

They all stood awkwardly, nobody quite able to land upon the right words. Jessie pulled out another floor wipe and ran it over her foot, then the soiled tile. The bin lid sounded again. Even the fish version of herself had been scared, literally, to death.

'It could've been any of ours, I guess, it's just bad luck it was yours,' Sofie eventually said. 'We should get a fish-bowl with a lid.'

Jessie nodded but didn't really care. Whether or not she owned a goldfish was hardly of pressing importance right now, but she was still unnerved thinking that some-body could have done it deliberately. Or was her mind just going into overdrive? It was difficult not to read mal-ice into it all, searching for clues, given that nothing much seemed to make sense lately: her phone temporar-ily disappearing; Priya's number being blocked; the mes-sages from Matthew; the attack; Magda going missing – and now this. In lieu of a better idea, she boiled the kettle and poured some penne into a saucepan.

'What are you making, Jess?' asked Sofie.

'Just dinner for me and Lauren.'

'Would it be okay if we join you? I can do a side salad. Henry's cleaner is over at the moment, so we figured we'd kill time here for a bit.'

As much as she wanted to, Jessie could hardly say no. 'Of course.'

Marcus sat at the table, wary of being in such close proximity to Henry, waiting for Jessie to finish cooking so he could make a start on his own food. He looked intently at the remaining fish. Interesting creatures. He envied their supposedly shoddy memories.

'Any idea where Lauren is?' Jessie asked Sofie a short time later. 'The food is almost ready.' Sofie shook her head.

It had gone seven o'clock so Jessie tried calling and got Lauren's voicemail.

'We could always leave some in the pan for her to reheat later?' Sofie suggested.

After Jessie had served dinner, Marcus put a cottage pie in the microwave and watched as the others started eating their pasta. Apparently, Henry couldn't even keep his mouth closed then. When Marcus's food was cooked, he joined them, eating the pie from the black plastic container with a layer of mayonnaise on top. Jessie frowned, looking at it. Despite having lived with Marcus for months, she still found that bizarre. She waited for somebody to mention Magda. Surely they must have seen the news? It was all over social media.

'Has anyone seen the news recently? About that local girl going missing. Apparently she lived in Brighton,' Jessie asked, trying to sound casual.

Marcus looked up. Henry shook his head.

'Who even reads the news these days?' laughed Sofie, as she helped herself to more salad. 'It's all so depressing, I just avoid it now.'

Her reply surprised Jessie.

'She's around our age and her name is Magda. It's all over Twitter.'

She could've sworn Marcus choked a little.

'That's sad, hope she turns up,' Sofie said disinterestedly. 'Is anyone going to use the washing machine after this or am I okay to put a load through?'

'Magda who?' asked Marcus.

Lauren walked into the kitchen, arms folded across her chest.

'It's Magda Nowak,'

She looked worried. Jessie put a forkful of pasta in her mouth but found she was unable to swallow.

'Remember? She used to live here.'

CHAPTER TWENTY-FIVE

'It's definitely her.' Henry shook his head in disbelief and turned his phone around to show the table the photo of Magda sitting in the café.

Marcus squinted and looked at Lauren, who had turned white, waiting for her reaction.

'What does it say?' Sofie stammered. 'Let me see.'

'Not much, just that she was last seen by a friend on Monday and that police are urgently appealing for her return. Nobody has heard from her since.'

Sofie's mouth dropped open.

'That's familiar,' she said, exhaling forcefully. 'So, she's been in Brighton this whole time? I presumed she'd gone back to Poland or something after she ran off and left us saddled with all her bills.'

Henry passed his phone to her.

'Looks that way.'

Jessie studied them all intently, quietly trying to draw clues from any flicker of movement on their faces.

'It's all over the news. There's a big search happening,' Lauren said, sounding upset. 'What if it's something bad this time and she hasn't just run away?'

Lauren was always on her wavelength, Jessie thought, nodding. Marcus stayed still and quiet, not taking his eyes from Lauren. It annoyed Jessie that he seemed so obsessed with her. In all her time at Maver Place, it was only ever Lauren that he bothered making an ounce of effort for.

'Are you all right?' he asked.

Lauren made a face that indicated she wasn't.

'Should we call the police?' she asked, looking at them all in turn.

Henry's lip curled in response.

'And say what? She used to live here and now she doesn't? You'd be wasting police time.'

'It's a joke!' Sofie spat abruptly, making Jessie jump. 'I can't believe she's got all these people out looking for her when she's probably just run off again. She's a thief and a liar.'

Jessie was shocked by the venom with which she spoke. Angry red dots appeared on Sofie's cheeks. Henry's face had clouded over too.

'I'll keep an eye on the news,' Marcus said pointedly, which made Henry laugh.

'Nice one, big guy. That'll help.'

'Well, if you've got a better idea I'd love to hear it?' Lauren snapped.

She had clearly been rocked by the news too. After a few seconds, Marcus took his plate over to the bin and threw the microwavable container inside, too lazy to put it in the recycling bin. He then busied himself with re-arranging the fridge. The whirring of the aged extractor fan became the only other sound in the room. More than anything, Jessie wanted to leave the kitchen which sud-denly felt cloyingly hot, and hide in her room, but some-thing about everybody's reactions made her feel as though she'd been nailed down to her chair.

'So, does anybody have nice plans for the weekend?' she asked timidly, moving the pasta around her plate with a fork.

Lauren knew how she felt; her appetite had upped and left too.

'Not really. I might go for a walk over the Downs,' she said, grateful for Jessie's attempt to normalise the sense of sticky discomfort coating the walls. 'How about you?'

The three remaining fish were now all floating at the bottom of the bowl.

'Nothing much either, probably just stay at Priya's when she gets back tomorrow.'

Lauren started drawing heavily on her e-cigarette, the familiar chocolate-box aroma overpowering the garlicky dinner smell. It only heightened Jessie's now-constant nausea and she couldn't stop a wave passing through her, causing an involuntary tremor.

'I'm going to the shop to get some real cigarettes,' Lauren said finally, throwing the vape pen onto the table and rubbing her temples. 'Jessie, do you want to come with me?'

'I'll stay and do the washing-up,' she replied, sensing that Lauren might need some time alone to gather her thoughts.

When the door slammed shut, it took a few moments before anyone moved, then Henry scraped his chair back.

'Shall we get going, then?' he ruffled the top of Sofie's head, making her new fringe stick out at a funny angle.

She looked like a helpless baby deer. Her slender arms were so delicate, it was a miracle they didn't snap as she went about daily life. Jessie often forgot how young she was too, having barely turned twenty-one. Henry scuffed his boat shoe on the floor impatiently. Sofie locked eyes with Jessie.

'I'm staying here tonight.' Her words were carefully considered.

Henry looked irritated.

'Why? It's so much nicer at mine.'

Sofie glared at him. Jessie immediately regretted not going to the shop with Lauren. She could sense an argument brewing.

'What's the point of me paying rent to live in this flat if I'm never in it?' Sofie replied. 'Hmm? Go on, tell me.'

Marcus stopped rummaging in the fridge. Henry said nothing; she had a point.

'I stay at yours basically every night, yet you're still too afraid to properly ask me to move in with you because of your bloody mother,' she continued. 'I've tried *everything* to make her like me, to feel like I'm worthy of being with you, but to be honest, my patience is wearing thin.'

Jessie looked at the doorway, desperate to leave the table. Could she just get up and walk out without saying anything?

'You know it's not as simple as that,' Henry hissed next to her. 'She's not well, Sofie. I don't want to upset her.'

Marcus shut the fridge and silently left the room. Jessie looked at the doorway again, then got up and left too.

'See what you've done, Henry?' she heard from the hallway.

In her room, Jessie sat cross-legged on her bed, then got up to double-check the door was locked. A minute or so later she jiggled the handle again. She felt similar to a spider trapped under a glass, in that her surroundings all looked the same, yet were slightly distorted. These were the same four walls that Magda had slept within. She wished Priya wasn't away, tonight of all nights, otherwise she'd have called a taxi and headed straight over to her place.

Jessie paced her room, then decided to try and distract herself by watching something quietly on her laptop. A comedy would be best; a bit of light relief was desperately needed. She'd never seen that side of Sofie before and it was unsettling; their youngest flatmate was usually so caring and compassionate and no matter how bad things had been left with Magda, surely Sofie would be concerned about her? She was beginning to resent how similarly Sofie was dressing like her too – the novelty had well and truly worn off and Jessie had noticed even her voice had changed now. It was creepy.

Eventually, Jessie drifted off to the sound of canned laughter. The room was dark, apart from the usual chink of moonlight that shone in through the gap in the curtains and the laptop switched itself onto a black screen-saver. A small clock in the bottom right-hand corner showed it was nearing midnight when the rattling sound started up. It worked its way into Jessie's dream at first, where she was frantically trying to figure her way out of The Lanes again, then tugged her back out of sleep. Was it happening in real life? She sat up and looked towards the door. The handle was moving – somebody on the other side was trying to get in. Then a knock came.

'Jessie, are you in there?' Sofie whispered. 'I just want to talk about earlier, about the way I acted at dinner. I'm so sorry for that.'

She sounded normal, but still … Jessie didn't move, not wanting to let on that she was inside and awake. She closed her laptop quietly and placed it on the floor, then drew the covers over herself, pretending to be asleep. She stayed as still as possible until she heard Sofie sigh and go back to her own bedroom.

CHAPTER TWENTY-SIX

Jessie struggled to get back sleep after that, her mind busy, fighting against her weary body. Somewhere in the early hours of the morning she decided a camomile tea might help. Throwing her gym hoody on and making as little sound as possible unlocking the door, she tiptoed downstairs. Reaching the last step, she stood opposite the junk cupboard in the hall and paused, considering taking a look inside. There could be more letters addressed to Magda in there, or something that might shed some light on her whereabouts. It was worth a try.

She slid the bolt over and stepped inside, leaving the door slightly ajar so as not to feel suffocated because it was only a couple of metres deep in there. She felt around for the light switch and clicked it on. It had been painted over with the same cream colour as the walls, meaning all the smeared fingerprints of other residents showed up prominently. The thought that Magda would have touched the same switch made Jessie shudder. She was echoing the life of a missing woman. She didn't believe in ghosts, but what if Magda had died and was watching her now, somehow searching for fragments of her old life? Jessie shook her head. It was too easy for her exhausted, overly medicated mind to get carried away. Jessie approached the box she'd found the letter in previously and realised a few words had been scrawled on the side in looped, permanent marker. It wasn't the neatest writing, but it looked as though it said 'Beth's stuff'.

Nobody had ever mentioned a Beth before. Another box, on the shelf below, had a label with 'Georgia' on it, another new name. Inside, Jessie found more letters addressed to various ex-tenants who'd since moved on, little paper reminders that renting is nothing but an endless cycle of living in a home that never really quite belongs to you. A home where you have to email a stranger asking for permission before you hang a picture up in 'your' living room, which you share with people you either found through a letting agent or online and took a gamble on. It was a thin thread that wove all these lives together and placed them under one roof. If she'd have gone for the basement apartment that smelled of rubber, at least she wouldn't be caught up in this Magda mess. Maybe she'd have never been attacked, either. Then again, if Matthew was involved, as she fretted he was, then perhaps things would still be exactly the same. Only her bedroom would be smaller. All these names, all these woman who'd passed through this flat before her ... why had none of them stayed? Suddenly the cupboard felt like a coffin and Jessie wanted out. But when she turned to leave she saw the door was no longer ajar.

'No, no it can't have,' she muttered to herself, pushing at it harder.

When it didn't budge, she began to panic. It was jammed. Jessie thought about banging on it loudly in the hope that Marcus might wake up and let her out – his room was just across the way, after all. But then she'd have to explain why she was looking through boxes of old possessions in the storage cupboard at three in the morning. Her phone was back upstairs so she couldn't call for help either. She thumped her fist against the wooden door again, with more force this time. The air tasted stale. She had to get out, there was no way she could wait until the morning to be found. Her panic levels were rising and it was getting harder to breathe by the second. Jessie crouched down and put her head between her legs, then tried to call for help.

'Marcus? Hello, Marcus?' she shouted, the walls eating her words, transforming them into useless muffles.

Jessie could feel her forehead had turned clammy. She banged at the door again and again and again, until finally, it swung open. She sagged with relief momentarily, then stiffened. Henry was there, standing in the dark, the moon shining in through the kitchen window highlighting one side of his chiselled face. He was naked from the muscular waist up, wearing only navy jogging bottoms, laughing.

'Your face is a picture right now.'

A typical school bully prank for him to have played, locking her in that tight space with the spiders and the damp, so soon after she'd been attacked too, when her nerves were so evidently in tatters to everybody around her. He probably got off on playing tricks like that.

'I didn't think you'd stayed here?' she asked, finally rediscovering her voice.

Henry grimaced.

'It didn't feel right leaving Sofie here to sleep alone. She's been so jumpy lately, especially since that day you all thought someone broke in.'

With that, he smirked. Jessie needed to get out of the confined space.

'So, no chance of a thank-you kiss for rescuing you, then?' Henry said, still obviously amused.

'You think that's funny?' Jessie said, pushing past him and catching her breath. 'Locking someone in a cupboard isn't a joke, Henry.'

She felt braver now that she was back in the hallway.

'*I* didn't lock you in.' He shot her a withering look. 'Sofie woke me up when she heard a noise and asked me to check downstairs.'

Jessie was about to walk upstairs without saying anything, but then stopped a few steps up and looked down on Henry.

'Doors don't just bolt themselves.'

She let her words hang in the air for effect, then headed back to her bedroom, making sure her own door was tightly locked.

Jessie awoke again a few hours later but stayed in her room, reluctant to go downstairs until she heard Sofie and Henry leave. She was still shaken from being trapped in the cupboard and couldn't handle the thought of having to make awkward small talk with anybody either. It was as though irate guard dogs were patrolling the corridors outside. Her stomach rumbled, demanding toast with jam. She was thirsty, too, but didn't want to leave the safety of her room. The atmosphere in the flat was extremely tense now and she just wanted to hide, blocking it all out. Jessie searched desperately through her handbag, hoping to find an old bottle of water, but had no luck. As her thirst grew, she knew she'd have to brave it. She put her headphones in for a boost of courage, a visual signal to show she didn't want to chat right now, and headed downstairs.

Reaching the kitchen and finding it empty, she breathed a sigh of relief and leant against the counter. A note from Sofie had been left on the table, reminding everyone to feed the three remaining fish. Lauren walked in.

'Morning, babe, how's it going?' She sounded downcast.

There was a little smear of paint on her nose so she'd obviously been working on one of her canvases. Jessie responded as she usually would. How ridiculous would it sound to bring up that Henry had imprisoned her in a cupboard in the middle of the night? Especially given that Lauren had seemed so rattled by the news about Magda yesterday.

'Not too bad; had a bit of a rough night's sleep so just getting some of this on the go.'

As Jessie raised her mug of coffee in the air, a bit of brown liquid dripped onto the floor. Lauren gave a small chuckle, but Jessie could tell it was forced.

'Is everything okay?' she asked.

Lauren gave a half-hearted shrug.

'It's such a stressful time at the moment. Seeing Magda all over the news, someone I lived with and was so close to ...' Lauren's eyes started glazing over. 'It's a shock.'

Jessie placed the mug down and wrapped her arms around Lauren in a hug. Her shoulders jerked.

'I can't imagine how it must feel and I'm so sorry. If you ever want to talk about anything, you know I'm always here.'

After the attack, Lauren had really been the one to step up and look after her when she had needed a friend the most. Lending an ear was the least Jessie could do in exchange.

'How about we head into town later?' Jessie suggested. 'Cheer ourselves up with a bit of retail therapy and grab a slice of cake.'

She didn't especially want to be out in a crowd, but felt she could manage it with Lauren by her side. Lauren reached for a sheet of kitchen roll.

'Sorry about this, I hate crying in front of people,' she sniffed, dabbing at her eyes. 'Sounds great. I think we could both use a bit of that.'

They decided to walk into the city centre. Jessie kept her hands buried deep inside her pockets and her collar pulled up, wondering how Lauren could stand to smoke and expose her fingers to the wind like that. She guessed her vape pen had definitely been set aside for now. As they began their climb of North Street, the large swooping road leading up to the Churchill Square mall, they passed a Subway sandwich shop. Sitting on the floor on dirty sleeping bags outside were two homeless women, one of whom was stroking a German Shepherd dog. A paper coffee cup containing a pitiful few silver coins had been placed next to their cardboard sign asking for change.

They looked bored and defeated, watching a crowd of people with weekend plans rush past them, barely pausing to acknowledge the two skinny figures. Jessie spotted them from a few metres away and realised she recognised the woman on the right, the one with the long dark hair. She was wearing the same beanie as she had on that evening when Jessie had stood under the Christmas lights and noticed her sitting on the steps around the Clock Tower. The image of the woman's sunken eyes contrasted against the twinkling decorations had stayed with her, along with the fact that she and the woman appeared to be close in age. It was upsetting to think how their lives had probably started off in a similar way but had turned out so differently. Really, homelessness was a misfortune that could befall anybody. She herself was only ever one missed rent payment away from having to move back in with her parents or crash on Priya and Zoe's couch. Not everybody had that support system. She didn't recognise the other woman with dreadlocks, who looked a lot older, petting the dog.

The younger woman connected with Jessie's sympathetic gaze, then moved her eyes over to Lauren. Quickly, she then looked down at her lap, trying to cover her face with her hair and whispered something to her friend.

'Evil,' the older woman rasped, pointing at Lauren, who flinched but didn't stop walking. 'That one is pure evil!'

A few strangers heard and turned to look in their direction. Lauren sped up and so did Jessie. She could hear the homeless women starting to argue with one another.

'It's really sad to see so many people on the streets, isn't it, especially when they're obviously on drugs and not with it,' Lauren said calmly, when they were far enough away not to be heard.

Jessie glanced back over her shoulder. The dark-haired woman was quivering. She didn't know what to think. But Lauren could be right; the woman with dreadlocks was under the influence of something.

'Can we pop into Boots quickly? I just need to grab a few bits,' Lauren continued, eyes facing forward.

'Sure,' nodded Jessie, as they approached the store.

She turned back again. The women had gone back to fussing over the dog. Once inside the shop, Jessie and Lauren went in separate directions, with Lauren heading towards the pharmacy section at the back.

Jessie wandered through the rows of neatly displayed toiletries. Something about the fact they were all new and untampered with felt like a head stroke to her. She appreciated order. A rotating display unit of pristine nail varnish bottles called her name and she picked out a pale pink one then put it back again. It'd be a tricky purchase to justify, given that she already had plenty in similar shades at home. She ran a speedy mental checklist of basic essentials and realised her shampoo was running low, so at least she could warrant buying a replacement for that. Perhaps a new sleep spray to relax her before bed wouldn't go amiss either.

Lauren found her in the haircare aisle, standing between the shampoos and a shelf full of dyes, looking at what was on offer.

'Maybe you should go blonde like me?' she suggested, picking up a box of at-home bleach.

The woman on the front of the box grinned inanely back at them.

'I can dye it for you later, if you want?' Lauren continued, picking up a small section of Jessie's hair and twirling it between her fingers. 'It's funny how you and Sofie have the same sort of hairstyle, yet *we're* the ones who are so close in the flat.'

She gave a laugh that sounded like a bark. Jessie was a little taken aback by the suggestion but tried not to let it show. She eyed Lauren, trying to work out if she was joking. But it quickly transpired she wasn't and was patiently waiting for an answer.

'I wouldn't suit hair like yours,' Jessie said, bewildered, which made Lauren frown.

'Of course you would. I wish you had more confidence Jessie,' she implored. 'I'll show you how to do your make-up like mine too, that'll help you get the look. Some proper bright red lipstick would definitely give you more self-assurance too.'

Jessie was beginning to feel uncomfortable. She did really admire Lauren's style but it just wasn't her. Lauren probably had good intentions to help build her self-esteem back up but it was an odd suggestion – she couldn't imagine Priya or Nicole ever saying anything like that. Maybe coming into town had been a mistake. Jessie longed to go home and curl up in bed alone again, to swallow enough pills to sleep away the rest of the weekend.

In all the months they'd lived together, she'd worried about coming across as a meek little loser chasing her flatmate around, looking for friendship, but now it felt that the tables were turning. Lauren was almost bordering on clingy.

'I'd be up for a make-up tutorial at some point, but I think the hair idea is a no go,' Jessie kept her voice airy. 'I'm useless at fashion and beauty, which is probably why I've been wearing the same stuff for years.'

That answer placated Lauren slightly.

'Let's buy some bits now then, we can do it when we get home! I'll get you them as a present.'

Lauren grabbed Jessie's hand and animatedly dragged her back to where the different beauty brands were housed by the entrance. She started gesturing wildly at the products, waving a black eyeliner pencil around, then took the cap off and drew a mark on the back of her hand.

'See the way it smudges?'

Jessie struggled to keep up with everything Lauren was saying, her brain feeling like a wrung-out sponge. She was chattering away at such a speed, throwing eyeshadows into the basket too, it was a miracle she could still breathe. It was starting to feel over-intense. Was Lauren trying to buy her friendship? What with the numerous takeaways, drinks on nights out and now this? If this was her way of trying to help Jessie forget about the attack, it was only making her uncomfortable.

'Really, it's not fair for you to pay,' Jessie insisted, folding her arms across her chest. 'And I don't want you to. I can buy my own stuff.'

Getting a round in was one thing, but splurging on unnecessary gifts was another. Jessie appreciated Lauren's generosity but didn't want to be thought of as a charity case.

'Sorry, you're right,' Lauren laughed, smearing a lipstick inside her wrist. 'Can we do the makeover when we get back, then take some photographs together? I need to show people on Instagram that not only am I still alive but I actually have friends too.'

Jessie found herself lost for words. Something about Lauren was off today. If she didn't know her better, she'd say she might even be drunk. She decided that she'd head to Priya's after the makeover. They needed to discuss Matthew anyway. Having kept her promise that she'd think things over before reaching out to him, Jessie had now decided firmly that she still wanted – no, needed – to do it. She needed answers from him and to fully draw a line under their relationship, because even when she wasn't actively trying to work out how he knew she'd moved to Brighton, or whether Matthew had been involved in her attack, his face still hummed in the back of her brain, like a neon sign in a late-night greasy spoon. A constant, dull buzz. Not always at the forefront, but present nonetheless. She was desperate for just one thing in her life to be clear-cut for a change, to destroy the last of her connections to him so she could attempt to start building something better for herself.

When she'd had enough of piling up a stash of products, identical to those in her own bedroom, Lauren walked over to the queue to pay for them, her movements jerky, like a wind-up toy, and unlike the other sauntering shoppers. Jessie followed her and withdrew a £20 note from her purse.

'Don't be silly, let me buy these,' she tried again, trying to push the note into Lauren's free hand.

'No, I want to get them for you. You've had a rough time and today is about cheering you up.'

Lauren sounded stern. She clenched her fist into a tight ball, so the money couldn't be placed in her palm and Jessie stopped protesting. By now she knew that when Lauren had set her mind on something, she rarely budged. She put the money back in her purse, vowing to secretly transfer it into Lauren's bank account later on, the details of which she already had saved from sending over her portion of the council tax, and watched her interact with the cashier. Lauren joked as the make-up was slipped into a carrier bag, along with the mandatory skincare vouchers you always seemed to be given in Boots but which nobody ever seemed to spend. Jessie's own purse had several expired ones in it. The shop assistant laughed along, clearly happy to have a customer not glued to their phone while paying for once. Lauren's gravitational pull was very much in full effect. Her charm and humour could draw in anyone she set her sights on.

As she waited, Jessie pulled up Twitter on her phone and began absentmindedly scrolling through. She laughed at a funny quip someone had posted, then caught up on the latest celebrity divorce announcement. Then she saw it. A tweet from the *Argus*. A dog walker had discovered a body washed up on the beach earlier that day. Before she'd even clicked the link to read the full article, Jessie's own body braced with anticipation. When Magda's photo loaded at the top of the web page, the room began to spin. The overhead fluorescent bulbs became blinding. She gripped onto a shelf of allergy medication and gasped so loudly that a nearby couple stopped their conversation and stared. Their toddler began to wail in its buggy, kicking her chubby legs around. Magda wasn't missing. She was dead.

CHAPTER TWENTY-SEVEN

'Are you okay?' Lauren touched Jessie's arm lightly, making her jump. 'You've gone all pale.'

Jessie steadied herself, wishing that the lingering couple would stop eavesdropping and soothe their screaming child instead. She threw them a condemning look and headed to the exit of the shop, needing to catch her breath. Once outside, she showed Lauren the news report and watched her read it, her eyes rushing from left to right, taking in each sentence as quickly as she could.

'It says that at this stage of the investigation the death is not believed to be suspicious,' Jessie blurted out, unable to wait. 'Suicide ... that's just so heartbreaking. Or do you think she was drunk at the time?'

Hopefully her own attack was unconnected. Maybe some of the guilt she'd been carrying around over the last few days would start to shift when the post-mortem results came in and ruled out any foul play. But if they didn't? Lauren's face remained blank, digesting the blow.

'"The police are awaiting the pathologist's report."' She read the last sentence aloud, then handed Jessie back her phone and reached into her handbag for her tobacco, attempting to roll with trembling hands.

Lauren coughed as she took a strong drag, the end of her cigarette glowing hotly.

'Are you okay, Lauren? And do you think Sofie and Marcus will be upset? It must be awful that this has happened to someone you know,' Jessie spoke slowly.

It felt too serious to post about it in their group chat, a space littered with emojis and passive-aggressive messages asking whose wet clothes had been left in the washing machine, stopping anybody else from using it.

'Even if they are upset it won't be to the same extent that I am,' Lauren said, looking stunned. 'Marcus was going through a real low point when Magda lived with us – he was in his room literally *all* the time – and it's not like Sofie was often around either. It was just me and Magda, we were best friends.'

Jessie couldn't imagine how Marcus could spend even more time in his bedroom than he did currently, forever locking himself away from the world, emerging only at mealtimes or to go to work.

'I'm so sorry this has happened, Lauren. If you ever want to talk about it with someone, you know where I am. My door is always open.'

The couple left the shop, their focus back on their toddler, who was enjoying being cooed at. Lauren and Jessie moved slightly to get out of the family's way.

'This feels like a bad dream,' Lauren replied, her features still unreadable. 'I think I'm going to head home, I don't want to stay out any more. Are you coming?'

Wanting to try and get hold of Priya first, Jessie decided to hang back in the city centre for a bit longer. She'd find a café and call her, preferring to do it outside of the flat.

'I just need to sort a few bits out first, then I'll get the bus back. Can you manage on your own?' she said, hoping Lauren might prefer to be alone anyway. 'If not, I can come now if you'd rather.'

She'd make it up to her later, by cooking a nice dinner and spending the evening with her, being on hand in case she wanted to talk about anything.

'It's fine, babe.' Lauren coughed again, almost sounding relatively normal. 'I could use a bit of time to myself. See you in a bit.'

A trail of smoke followed Lauren down the hill, as Jessie headed in the opposite direction towards a coffee shop. It was a small boutique one with bunches of fresh flowers lining the outside (and therefore bloggers too), just past the point on Western Road where Brighton 'ended' and Hove began. She hadn't been in the coffee shop since university but suddenly found herself yearning for one of its famed hot chocolates, hoping a sugar hit might help her feel less spaced.

Images of Magda floated through her mind as she walked. Magda taking in her last breath. Was it an accident? Had she screamed? Would anybody have heard? She could see glimmers of the sea that had swallowed her up just peeking out from the end of the road leading down towards the beachfront. How awful it must have been for the unfortunate person who had discovered Magda's lifeless body too. Jessie entered the coffee shop, allowing the warmth of it to embrace her, feeling dazed. She ordered a drink and the server behind the till, a beefy man with a wiry beard and sailor tattoos, promised to bring it over. Taking a seat by the counter, just in case he forgot what she looked like, Jessie pulled out her phone. Priya answered after two short rings.

'I've seen the news,' she said immediately. 'I can't believe it – that poor, poor woman. She was training to be a midwife, what a waste of a life. Imagine feeling so trapped that ending it all was your only way out.'

'It's heartbreaking, isn't it?' Jessie agreed, shaking her head even though Priya obviously couldn't see. 'She said there was something she wanted to tell me, that evening we were meant to meet so I could return the necklace to her. Now I'll never know what it was.'

There was silence on the other end of the line.

'To be honest, Jess, you have so much other stuff to be dealing with right now that I'm not sure it's a good idea to invest much more of your energy into this,' Priya said eventually, exhaling loudly at the end. 'I know it's really upsetting but try not to think too much about it. You know Lauren, you trust her, and she says this

Magda was messed up and left them in a bit of a financial fix. It sounds like she could have been caught up in all sorts.'

The man with the beard placed the hot chocolate down on Jessie's table atop a small china saucer. She nodded thank you in his direction and he smiled back, then returned to his usual post behind the counter, wiping down the nozzle used for foaming milk on the coffee machine.

'I hear you. It's just all so surreal ...' She paused, taking her first sip. 'But what do I do with the necklace I found now? It was obviously important to Magda; maybe her family would want it back?'

The drink scalded her tongue.

'Wasn't she from Poland? I thought the news reports said her family don't live in the UK?' Priya replied. 'Look, I know you care and it's amazing that you do, but you can't take in every stray dog and take on every stranger's problems. Give it to Lauren or Sofie, maybe one of them would like something to remember Magda by.'

Jessie decided to sleep on it. Perhaps she could contact Magda's friend who had been quoted in the newspaper and return the jewellery to her? Anything to get it out of her own bedroom, where, even though it was small, it seemed to dominate a lot of space.

'I have something I wanted to tell you,' Jessie said, suddenly remembering the purpose of their phone call. 'I've been thinking about your advice, how you said I can't let Matthew ruin my life, and having really considered it, I'm going to message him. I wondered if you would help me work out what to say?'

She blew on the hot chocolate before taking another gulp. It was so thick, almost like drinking a sauce, coating her throat in a dense layer on the way down. Priya gave a heavy sigh, making the call crackle and Jessie's ear tingle involuntarily.

'Well, I don't like this idea but you know I'll back you. If you really think it's for the best?'

Jessie felt something rise up and strengthen within her; it was a feeling she hadn't experienced in a long time, something close to a shred of fighting spirit.

'I do. I need to try get and get closure over everything. I need so badly for there to be a definitive end point to all of this; I feel like I can't truly start my life over until there is.'

Priya stayed silent.

'I've started to realise that life is too short to be afraid of your past. Look at Magda – nobody knows when their time is up. I've spent too much of mine looking over my shoulder and jumping at my own shadow, I need to start rebuilding myself.'

There was a change in Jessie's voice, a determination that Priya hadn't heard before.

'Why don't you come round mine and we can figure out the best approach?' she offered.

'Can we say seven? I should spend some time with Lauren first and make sure she's handling the news okay; she was acting really strangely today,' explained Jessie.

'Would you mind if I stay over too? It would feel weird sleeping in Magda's old room tonight.'

They said their goodbyes. Jessie finished the last of her drink, pushed her chair back and walked to the bus stop.

Back in the flat, Lauren stood in her bedroom, painting. Pulling the deep red strokes of oil across the canvas helped to dispel some of the unidentifiable emotions she'd been feeling, ever since Jessie had shown her the article. She mixed a blob of black into the crimson, turning it an even bloodier shade and swiped again. The artwork was coming together nicely and would soon be finished. There was a knock on the door. She balanced the messy palette precariously on the edge of her easel and opened it to find Jessie standing on the landing, holding a family size bar of Dairy Milk.

'Just to say thank you for the make-up,' she explained, handing the bar of chocolate to Lauren. 'And maybe cheer you up a bit.'

'That's so sweet,' Lauren replied, stepping aside, allowing Jessie to enter. 'Sorry, it's a bit of a mess in here.'

Jessie looked around, taking in the clothes strewn over Lauren's floor and piled on a beaten-up leather chair in the corner. The last time she'd been in here, Lauren had seemed cagey about letting anyone in her bedroom. She noticed that the photos previously stuck to the walls by Lauren's bed had been taken down, small shadows of Blu Tack being all that remained. Lauren saw her staring.

'Probably get charged for those marks if I ever move out,' she laughed unnaturally. 'Maybe it's time I painted these old walls up anyway. I hate that we have to live in this magnolia box where there's no space for expression.'

Truthfully, Jessie didn't mind her plain walls. She was used to them now and her room felt more her own. Then she remembered that it used to be Magda's and felt ill. She was grateful to be staying at Priya's tonight, but what about all the other nights? She could hardly move in with her and Zoe, their flat was already cramped enough as it was.

'How are you feeling?' Jessie asked. 'About it all.'

Lauren was hunched over her laptop, queuing up old house songs on iTunes. They were mellow in tempo, the type of songs that Jessie imagined people who had defined back muscles and who wore white crochet dresses listened to as they watched the sun set in an Ibizan café. She hadn't been allowed to go on the girls' holiday with Nicole and the rest of her friendship group at the end of sixth form, on Matthew's orders. She thought about sharing that with Lauren, maybe suggesting they plan their own trip, but it didn't feel the right time to start talking about herself.

'It's been on my mind all afternoon,' said Lauren, looking up and meeting Jessie's eyes. 'But I've had some serious losses in my time and I'm not going to force myself to feel worse about this one than I need to, when it can't compare. If that makes sense?'

Jessie looked at Lauren, really taking in her peaches and cream complexion, the tiny tattoo on her wrist, and thought about how close they'd become in just a few short months. How nice it was to just hang out in Lauren's bedroom together, even though the circumstances were less than ideal, the air heavy with confusion over Magda's death. They'd reached a stage where it felt weird being in the flat at the same time and not spending almost every minute of it together. Even when they were apart, Lauren was forever messaging her funny takes on whatever the day's big celebrity news story was or making quips about Marcus.

'Shall we try out some of these new make-up bits, then?' Jessie suggested, spotting the Boots carrier bag on Lauren's windowsill and thinking that doing something relatively normal would be a welcome distraction for them both. Lauren's eyes lit up.

'Definitely!'

She began moving the mound of clothes from the leather chair, then signalled royally to it.

'Take a seat. I found this at a car boot sale for a tenner – not bad, eh?'

Jessie shut her eyes as Lauren blended a golden-brown powder over her lids, taking the time to think more about what she might want to say to Matthew later. The make-up brush tickled but the majority of her swelling had gone down now, so at least it no longer hurt to apply make-up. She was healing. Jessie could smell the chewing gum in Lauren's mouth; it was a sweeter kind of mint than the brand she kept in her own handbag. Less medicinal.

'This is so fun for me, therapeutic almost. It's like getting to paint a picture on someone's face.'

Lauren hummed as she worked, layering up creams and gels on Jessie's eyelids, cheeks and, finally, lips.

'I'll do your hair too. Just make sure you keep your eyes shut the entire time, otherwise you'll spoil it.'

She could hear Lauren tidying up as she went, putting things into drawers and opening the wardrobe once or twice. Lauren made sure to explain each step of the process, even when she used heated irons to create soft waves at the back of Jessie's head – not that Jessie was really taking any of it in. She pinned lengths of her hair up into a makeshift messy bob.

'Open your eyes.'

Jessie looked in the mirror Lauren was holding up for her. Suddenly she had deftly sculpted cheekbones that made her appear harsher, edgier and the cat flick of eyeliner was so precise she was compelled to pull the mirror closer to inspect it. Shimmers of highlighter had been placed along the upper arches of her eyebrows and on the end of her nose. They caught the light when Jessie turned her head.

'How have you managed this?' she gawped, wide-eyed, not quite able to believe the reflection she was seeing. Her face had changed entirely; she could barely recognise herself.

'We look like twins,' Lauren laughed, smoothing down a piece of Jessie's fringe again. 'Let's take some replacement snaps for my wall.'

She laughed again, a deep laugh that crawled its way out of her belly, and clapped her hands together gleefully, admiring her handiwork.

CHAPTER TWENTY-EIGHT

They stayed in Lauren's bedroom for a couple of hours, Jessie curled up in the leather chair, touching her face every few minutes in disbelief, Lauren idly painting at her easel and controlling the playlist.

'I need to head off,' Jessie said eventually, heaving herself up and out of the chair. 'I've arranged to meet Priya.'

A smear of make-up had rubbed off on the chair's high curved back, where her cheek had leant against it. The afternoon had passed by with the speed of a freight train.

'What was that?' Lauren asked, peering out from behind the canvas.

'I've arranged to catch up with Priya tonight,' Jessie repeated, heading to the door, smiling to Lauren as she did. 'I'm glad you're okay.'

Lauren put the paintbrush down.

'I'm not really,' she said, suddenly quiet and serious.

Jessie wavered. Lauren had seemed fine only a minute ago and hadn't mentioned Magda at all for the last few hours. But, Jessie considered, whereas Lauren had surprisingly implied she was a bit of an expert on grief,

Jessie had only ever spent her life living in fear of it. Her grandparents had either died before she was born or were still alive and well. The most loss she'd suffered was the odd family pet. Not knowing the 'appropriate' response to this situation, she would have to follow Lauren's lead.

'You're *not* okay, do you mean?' she asked.

Lauren shook her head vigorously in response.

'I'm not okay at all.'

She stepped away from the easel.

'Can you please just stay here? I really don't want to be alone.' Her voice was high, almost pleading. 'I hate being on my own.'

A pang of guilt struck Jessie. She already felt bad for keeping a huge secret from Lauren, pretending she knew practically nothing about Magda when in reality they'd arranged to meet. But still, Jessie needed to speak to Priya about how to approach Matthew. She was torn.

'Is Sofie coming back tonight? I'm sure she would if you asked her to,' she tried to reason. 'I can ring her now, or Marcus. You and him both knew Magda far better than I did. I never actually met her.'

There hadn't been a need for her to add that last part on. Lauren looked at Jessie strangely, clearly thinking the same thing.

'I know you didn't, but you do know *me*,' she pushed again. 'Can't you tell I'm upset? You're my best friend, Jessie, and I really need you to stay with me tonight. I can't stand the thought of being left alone.'

Lauren's mouth wobbled as she spoke and Jessie's hand hovered over the door handle, unsure what she should do with herself. It had to be Priya she spoke to about Matthew because she needed advice from somebody who knew their history and could verify her own memories of it. She could meet her just for an hour, then come straight back? Jessie was also desperate to talk about Magda without having to be on guard over her words. She submerged Lauren in a hug.

'I promise to be so speedy you won't even realise I've gone.'

Lauren clutched her tightly back. After a few seconds Jessie tried to wriggle free, but the vice-like grip only became stronger, like a tightening belt. Then the prison slackened and Jessie slipped out, a little breathless. Lauren's eyes were vacant.

'Sure, just go then,' she sighed. 'I see where your loyalties lie.'

It was a comment designed to make Jessie feel awful. She'd vowed to be a good friend but was about to do the opposite by leaving.

'I'm so sorry, Lauren, it's just that I want to speak to Priya about my ex-boyfriend. The one I told you about when we were watching the music channel downstairs. Do you remember?' Jessie felt a familiar sensation of remorse mixed with dread as she spoke.

It was the same feeling that Matthew used to give her, whenever they argued and he told her that all the bad things that had happened in his life were her fault.

'Why can't you talk to me about that?' Lauren asked, her nostrils flaring.

The music on her laptop finished but Lauren didn't move to queue a new selection of tracks. They both heard Marcus enter the flat downstairs, dump his bag on the hallway floor and head into the kitchen.

'I can, and I know we can talk about anything. It's just that Priya actually *knows* him so she understands the situation better,' Jessie explained as patiently as she could.

Lauren shrugged defeatedly and looked at her feet, uncomfortable with how much emotion she'd let herself disclose. When would she learn that when she acted in that way it scared people? She was desperate not to lose Jessie as well. Having her close by helped to silence some of the snickering voices in her head that jabbed and teased, telling her she had no true friends, that nobody earned for her. The stress of Magda's death was making them louder than ever.

'Sometimes a fresh perspective is good, but I get it. Don't worry about me, I'll just stay here and paint,' she mumbled, closing her eyes.

Jessie checked her watch and gave Lauren one last quick hug. She was running late and would have to catch the next bus if she were to make it to Priya's for seven.

She slammed the front door shut and bounced down the steps, glad that the bus stop was only a short walk away. It was still early enough to mean she could avoid sharing the journey with hyperbolic groups of students, hiding half-drunk cans inside their coats. Their chants and cat-calls put her on edge nowadays. As she walked, Jessie became aware of a second set of footsteps behind her. She instinctively tightened the grasp around her phone and took a sharp intake of breath, as though she were about to have her head dunked under water. Act normal. That sound of footsteps was familiar. She waited for them to overtake her but instead, they halted right behind her.

'Do you have a minute?'

Jessie froze, then turned her head around. It was Marcus. Had he been following her? His dark eyes met hers.

'I'm actually running late – I should already be some-where,' she said, making a show out of checking her watch.

'I wouldn't ask if I didn't think it was important,' Marcus replied, unsmiling.

Jessie dithered.

'Okay, but just give me a moment to text my friend to let her know I'll be late.'

She reached into her bag for her phone and Marcus glanced up at the flat windows that faced the street. They were shrouded in darkness.

'Of course,' he said quietly. 'But I think we should move away from the flat. Let's try the place on the corner.'

As they walked together, Jessie got a reply from Priya, saying she was free to head round whenever she was ready, then started to second-guess what Marcus might say. He looked serious. But then again, he always did. Could he somehow know that she'd been in contact with Magda? Jessie swallowed hard, then remembered she could always use the necklace as a perfectly plausible excuse. She needn't mention that Magda had also wanted to speak to her about why she'd left Maver Place.

When they reached the wine bar at the end of the street, Marcus let Jessie pass through the door first. It was a dimly lit venue with slim, leather-bound menus and attractive waiting staff. For a split second she wondered if he was about to confess he'd been harbouring feelings for her. Maybe it wasn't Lauren he had his eye on after all? She had no idea how to respond if that were the case, as those feelings certainly weren't mutual. They heaved themselves up onto stools at the bar and a waitress immediately poured out two glasses of tap water and placed a couple of menus between them. Without looking, Jessie ordered a glass of the cheapest red wine and Marcus asked for a lager. He looked agitated. She waited for him to start speaking.

'I'm worried about Lauren,' he said eventually, picking at his nails.

It was a nervous tic he had. Jessie had noticed him doing it a few times in the flat too, usually when they all ate dinner together or if Henry was around.

'Because of Magda?' she asked, leaning forward to hear him better.

A birthday party cheered loudly at the far end of the room. A woman with a holographic badge pinned to her shirt blew out the candles on a cake, then fanned away the smoke, laughing. Her friends all clapped.

'In part, but I'm also worried that her behaviour is becoming a bit ...' He paused, searching for the right word. 'Unpredictable.'

Grief was an intensely personal thing; it was to be expected that Lauren might have a few up and down moments while they waited for the police to announce the results of the post-mortem. The whole of Brighton seemed to be on tenterhooks – Magda's story had garnered a lot of attention. Jessie waited for him to continue, unsure as to what he meant.

'She might be more upset about Magda than she's letting on,' Marcus continued. 'The two of you are obviously very close, but you don't know her like I do, she keeps a lot bottled up.'

Marcus studied Jessie's face, as if suddenly realising it looked different today. She felt her cheeks blush under the thick layers of make-up she was wearing, suddenly feeling stupid.

'How do you mean?' Jessie asked, a crinkle forming over her brow.

He evidently didn't like that they'd become such solid friends. That Lauren now seemed to prefer spending time with her, rather than with him.

The same waitress carefully offloaded their drinks from a tray and asked if they'd like anything to eat. Both

Marcus and Jessie shook their heads, then waited for her to leave before resuming their conversation.

'We used to be close too, believe it or not,' Marcus said, his eyes looking tired. 'I know she doesn't handle stress like this very well. I just want to make sure she's taking care of herself?'

Jessie didn't respond. Was he implying she wasn't being a good enough friend? She'd be heading back to Lauren as soon as she'd finished at Priya's, despite dreading the thought of sleeping in her own bedroom. Magda would still be dead by the time she got back. Maybe she ought to crash on the sofa.

'To be honest, Marcus, I don't really think what you're saying has anything to do with me. It's pretty obvious that you have feelings for Lauren, right? It's not my fault if they aren't reciprocated.'

Marcus lowered his beer and leant back.

'That couldn't be further from the truth,' he said drily. 'I don't have a crush on Lauren.'

'So why are you always staring at her like a lovesick teenager across the dinner table?'

'I don't. She's just a friend.'

'Of course, just a friend.' Jessie's voice had taken on an irritated tone.

'I've lived with her a long time and I care about her, but my feelings aren't romantic in any way,' Marcus continued, unconvincingly. 'I don't know how much she's told you about her past, and it's not my place to, so I won't, but she's had a difficult life. She also mentioned that you were out with some people she used to hang around with the night you were assaulted?'

Jessie widened her eyes. Marcus was the last person on earth that she wanted to talk to about her attack, which had flipped everything she thought she knew about the world and humanity on its head.

'I'm sure if there's anything that Lauren wanted me to know about, then she would have told me by now,' she replied, mentally checking out of the conversation and shutting down.

She drank her wine greedily, feeling it burn first her throat and then her chest. Jessie wanted to get going, to speak to Priya, not Marcus. He was evidently uncomfortable too. She took a took a £5 note out of her purse and laid it on the table.

'Sorry, but I really need to head off now, unless there's anything else?'

Jessie looked at him hesitantly, hoping that they were done.

'No, nothing else,' Marcus replied defeatedly, reaching for his phone, wanting something to do other than stare at Jessie as she left the bar.

That conversation couldn't have gone any worse. But what else could he do? Lauren had built up a wall around herself and it seemed Jessie was the only one she now allowed in. He, on the other hand, was left shut out on the other side, worrying and trying to fill in the blanks himself.

Outside, the cold air felt good against Jessie's flushed face, but it was dark now. She'd have to call a taxi. As she waited for it arrive, she watched the back of Marcus's skinny frame through the window, dejectedly hunched over his pint glass, fringe narrowly avoiding the liquid inside, shoulders slumped.

CHAPTER TWENTY-NINE

Stepping out of the taxi, Jessie internally groaned as she handed over the fare. Being afraid of walking through the city alone was putting a real dent in her pocket. She watched the large white moon shadow bounce off the dark sea and thought about Magda – Brighton had a strange air about it tonight. Pushing the noisy buzzer for Priya's flat made her involuntarily jump, which annoyed her; she was coming to realise that she didn't want to exist as a timid half-person, who flinched at the sight of their own shadow or at a doorbell they'd rung themselves. Where was that person she used to be, the one she was before meeting Matthew? Who loved going to new places, who painted their nails bright colours and easily cracked jokes with friends over coffee, without second-guessing herself? How much harder did she need to try to become that person again? Brighton was supposed to be a new start. She couldn't let it slip away, this chance at happiness, and willed the black clouds that had taken up residence in her mind to shift. The door opened.

'Come on in,' Priya said, smiling, her ponytail swishing behind her as she led Jessie inside the flat. 'Zoe's out with her work lot, so we've got the place to ourselves. Your make-up looks different.'

The bright moon outside and a chunky television in the corner were the only sources of light in the room. Priya fumbled with the switch of a copper floor lamp as Jessie perched on the edge of the windowsill, gazing out at the ruined pier and leisurely moving water down below. She unpinned her hair, letting it tumble back over her shoulders, and lined the grips up in a neat row.

'Sorry, didn't realise how gloomy it was in here,' Priya said, her eyes adjusting from sitting in darkness all afternoon, absorbed in Netflix documentaries. 'Drink? I've got lemonade, water, tea ... whatever you like.'

Jessie had spotted bottles of wine in a rack on top of the fridge.

'Maybe something a little more alcoholic?' she replied, continuing to stare intently out the window.

The sea looked misleadingly gentle and calm, yet if the papers were to be believed, a woman had committed suicide in there just days ago. They claimed that Magda had deliberately chosen to let the waves drag her under, filling her lungs filled with salt water, rather than stay alive. Jessie shivered and turned away, closing the curtains. Life felt so fragile. You didn't get a second go at it either.

'How are you feeling? About it all,' Priya asked, obediently fetching a couple of wine glasses.

On the taxi ride over to Priya's place, Jessie had thought long and hard about what she wanted to do. The conversation with Marcus had got her mind whirring. She thought about how she'd survived being physically attacked. Yes, her attacker had left her afraid and bruised, but so had Matthew – and the key word was survive. She had made it through both ordeals. Finally, she saw the power in recognising that she'd overcome them both. She didn't want to let her demons overtake her, as poor Magda's supposedly had. Instead, she was still standing and no longer prepared to give anybody a reason to see her as a walkover.

'I still feel on edge – it's almost become second nature to look over my shoulder now. But I've realised I don't want to – no, I don't *have* to – any more.'

Priya listened and nodded as Jessie recounted her revelation.

'I'm not made of glass,' she said firmly. 'It took being mugged by a stranger, years of mind games from Matthew, never mind Rob the Tinder twat, but finally, I get it. Life is too short to be trapped in a prison of anxiety all the time.'

Jessie could feel herself getting stronger with every word.

'That's amazing to hear,' Priya enthused: she'd never heard her friend sound so resolute.

'I'm going to rip the plaster off and call Matthew. He needs to hear it directly from me that whatever he tries to do next won't hurt me.'

It was frustrating to Priya that her years of endlessly advising Jessie to cut ties with Matthew hadn't made the slightest bit of difference, but she understood it was a conclusion she had needed to reach by herself. It was better late than never.

'To tell you the truth, I was a bit worried that you still had feelings for Matthew,' Priya confessed. 'And that if he suggested giving it another go you'd drop everything here and run back to him.'

She felt bad for saying it, but Priya had watched Jessie live under Matthew's spell since the first day they met at university and that relationship had never been a balanced one, or a source of joy, it was only anguish, willing the phone to ring (or not ring) and long car journeys across the country.

'That's fair,' Jessie conceded. 'A few months ago, I probably would have.'

There was something else still worrying Priya.

'What about that video he has of you, though?'

It was another problem Jessie had turned over and over in her mind. Eventually, she'd reached the conclusion that really, if Matthew decided to share the explicit clip around social media – and she wouldn't put it past him – what could she do, other than report it to the police? Who were unlikely to be able to help and by that point it could have already been seen by hundreds of people, maybe even members of her family.

'Of course I'm still worried about him sharing it, but I can't stop him,' Jessie replied, closing her eyes. 'The police weren't able to do anything last time, so I'm trying to reframe my thinking instead – which is the one thing I do have control over. Shit things happen to people all over the world every single day; it's how you respond to them that matters the most.'

She was trying to be brave and the more she faked it, hopefully, the more genuine a reaction it would become.

'The people I care about won't watch the video if I tell them not to.'

Priya stayed quiet. She worried about how Matthew might respond over the phone and whether Jessie should really be calling him.

'Do you mind if I ring him from your bedroom?' Jessie asked, as if reading her mind. 'I think I need to be alone, but it would be reassuring to know you're just in the other room.'

'Go for it, I'll be right here. I'm really proud of you, Jess,' Priya replied, crossing her fingers in solidarity.

Jessie sat on the end of Priya and Zoe's bed. It was one of those cheap divan bases that looked like a giant quilted mattress, with an actual mattress on top and sliding drawers on one side. After a few deep breaths, in through the nose and out through the mouth, she searched through her blocked list for the number Matthew had last contacted her on and pressed 'call'. She could feel her temples pulsing harder with every ring. Why wasn't he picking up? He'd been plaguing her for months, requesting that they talk. She couldn't wait for it to be over with, once and for all. Nothing. She went back to her blocked list and tried his old number, the same one he'd had when they were together.

'Here she is.' Matthew sounded as though he was smirking down the line. 'I wondered when I'd be hearing from you.'

Jessie felt her legs go numb. His voice still made her nervous, but she knew she had to push past it. The fact he'd dared to greet her so casually had knocked her sideways. A pool of rage began to bubble.

'This is the last time you'll be hearing from me,' she said hard-heartedly, which only made him laugh.

At least it sounded quiet wherever Matthew was. Jessie had worried she'd catch him while he was out with friends as it was a Saturday night, and that he'd put her on speakerphone, letting them all have a good laugh over her.

'How did you know I moved to Brighton?' she asked, already dreading the answer before it came.

Maybe he'd tracked her phone – she hadn't considered that until now. Matthew wasn't all that technologically advanced but he could have asked a friend to do it, somehow. Jessie could feel her resolve crumbling away and the paranoia creeping back in. How foolish she had been to think she could sweep years of psychological torture under the rug and scare Matthew off with a simple phone call.

'Nicole's sister,' he said flatly. 'I've been seeing her since you left.'

His words were like a punch in the gut. She'd seen Demi-Leigh, Nicole's younger sister, over Christmas in the pub. On the same night that she'd last seen Matthew. They'd sat around the same table and clinked glasses, shared a taxi home. Demi-Leigh had always been a sweet girl, quiet, and as far as Jessie knew, had never had a boyfriend before. Exactly like her when she'd first met Matthew. Demi-Leigh must have kept the fact she was sleeping with him from Nicole, otherwise she'd have definitely put a stop to it.

'If you're with Demi-Leigh, then why are you still h-hounding me?' Jessie stammered, her mouth dry.

She imagined Matthew back in the flat they'd shared together and wondered how different it must look now. Did Demi-Leigh stay there often, in the bed she used to sleep in? Would she sit docilely by his side as he played video games, too?

'She doesn't mean anything, Jess. You know it's always been me and you,' Matthew said, gently this time. 'So you can stop with your big adventure by the sea and come back now.'

Jessie wasn't sure whether he genuinely believed that she had planned to come back all along or if he was just trying to tug at her strings, testing to see if he could still make the puppet dance. Either way, it didn't matter. She'd accepted that she'd never get closure from Matthew himself – he probably didn't even know how cruel he'd been throughout their relationship, so she'd have to find closure alone – by letting go of all the pain he'd caused that she'd barricaded within her, and start moving forward, forcing it out of her system.

'I'm never coming back,' she said, with more conviction. 'You're pathetic.'

It was a sentence she'd rehearsed in her head countless times, after opening every email or text, seeing every withheld number call from him, and especially when she struggled to sleep. It was exhilarating to finally say it aloud.

'Hey, that's not fair,' Matthew sounded surprised. 'I haven't got a bad bone in my body, not really. We had our ups and downs but—'

'Which is why you've been threatening to leak a video of me, a video I never consented to being in? And sending me emails from weird, anonymous accounts, saying I make you sick?' Jessie was almost shouting now. She'd found her flow and was on a roll with it. 'I was attacked recently, Matthew, near enough left for dead. Did you know that? Were you involved? All I ever did was love you and all you did was hurt me, so I wouldn't be surprised. You've turned me into a fucking wreck and I can't live like this any longer.'

She took a deep breath, then went back for more, trying to ignore the sense that her legs were so numb she could jam a fork into them and not feel a thing. Her body's visceral response felt treacherous.

'You never loved me, not really. You might think you did, but you're incapable of it. Your psycho text messages are the last thing I need too.'

In all the time he'd known her, Matthew had never heard Jessie raise her voice like this. A few times she'd feebly tried to push him back when he'd got a bit rough with her, but nothing like this. He sat up straighter on the sofa. She was making him uncomfortable and he didn't like it. She shouldn't be allowed to speak to him in this way, with such little respect.

'I didn't email you saying you make me sick,' Matthew said, sounding genuinely confused. 'And what do you mean you were attacked?'

Jessie felt her chest rapidly rise and fall. At least she could definitely cross him being involved with that off her list.

'I haven't messaged you since Christmas either, and never from another number. Only this one.'

Matthew looked around his empty living room, at the games controller abandoned on the floor and piles of washing-up by the sink. He thought about all the other women he'd brought back here, and then the nights he'd come home alone over the last few months. He'd always expected Jessie would come back eventually. Things had got heated, but they'd never gone this long without speaking before. Maybe she was right, perhaps he hadn't been totally fair throughout their relationship.

Jessie had always been a constant in his life, the first since his own mother had left after divorcing his father. The same father who barely acknowledged him growing up, other than to ask him to buy more Jack Daniel's from the corner shop, despite him being nowhere near old enough to get served. The thought of Jessie being far away like his mother, out of his control, had always been his biggest fear. He'd driven her away, then started lashing out. All the anger he'd unwittingly injected into his veins when his family split apart had constantly fired out in Jessie's direction. He'd enjoyed damaging her because he'd been damaged. He held onto the moment of clarity that had arrived too late.

'I did love you,' Matthew said quietly. 'Just not in the right way. I'll delete the video, it was stupid of me to dredge that up.'

There was so much more that Jessie wanted to say to him, but at the same time, she'd heard enough. Something within her still ached at the familiarity of his voice, to hear it call her beautiful, but she knew she was setting herself free. Her own experiences of growing up had been a dream in comparison to Matthew's, something he never let her forget. Memories of freshly ironed school uniforms, neat packed lunches and bedtime stories became shrouded with guilt after she listened to him talk about his own childhood in contrast, but no matter how bad Matthew's had been, it still wasn't an excuse for him to treat her so badly. All those allowances she'd made for him, because of his challenging past, had been a mistake. There was a glimmer of remorse in Matthew's voice that she'd never encountered before. If she'd heard it a few weeks previously, it would've sent her back down the path of raking over every detail of their relationship. But not now. She'd also be phoning Nicole first thing in the morning, to ensure Demi-Leigh stopped having any involvement with such a narcissistic monster. Jessie couldn't go back in time and tell her younger self to run fast and far away from Matthew, but she could at least try to stop history repeating itself.

'You need to leave me alone,' she said, her voice quiet and firm, brooking no argument.

Then she hung up the phone and her body flooded with relief.

After a few minutes of sitting at the end of the bed in silence, Jessie walked back into Priya's living room and nodded. She doubted that any combination of words she could say to Matthew could ever really summarise or immediately quash all the knock-on effects of their monumental, life-altering relationship. That would take some time. But at last, she felt done.

'Do you mind if I crash on the sofa again?' Jessie asked quietly.

Any strength had all but left her body.

'You don't need to ask, of course you can.'

Jessie's phone bleeped. She looked at it apprehensively. It was Lauren, asking where she was.

CHAPTER THIRTY

Judging by the lack of sad music piping through the corridor the next day, Marcus was out when Jessie got home. She was glad about that. She headed straight up to Lauren's bedroom and knocked on the door, then pushed it open.

'Oh look, it's the dirty stop-out.' She shot Jessie an accusatory look and closed the magazine she'd been flicking through. 'You've been gone all night.'

Lauren clearly hadn't slept. She was sitting in the same leather chair that Jessie had been curled up in herself, only the day before, wearing the same clothes.

'I know, I'm sorry. Last night ended up being really draining,' Jessie explained, meaning it. 'I called my ex.'

Lauren's face thawed a little at hearing that.

'How was it?' she asked, rubbing at her tired eyes.

Hearing that question was the straw that broke the camel's back. The floodgates opened. Jessie started to cry, tears that were a mixture of both liberation for cutting all ties and fury that it had taken her so long to reach this point.

'Oh no, not good?' Lauren consoled, walking over and rubbing Jessie's back.

Jessie wiped away a small slither of snot that had escaped her nose.

'Really good, actually. I needed this to happen,' she laughed, sniffing.

She looked at Lauren, whose face was so full of concern, and felt grateful she had women like her and Priya around. These were the relationships that would see her through while she rebuilt herself.

'Shall we make some brunch and you can tell me all about it?' Lauren asked, smiling with bloodshot eyes. 'I think we're home alone and I've got some charcoal facemasks we can do.'

It sounded like the perfect way to spend the rest of a lazy Sunday afternoon and Jessie was already more than keen to draw a line under the entire weekend. She headed across the landing to change, then met Lauren on the sofas downstairs. The facemask packet promised to cleanse, soothe and renew her from the outside in. She hoped it would. That night, she slept more soundly than she had in a long while.

The next morning, however, Jessie awoke to an ice pick smashing through her right eyeball. She hauled herself out of bed and squinted. Next would come the shooting stars that had terrified her so much the first few times she experienced them, tricking her into believing that she was going blind or mad, until a doctor explained that she was having a migraine. She knew she needed to heed the warning signs and make her bedroom darker, immediately. The gap in the curtains that she could usually ignore suddenly became her sworn enemy, mocking her with a stray sunbeam. Jessie dragged the chair out from underneath her dresser, picked up the silver metal clip she secured her hair with in the shower, and used it to pin the fabric together, then flopped back down into bed with relief. Her migraines were usually the result of stress or strong coffee – both of which she'd consumed far too much of lately. She emailed Pamela to explain she wouldn't be in, then took some of the sleeping pills stowed away in her top drawer and hoped they'd kick in fast, knocking her out before the worst took hold.

After a couple of hours' rest, Jessie came to, still feeling drained. Although the migraine seemed to have passed, her body was weak from it and the lack of food. She pulled on her old dressing gown, which smelled of clean detergent, something she always found a comfort, and made her way downstairs slowly, gripping onto the bannister as she went. This was the start of her living as her new self so maybe after some toast she'd get back on Tinder again, see who else was out there. Reaching the fifth step, she paused, convinced she could hear a rustling sound coming from the kitchen. A mouse? Maybe next door's cat had wandered in somehow? Because it sounded like a hungry animal making its way through the bin in search of scraps and Lauren had definitely said she had an early morning shoot today. Marcus and Sofie usually worked Mondays too, so today was one of those rare ones when she had the flat to herself.

The rustling started again. Her heart began beating a little harder as she rounded the corner – one more step and she'd be able to see into the kitchen. This time she knew it was real. Her legs stiffened. It wouldn't be surprising if they had a mouse, due to Marcus's inability to ever scrape a plate clean properly, but surely they weren't this loud? Jessie dared to look directly into the kitchen. She saw a flash of long, dark hair. A woman, a stranger, was in the kitchen – in her kitchen – reaching up into a food cupboard. Her face was hidden by the open door, but Jessie could tell that she was loudly shovelling handfuls of cereal into her mouth, crunching them down hungrily. Jessie couldn't move, rendered immobile from fear. She had to get back upstairs without being heard and call for help. That was the only option. The crunching was replaced by a tuneless whistle, as the woman performed a slow and lazy song to herself. Goosebumps prickled at the back of Jessie's neck and ran along her arms. Trying to move as silently as she could, she turned and placed one foot lightly on the ascending step. Her palms were sweating. So long as the off-key whistling didn't get any closer, she'd be fine. Just keep going, walk back up to safety, she repeated silently to herself. Until a high-pitched jingle shot through the air. Her phone! It was in the pocket of her dressing gown; she patted herself desperately then pulled it out. 'Mum mobile' was calling.

The whistling stopped and something clattered to the floor in the kitchen. Jessie's phone continued to chime as she jabbed at the side buttons, desperately willing it to stop. Not that it would make a difference; it was too late for that. The animal had already seen her and was coming to pounce. As it ran towards her, Jessie clenched her eyes tightly closed, waiting, having already surrendered to it. The footsteps kept running. They ran all the way to the front door. The woman turned to look at Jessie on the way out. Her eyes, two dark coals pushed deep into a skull, sat above hollowed out cheekbones. Her skin was marked with pocks. Jessie screamed, the sound that had been forming in her throat over the last few minutes, finally erupting like a tin kettle on a stove. The intruder screamed back, looking equally as terrified.

'It's not …' came a strangled, stuttering voice, 'it's not what it looks like. I'm so hungry and …'

The smell of stale sweat assaulted Jessie's senses. She noticed the woman had stains all over her grey tracksuit bottoms too and her face was familiar.

'Get out,' Jessie cried, utterly horrified. 'Get out, get out!'

She couldn't stop shouting that same sentence over and over, until long after the bony figure had disappeared, leaving the front door swinging in her wake, Cheerios scattered all over the tiled kitchen floor. Jessie's thumb was rigid as she tried a couple of times to slide it across the screen to answer when her mum called again.

'Hi darling, how are you?'

All Jessie could do was wail down the phone, failing to form any words that made sense.

'Someone – someone in the flat! Mum, there was someone here,' she eventually managed to garble. 'I just saw someone who'd broken in run away.'

Her mum, sat behind her desk over a hundred miles away, pushed the volume on her phone up as loudly as it could go.

'Jessica, are you sure?'

'I'm sure,' Jessie whispered hoarsely.

'Then call the police – and leave that flat right now.'

Jessie's mother gritted her teeth together and shot a worried look at her colleague, who had walked over and was hovering nearby with concerned curiosity.

'I'm in pyjamas,' a quiet voice replied. 'I need to change.'

'Then lock the door. Can you at least do that?' her mother implored. 'Do you know your neighbours?'

'I'll call the police and phone you back,' Jessie replied, clawing back some control.

The woman was gone, she was alone now. Hearing her mum panic had given her a renewed determination to stay calm. They couldn't both lose their heads at the same time.

Sergeant Fiona Langley knocked on the door just after Jessie had zipped her jeans up. She was a woman in her late thirties with sandy blonde hair and a ruddy complexion. Her colleague, PC Oliver Phillips, a younger man with a stubbly jawline and kind eyes, stood next to her, arms folded. They'd received a call from a distressed woman who said she'd come downstairs to find a stranger in her home with no signs of a forced entry. It was as though whoever it was had let themselves in using a key.

A brunette with a blunt fringe and pleasant face opened the door, clearly shaken. Her slim-fitting jeans were neat, as was the casual silk blouse she'd thrown on over the top, with a tiny polka-dot pattern. The officers introduced themselves and Jessie let them into the house, leading them into the kitchen to take notes and ask questions.

'I'm sorry to have called. I feel like I'm wasting your time,' said Jessie, ever conscious of being a nuisance.

She knew what had just happened was by no means normal, but this woman hadn't actually stolen anything apart from food, which probably meant she was desperate. Her previous dealings with the police had left her unsure whether they would be able to help.

'We're glad you called, Miss Campbell,' Sergeant Langley reassured her. 'Please tell us again exactly what happened.'

Jessie went into detail, mentioning the possible break-in she thought had happened a couple of months previously which they'd all dismissed as someone having not locked up properly. She then described the woman's dirty clothes and wild, glittering eyes, the bruising on her hands and wrists too. And her face, it was one she recognised. Why did she know her face?

'I think,' Jessie said, thoughts knitting together as she spoke, 'I think it might have been a homeless woman I've seen around town. She sometimes sits outside Subway.'

Sergeant Langley glanced across to her colleague, whose interest had clearly been piqued.

'Do you have any connection to this woman?' PC Phillips asked, leaning forward. 'Can you describe her in more detail for us? Height? Colouring?'

He held a small notepad in his hand and a miniature pen in the other, and resumed scribbling notes down.

'Not at all; I think I just remember seeing her begging in town. She shouted at my friend in the street once too.'

The police officers nodded, looking thoughtful.

'Can you tell us about the security of this flat? And the other people who live here?' Sergeant Langley pressed.

She was due to start her detective training soon and relished a challenge. It was intriguing that the entrance lock didn't appear to be at all damaged and yet this young woman, who upon first impressions seemed to have it relatively together, was certain the front door had not been left open.

'The front door is one of those that locks when you slam it shut. There's a tiny balcony off of the kitchen but that's always locked too – it's only really my housemate, Lauren, who goes out there to smoke,' Jessie continued, smoothing down the non-existent creases in her silk shirt. 'She and the others who live here are out at work.'

PC Phillips read back the description Jessie had given of the young woman she'd found in the kitchen once more. Sergeant Langley's eyebrows shot up. She was often called to incidents involving Brighton and Hove's homeless community or chatted to them on her rounds. A picture had formed in her head.

'Excuse me for a moment, I'm just going to call one of my colleagues at the station and ask them to run a name through the system,' Sergeant Langley said, heading out into the hallway for some privacy.

Jessie and PC Phillips sat on the sunken sofas as they waited. The policeman gave her another of his supportive smiles.

'It's a nice place you have here,' he lied.

'Thank you,' Jessie replied. 'It'll do for now.'

He pretended to read back over his notes until Sergeant Langley returned a couple of minutes later, with a triumphant look on her face.

'Does the name Elizabeth Holliday mean anything to you, Miss Campbell?'

CHAPTER THIRTY-ONE

'What's going on? Jessie, are you okay?' Lauren asked, sounding alarmed.

She stared at the two police officers who'd stood up when she came into the kitchen and tried to remain calm. They weren't necessarily here about Magda. She had to keep a cool head.

'This is Lauren,' Jessie said after introducing Sergeant Langley and PC Phillips. 'One of my flatmates.'

The ruddy-faced woman regarded Lauren carefully. Sergeant Langley had a photographic memory and a keen eye for faces. There was something about this flat that just wasn't sitting quite right. She couldn't put her finger on it yet. But she would. She always did. It's why she was so excited to start her detective training.

'We received a report from a resident here ...' PC Phillips looked down at his notepad, having already forgotten the address of the flat. 'Here at 4 Maver Place, saying an unknown person was in the kitchen area of the flat, possibly attempting a robbery. However, there are no signs of a break-in. Is there any chance you might have forgotten to close the door earlier on your way out, Miss …?'

Jessie's face was still alabaster white. The female police officer had narrowed her eyes when she'd denied the name Elizabeth Holliday rang any bells.

'Miss McCormack and I definitely would've shut the door,' Lauren confirmed. 'We've all been hyper-vigilant about it since someone accidentally left it open not long after New Year. Nothing was taken, though.'

Realising she'd been holding her breath, Jessie exhaled.

'Have you lived here for a long while, Miss McCormack?' Sergeant Langley queried. 'Might the name Elizabeth Holliday be recognisable?'

Lauren nodded, slowly at first.

'No … I do know a Beth Holliday though, if it's the same person. She lived here before …' Lauren stopped herself. 'But that was a couple of years ago. I don't understand why she'd come here.'

Now that Lauren had referred to her as Beth, Jessie remembered the box in the storage room with 'Beth' written on one side. She hadn't put the two together. Had Lauren just deliberately stopped herself from mentioning Magda? Jessie looked at her again. She was clearly uncomfortable with the police being in the flat and bringing up the name of a possible suicide victim who also once lived there presumably wouldn't help to alleviate the tension. Maybe calling the police had been the wrong thing to do.

'I haven't seen her in years,' Lauren added swiftly. 'We're not in touch.'

'Mind if I take another little look around the place?' Sergeant Langley enquired. 'Just to check there are no other signs of forced entry that we might have missed. We'll have a chat with your neighbours afterwards too.'

Lauren looked startled, but Jessie nodded, grateful that she'd given her bedroom a tidy earlier on.

Sergeant Langley poked her head into Marcus's room and grimaced at the smell. This occupant clearly didn't open the window all that often and there was minimal floor space available for her to walk on, but nothing looked obviously amiss. There were lots of photos on the wall of that blonde woman in the kitchen, Lauren, only her hair was darker and she looked much younger in them. In the storage cupboard, Sergeant Langley rummaged through the bags and boxes of leftover possessions, drawing a blank, then headed upstairs. Lauren bit her lip.

'Why would this girl be in our house?' Jessie asked Lauren, who took a seat next to her on the sofa. 'Could she have left something here?'

There was an intensity radiating from Lauren.

'I don't know,' she muttered in response, avoiding eye contact. 'Beth was horrible to live with, always coming into my room off her face.'

'Might she still have a key?' Jessie pressed.

'I-I'm not sure, there are always so many sets with people coming and going, it's hard to keep track.'

Sergeant Langley called down to PC Phillips, asking him to join her. He returned to the kitchen a minute later to ask if they could be granted access to the bedroom opposite the bathroom. Lauren's bedroom.

'Is it really necessary?' Lauren asked politely, after what felt like a minute of silence.

PC Phillips gave her a kind smile. If he thought something was awry, he hid it well.

'We'd really like to be able to say we've done a clean sweep of the place.'

Lauren, who'd dropped her keys onto the table when she'd walked in, stood up and handed the bunch to him.

'It's the one with a blob of red nail varnish painted on it.'

'A very clever trick,' he said, giving another smile. 'Please don't worry, this is all routine.'

Jessie and Lauren heard the two police officers' footsteps creak on the floorboards overhead and a lock click open.

'I just don't like the idea of strangers going through my stuff,' Lauren said. 'This is completely bonkers.'

Upstairs, PC Phillips checked the windows in Lauren's bedroom. He didn't really think they'd find anything in there, but was interested in Lauren McCormack's reaction when they'd suggested looking around the rest of Maver Place. The other flatmate didn't seem to mind – then again, she'd been the one to make the call, after all. But if there was one thing he'd learnt during his time on the job, it was that people are full of surprises. Hidden behind a curtain on the windowsill was a small silver object. A phone, plugged in to charge. It looked too dated to be anybody's primary phone. If he had to guess, he'd say it was a burner. The type of phone he'd seized from people's homes who were making calls they shouldn't be. Phillips scribbled something on his notepad, then stopped in front of Lauren's easel and stared at the paint-ing attached to it. He was no art critic but he could tell a lot of hard work had gone into the piece. The subject of the painting had a mouth twisted in horror and it was incredibly lifelike. He touched a finger lightly to a splatter of crimson oil paint in the right hand corner which hadn't yet dried. There was an artist's signature on it: *Truth Teller*.

Sergeant Langley tapped his shoulder.

'Here's a photo of Elizabeth Holliday. Surely you rec-ognise her too?'

Sergeant Langley had pulled up an old news report on her phone, which had a picture of a young woman with dark, sunken eyes.

PC Phillips took the phone and used two fingers to zoom in on the image. Yes, it was a face he knew well. He'd seen it on his patrols around the city centre numer-ous times. Elizabeth Holliday was a particularly sad case, a twenty-something who'd become well-known to him and the other guys down the station, for being locked in the vicious cycle of petty crime, prison and begging on the streets. Elizabeth, or Beth, as she was also known, had some nasty habits to feed. The report was about her ban from the local shopping mall, having being caught shoplifting. Phillips always felt a little callous arresting women like her, who had nothing, and who hadn't com-mitted a violent crime, until they started screeching and scratching at him with their dirty nails. Then, he didn't mind roughly pushing their heads down and telling them to get in the back of the police van.

'Should I put the kettle on?' Jessie asked, desperate for something to do while the search took place upstairs.

Lauren's stunned silence was only adding to her anxiety and Jessie really wanted to call her mum back. Sergeant Langley reappeared in the doorway.

'Thanks, ladies,' she said, deliberately neutral. 'We'll be referring this on to the investigative team back at the station. They'll be in touch soon.'

She handed Jessie a card with something handwritten on the back.

'Here's your crime reference number and my contact details. If you think of anything else that might be helpful, please don't hesitate to get in touch.'

PC Phillips stepped out from behind her.

'Someone will be round either today or first thing tomorrow to dust for prints which we can then run through the system, to see if there's a match with anyone on our database. We'll let ourselves out.'

Jessie took care not to step on the cereal which was still scattered across the floor.

'We need to get the lock changed,' Lauren said, lips pursed. 'I can't believe it. Let's call the letting agent now.'

Jessie poured the boiling water into two mugs and added a teaspoon of sugar, the way Lauren always did for her when she was hungover. She hoped it would help lessen the shock.

'I wish they'd send someone round to do all those tests quicker.'

Jessie took a sip, gearing herself up.

'When did Beth live here?' she asked, choosing to sit on the sofa opposite Lauren rather than next to her.

The sofa she'd lain semi-conscious on following her attack. She looked around the kitchen, a room she'd spent so much time in over the last few months, and felt her stomach tighten. This flat-share had been nothing like she'd hoped it'd be when she first moved in. She'd wanted to slot herself into a bustling, ready-made home full of exciting twenty-somethings like her, who she'd become good friends with. Apart from Lauren, she rarely saw anybody else. It felt like the walls were mocking her for making the wrong move. She replayed the horror that she'd felt coming down the stairs and seeing that strange, uninhibited woman in her kitchen. Maver Place was cursed.

'Well, I've been here for four years and she was there in the beginning, when there were just three of us. Me, her and Georgia.'

Jessie nodded, Georgia must have been another flatmate who'd long since moved on. She couldn't fathom why Lauren still lived here four years later. The flat was okay, but little more than a stopgap. Then again, what were the alternative options? Jessie thought back to all the countless other places she'd viewed before moving in, the one with the landlord who clearly wanted more than her rent money, the one with the hole in the floor. Even Priya and Zoe's flat, which was far smaller than theirs, was just as expensive.

'Just three of you?'

'Yeah, Marcus's room is the old living room. When the landlord put the rent up we had to figure out a way to cram one more person in here,' Lauren lamented. 'I really didn't want him to live here at first, and he changed everything. The whole dynamic.'

That seemed fair. She certainly wouldn't have chosen to live with Marcus if she could have helped it either. Jessie thought about the last time she'd seen Beth, prior to this afternoon's events. When Beth's friend had shouted something at Lauren. Was it really possible that Lauren hadn't known it was her former flatmate sitting in the street?

'Lauren, there's something I don't understand,' Jessie began, pulling her mug closer to her chest. 'Why is Beth homeless now? I'm sure she was with that homeless woman who shouted at us in town when we walked past.'

Lauren considered her words for a while before speaking, not wanting lie but equally not wanting to scare Jessie with the truth.

'Towards the end she was very unwell. It reached the point where she was taking drugs most days, then twice, three times a day.' Lauren looked visibly upset. 'It was horrible watching her turn into this shell of a person and being unable to do anything. We both went down a bad path together.'

All those references Lauren had made to her 'old crowd'. This must be what she meant. There was so much more to her past than she'd ever let on.

Jessie gulped.

CHAPTER THIRTY-TWO

The following day, Jessie returned to work. Lauren's studio didn't have any major shoots booked in, so she had volunteered to wait around for the locksmith. Marcus had offered to swap his shift to keep Lauren company. What a surprise, Jessie thought to herself. Sitting at her desk, Jessie knew what she was about to do was wrong – on par with watching a neighbour undress through a crack in the curtains, sneaking a look at the most shadowed parts of their lives. But she needed to know who she was living with. She had a *right* to know, she reasoned to herself. Everything that had happened lately, her attack, Magda going missing, the break-in – all the bad things that had gone on seemed to lead back to Maver Place in one way or another, not Matthew after all.

Jessie's finger hovered over the 'M' button of her keyboard, the monitor beaming out its usual blue welcome message and the Sussex NHS Trust logo. If anybody caught her searching for Marcus Ratcliffe's name without a valid reason, she knew there was a high chance of receiving a disciplinary. Breaching patient confidentiality was a massive no-no. Pamela had drummed that into the head of each and every member of staff before they'd so much as taken their coat off on their first day. So, looking up her housemates in order to see whether or not any of them had ever been seen by a member of the psychiatric team or received treatment was most definitely against the rules. But something wasn't right. Only a few months ago these people were relative strangers to her and now, having lived so closely with them, she was left wondering what secrets they might possibly be hiding. Even Lauren. She needed answers.

The radio chattered away in the background, announcing it would soon be time for the three o'clock news, before launching into a jingle about a mattress warehouse. Jessie tried to remember the last time she'd managed to sleep soundly since moving into Maver Place, but couldn't. Her body seemed stuck in a permanent state of fatigue, eyelids constantly threatening to close whilst she sat at her desk, sipping on yet another stale coffee. She'd spent most of the day deliberating looking her flatmates up on the database, not only put off by the thought of losing her income if she got caught, but also of what she might find. Who was she really living with? How well did she actually know them? She had thought she and Lauren knew one another intimately – they shared everything from dinners to a tube of toothpaste, for God's sake – but even Lauren was starting to act shiftily and her behaviour around the police yesterday was odd.

Jessie knew exactly how dark and tangled the human mind could become; it surrounded her every day in this very office. She'd recently processed admittance reports for a woman who started her day off by drinking a bottle of vodka, before smashing it and pushing fragments of the fractured glass deep into her vulnerable wrists. She'd typed letters to general practitioners informing them that a patient registered with their surgery was convinced that the devil was trapped inside their head, and that they'd been prescribed a hefty dose of Chlorpromazine for the foreseeable future. Jessie had covered for Cheryl on reception, looking these people in the eyes, sometimes unable to distinguish who was a client and who was the supportive family member. It often came down to the most subtle of signs that somebody was seriously unwell, their body language, the pitch of their voice. She knew more than most that bad thoughts and harmful actions came disguised in all shapes and sizes. The newsreader on the radio moved on to a story about a car accident at the bottom of Elm Grove, killing a pedestrian earlier that morning. Lately the news felt more sinister than ever, or perhaps she had just begun to notice it more. Jessie listened hard for an update on Magda's case but there wasn't one; then, slowly, began to type Marcus's name into the search bar of the patient database. She held her breath. No! There were no matches, which came as a surprise. She double-checked the spelling of his surname. R-a-t-c-l-i-f-f-e. Still nothing.

She leant back on her chair. Who to try next? Sofie Chang. Sofie, the woman who had steadily been stripping off bits of Jessie's identity and absorbing them into her own. The hair, the outfits, the mannerisms. Was it possible she could have some kind of personality disorder? Jessie typed Sofie's name in and a file flashed up. Her heart jumped, until she realised the date of birth didn't match up. The Sofie Chang on the system had been born in 1976. Jessie's jaw was beginning to ache from clenching. She'd try Henry next. Jessie had already seen his file on Juliette's desk once before, so she knew that there'd definitely be something to unearth about him. She typed his name deliberately, then watched the system load up. Henry Goldsmith-Blume, there he was. Right in front of her, his file waiting to be opened. Jessie peered over the top of her computer. Juliette was busy reading case notes, humming along to a Simply Red song through a mouthful of Jaffa Cake. Jessie's eyes scanned the latest entry on Henry's file. He had been receiving therapy, it said, for mild depression stemming from *difficult familial relationships, most notably with his father*. She was on guard for Sofie's name, or her own, but there was no mention of either. There were, however, lots of mentions of him repressing his emotions, feeling like he had to be strong for his mother. Nothing relating to Maver Place. She sighed. All this power she'd thought she had at her fingertips? In reality, it amounted to nothing so far. And the only person left to look up on the database was the last person on earth that she wanted to.

A file with Lauren's name and a matching date of birth appeared. She closed her eyes for a few seconds, then tentatively double-clicked on it. The rainbow-coloured pinwheel indicated that the information held within was probably extensive so Jessie checked again that Pamela was nowhere to be seen, ditto any of the doctors. The most recent entry had been made just a few weeks ago – a letter to Lauren's GP added onto the system by Dr Statham. Jessie clicked the 'read more' button and scanned the page, her heart racing, stomach plummeting. The words 'obsessive' and 'violence' leapt out at her. Her eyes blurred, trying to take everything in at speed, while remaining on guard. As she read on, her body became bloodless:

This female patient, aged 27 years of age, with no physical ailments, experiences intense depressive, manic and violent episodes. She reports symptoms of psychosis and aggression and is prone to high-risk behaviours (including substance abuse), and was previously an in-patient at Mill View Hospital following the death of her sister. She has been known to form unhealthy attachments to romantic partners and obsessive friendships, fearing rejection and loss of the other party, and admits to being manipulative.

In the past Miss McCormack has undergone talking therapies and has been recommended further grief counselling. However she has since been dismissed from these services following a succession of missed appointments. We have been unable to contact Miss McCormack despite numerous attempts. It's also of primary concern that her latest repeat prescription has not been collected from—

Pamela's hand met Jessie's upper back.

'Have you seen my email?'

Jessie quickly clicked off the screen, then cursed herself for making it so obvious that she'd been looking at something she wasn't supposed to be.

'S-sorry. Which one?' Jessie replied, hoping her manager wouldn't notice the sheen of sweat that had sprung up above her top lip.

Lauren had never mentioned having a sister before. A sister who'd died. That wasn't normal. Did Marcus and Sofie know? Substance abuse. Violence. Aggression. Jessie thought back to the Christmas present Lauren had given her, addressed to 'my little sister' and a shockwave passed through her. That wasn't normal either. She wiped the sweat away with the back of her sleeve, the same silk shirt she'd put on when the police had arrived yesterday. They hadn't called with any more news yet. She almost didn't want them to now.

'About the bake sale, naturally! All for a good cause,' Pamela trilled. 'Will you come and give me a hand setting up, please? We'll miss cashing in on the mid-afternoon sugar slump if we don't get a wriggle on.'

Cheryl had coerced them all into selling lacklustre cupcakes to other members of staff to raise money for a local hospice. Last week Jessie had promised to whip up a load of brownies, but with everything that had happened yesterday, she'd clean forgotten.

She followed Pamela into the open space behind the reception area, where a spare desk had been covered with a disposable tablecloth, and began unpacking the multiple Tupperware boxes that Pamela had bought in from home, packed with flapjacks. The scent of golden syrup wafting out of them made her feel sick. Everything was moving in slow motion as she tried to piece her thoughts back together. The word violent resounded over and over. But Lauren would never do anything to hurt her. Would she? Pamela tutted and handed Jessie some of the shop-bought cookies that someone else had donated – probably one of the doctors, who also didn't have time to pull anything together from scratch either.

As she tried to arrange the biscuits somewhat artfully onto some paper plates, Jessie ran through everything she knew about manic episodes, which often saw patients go on shopping sprees and spending money they didn't have. She thought back to the charm bracelet Lauren had bought her for Christmas, all those takeaways, the beauty products she'd been so insistent on buying, and realised that actually, Lauren had never let her pay for *anything*. She remembered the way Lauren's hand had moved so deftly, throwing all those items in the basket, without pausing for a moment to tally up the cost, the way her words had fired off at a thousand miles per hour as she described everything she wanted to purchase too. Jessie had never seen her like that before. Sure, Lauren was chatty, but that had been something entirely different.

'Lazy, isn't it?' Pamela whispered, with a conspiratorial chuckle.

She was wearing a powder-blue mohair jumper today, her hair as coiffed as ever.

'What's that?' Jessie replied, blinking herself back into the room.

How could she go back to Maver Place after work? Knowing that she would have to sleep mere metres away from somebody like Lauren, who, according to what she'd read in the file, could fly off the handle at any moment. Somebody refusing to take their medication and missing appointments. No wonder Magda had left. Maybe *that's* what Magda had wanted to talk to her about, not Marcus. The penny was finally starting to drop. Could Lauren even be behind the attack somehow? Jessie touched the lump on the back of her skull, where the fracture was still slowly healing, and felt sick to her stomach. At this stage, she couldn't confidently rule anybody out.

'The packet of Maryland Cookies.'

Jessie looked at Pamela blankly, and she frowned slightly in return.

'Dr Statham has only donated these,' Pamela clarified.

Who cares? The man works unrelenting hours, she wanted to scream. Jessie battled the urge to overturn the table and race towards the exit. She'd have to stay at Priya's tonight. Or maybe getting out of Brighton altogether would be a better idea? She desperately wanted to run towards the fortress of her parents' house and be a little girl again, who slept under sheets that never smelled of damp because they'd been dried in a flat with crap ventilation. She longed to walk into a kitchen and not be faced with an overflowing bin that other people had continuously tried to squash more rubbish into, rather than bothering to empty. She missed having a shower curtain that wasn't streaked orange with mould and a home where she could fully relax, no matter who else was inside it. A home where people don't lie about who they are.

CHAPTER THIRTY-THREE

Jessie pushed her way to the front of the bus queue and watched her knees jitter throughout the duration of the journey. It was starting to get lighter again in the evenings and the sky was just about clinging on to the last remains of the day. Stepping off the bus, she froze. Was it worth going back to the flat to grab some clothes, or should she just head straight to the station and jump on the first train heading in the direction of her parents' house? She could phone them on the way, frame it as a surprise visit. She still had plenty of clothes in her old bedroom there that she could wear over the next couple of days, having been unable to fit them all under her bed at Maver Place. It'd be easier to not let on that anything was amiss – if she divulged any of what she'd come to learn about Lauren, her mum would never let her flat-share, or leave home, again. She was an only child, her parents' pride and joy. That was why she'd never fully disclosed how bad things had become with Matthew either, never wanting to upset them or reveal the terrible choices she'd made. Her mum would only find a way to shoulder the blame herself. There were plenty of other people she needed to call, too. Nicole, her oldest friend, for starters, to talk to her all about how Matthew had been seeing her younger sister, Demi-Leigh. Then Sofie, who she wanted to grill about Lauren. Had she known about their flatmate's history of violence and obsessive nature? Then Marcus, for the same reason. It was entirely possible that they were in the dark too. Lauren was obviously very adept at keeping her problems well hidden, which was as pitiable as it was terrifying.

Brighton's main station, which had trains direct to Chesterbury, was only a fifteen-minute walk away. Jessie knew she could do it in ten if she upped her pace and used a shortcut that led her to the back entrance. She kept her eyes down as she ran, wishing she'd worn more layers to work that day. Her trench coat, more fashionable than practical, gaped open in the wind. She put her card in the ticket machine and bought a single, not return, ticket, her head still swimming from the revelations about Lauren, thoughts all jostling for space. Jessie needed to get out of the city to think about what she really wanted. Did she even want to stay in Brighton at all? Perhaps it had never been a good idea moving there in the first place. Going to her parents' house would buy some time to figure it all out. The machine hummed from deep within, in no real hurry to spit out her orange ticket and receipt. She could hear the man behind her, next in the queue, tutting loudly. He was doing it on purpose, tapping a shiny brogue impatiently. The ticket dropped into the glass window in the bottom of the machine. Jessie snatched it up, shot the man a disdainful look and put her hand over her eyes, in the hopes it would help her see the departures board. She stepped closer and saw it was a half-an-hour wait until the next train home. She rummaged in her bag for her medication and dry-swallowed another tiny anti-anxiety tablet, desperate to find some calm.

It was cold in the station, even colder than outside somehow. Jessie sat on one of the wooden benches and watched a man attempt to play something on the infamous piano positioned by the entrance. It was open to all who were so inclined, an initiative by the council to 'raise the spirits of commuters'. The man wasn't very good. Pigeons bobbed their heads in time to the haphazard melody, an interpretation of an old nursery rhyme, and pecked at the crumbs of a forgotten croissant on the floor. Jessie grew restless. Now that she had decided to leave town, she wanted to get the literal wheels in motion, to be sitting on a speeding train. She debated buying a Cornish pasty, just to have something to occupy her mind and hands with for a while, then her ringtone sounded. It was a call from a withheld number. She ignored it. No good news has ever been shared via a call from a withheld number. A text from Lauren appeared.

Hey babe, call me when you can! What shall we make for dinner tonight?

Jessie felt the hairs on her neck stand on end and put her phone away. Eventually the announcement for her train to Chesterbury was called, and she watched the green and white string of carriages pull in. Salvation. She took a seat opposite a pregnant woman with tight ginger curls and considered all the things she'd left back at Maver Place, things that she would really need. Her laptop and jewellery, for starters. She batted those thoughts away. Blurred snapshots of countryside soon started whizzing past the window and Jessie took her phone out and searched for Sofie's number. It was time to start getting some answers.

'Hey, Jess,' Sofie answered in her usual sing-song. 'How's it going?'

Jessie wasn't sure how to begin. She couldn't accuse Sofie of keeping potentially life-threatening secrets from her straight away. She needed to suss out how much she knew, work out who had really betrayed her trust the most.

'Are you in the flat at the moment?' she asked, her tone serious.

Sofie immediately recognised that something was wrong. She put down the dishcloth she'd been using to wipe a counter in the café. The last customer had just left, leaving her alone to lock up and tally up the day's takings.

'I'm just wrapping up at work. You sound a bit stressed?'

Sofie blew heavily into the air, making her fringe flutter. She'd fast developed a hatred of it and couldn't wait for the damn thing to grow out. There'd been a breakthrough: she and Henry had spoken at length the previous night about how she shouldn't feel the need to change herself to please him. He'd cupped her chin and looked her square in the eyes and told her she was perfect, exactly as she was, no matter what colour her hair was or how many tattoos she had on display. In fact, they were just a couple of the things he liked about her, out of a very long list. He didn't want anybody like his sister's friends. He just wanted her. She'd spent the day feeling grateful for him and foolish for ever having assumed he'd love her more for wearing roll-neck jumpers. Her tattoos were little works of art, she was proud of them, and even though Henry would never dare to get one himself, he loved them too, because they were a part of her. And so what if his mother made it clear she found them repulsive? She didn't like Henry's mother all that much herself, truth be told. But finally, it seemed that he was ready to move out of his bachelor pad and look for a home of their own together. Mrs Goldsmith-Blume was never going to get better, Henry understood that now – he'd started meeting with a counsellor and recognised that he needed to start putting his own needs first. Start dealing with his emotions more head-on. Doing that didn't mean he was 'soft', or that he didn't care for his mother still, just that he had to take care of himself too.

'I am,' Jessie said, feeling her upset and anger at the thought of being lied to rising within her. 'I know I shouldn't have, but I read Lauren's file at work today. I know all about her history.'

The other end of the line fell silent.

'However, the thing I want to know now is why *you* didn't tell me about it? You and Marcus both let me move in with a woman who is severely mentally unstable. How could you have kept this a secret from me for so long?'

The pregnant woman sitting opposite Jessie looked up from her crossword puzzle and adjusted her glasses.

'I don't know what you mean,' Sofie finally said.

It was true. She spent the majority of her time at Henry's or at work, trying to scrape together enough money to maybe put a deposit down on her own place, somewhere she could burn incense without receiving a text from anyone about the flat starting to smell like a shop that sells crystals.

'I knew she was in absolute bits after …' her voice trailed off.

'It's okay, Sofie. You can say it. After her sister?' Jessie persisted.

'Yes, after Georgia died,' Sofie said, worried that she'd really upset Jessie. 'Sorry, it just feels rude talking about someone else's bereavement. I wouldn't like it if I heard that my flatmates had been discussing my personal life behind my back.'

Jessie felt guilty for having gone in all guns blazing. Sofie was sweet and she was naïve; it was also true that she was hardly ever home and was a permanent optimist and peacemaker. Of course, she hadn't known the extent of poor Lauren's vulnerable mental state – which she was obviously very good at keeping hidden. There was one more question she had to ask, all the same.

'Do you think Lauren is really capable of hurting someone?'

Silence again.

'I've never felt worried about living with her,' Sofie spoke carefully. 'I know she's had her issues to deal with, but I genuinely believe that Lauren is a nice girl – and she's been an especially good friend to you, hasn't she?'

Jessie swallowed hard. Was running back home an overreaction? She hadn't actually managed to read any of the nitty-gritty details in Lauren's file – and this was someone who'd been there for her during her lowest ebb, who'd made her tea and toast when her heart was broken and her body had doubled over in physical pain.

'If anything,' Sofie continued, 'I would say Lauren is more likely to hurt herself than anybody else. But to be honest, even though we've lived together for a long time, I still wouldn't exactly say we were all that close. So, I really don't know.'

'I don't know' wasn't enough of a reassurance.

'Maybe you should stay at Henry's tonight,' Jessie said, in what she hoped was an authoritative tone. 'Just until we work out what's going on here.'

Sofie gave an awkward laugh.

'Unsurprisingly, I was already planning to. What about you?'

For all Henry's faults, he was at least a good person to have on side in this scenario. Jessie was glad that

Sofie would be out of Lauren's firing line should her mood flip.

'I'll think of an excuse to give Lauren about why I'm not in the flat tonight and be back in touch when I've figured out what I'm doing. Take care, Sofe,' Jessie said, then cut off the call.

She was utterly exhausted, the lure of sleep calling. A red dot had appeared next to the voicemail symbol on her call register but she didn't want to listen to it, she wanted to shut her eyes and pretend that everything was normal, nap until the train pulled into Chesterbury. The woman opposite had given up on the book of puzzles she'd been filling in and was resting her head against the window, cupping her bump tenderly. Jessie's eyelids fluttered closed. She'd let herself take a short rest and call her mum when the train was a couple of stops away from Chesterbury and she could give her a rough arrival time. That made more sense. She was sure her parents would be at home tonight anyway, as they rarely ventured out on a Monday evening, other than for a quick visit to Sainsbury's. Just as the train approached Little Brownshire, a text flashed up from Priya.

Your flatmate Lauren has just messaged me on Instagram asking if you're at mine. What's going on?

CHAPTER THIRTY-FOUR

In Chesterbury station car park, Jessie slid into the passenger seat beside her dad, pecking him on the cheek. The car had trapped the strong scent of his ancient cologne, the one that his wife, Jessie's mother, was always nagging him to update. But for Jessie, it was comforting to be around. It made her feel safe. For the first time in weeks she could stop looking over her shoulder, expecting to be followed.

'Well, this is a bit of a surprise but it's nice to see you, sweetheart,' he said, putting the car in gear and reversing out of the parking space.

Jessie yawned loudly.

'A good surprise I hope. Sorry, for the short notice. I just really need a break and some peace and quiet. Given that Christmas was so busy, I feel like I've not had any proper downtime since I moved away.'

Her brain felt like scrambled eggs that had been blasted through the microwave on too high a heat. Her dad lowered the radio and smiled, but said nothing, keeping his eyes firmly on the road. Their relationship was one of quiet understanding. He wasn't the type to check in with her constantly, usually hearing news about her life second-hand via his wife, but they were close, and he loved having his daughter home. Back at the house, Jessie's mother hovered behind an ironing board in the living room, nervously awaiting their arrival. She'd been fretting about Jessie ever since that worrying phone call the day before. The door opened. She immediately engulfed her daughter in a hug and hair stroke.

'Tell me again, what happened yesterday, love? Your text wasn't entirely clear,' she fussed. 'The break-in turned out to not really be a break-in after all?'

Jessie's mother could always tell when something wasn't right with her. She looked so worn out and painfully thin.

'Honestly, it's fine, Mum. Please stop flapping.'

Her voice sounded thick with cold. That always happened when she was getting rundown. When Jessie was smaller she was forever coming home from sleepovers with a runny nose, so she obviously hadn't been taking care of herself. What was that mark on her forehead too, just visible through her baby's neat fringe? More than anything, she hated that she couldn't be there to look after her on a daily basis any more. In a funny way, it had been even tougher watching Jessie leave home the second time around. At least when she was at university – and still in a relationship with Matthew – she had come home at the weekends.

'Jessica, you need to tell us. What happened with the police? Your message wasn't clear?'

Once Sergeant Langley and PC Phillips had left, Jessie had texted her mum playing down what had happened, bluffing that she'd simply panicked and jumped to conclusions. Her mum had phoned several times, but she hadn't picked up.

'The woman in the kitchen was a friend of Lauren's who I've not met before and I didn't realise she was staying with us,' Jessie laughed, slapping on an 'oops, aren't I silly?' smile.

Her dad chuckled. Typical Jessie. She'd always been a funny little thing growing up, afraid of witches living under the bed or ghouls escaping from the inside of her wardrobe. He couldn't understand why she created such unnecessary anxiety for herself, or why his wife seemed to either, for that matter. Must be a woman thing. He resumed flicking through the channels: if he was lucky he might be able to catch the end of the news.

'How long will you be staying for? I've made your bed up and left some clean towels out for you,' Jessie's mum said. 'No rush, of course; you know we love having you here.'

It wasn't like Jessie to be so vague about her plans.

'If we'd have known you were coming I would've done a big shop and got all your favourites in,' she added, hoping she didn't sound overbearing. 'I could've made one of those Mary Berry lemon drizzle cakes I know you love.'

She knew if she pushed too hard that Jessie would clam up completely.

'Probably just a few days. I thought it'd be nice to surprise you,' Jessie replied, taking a seat on the sofa. 'Plus, I was feeling like a little break from Brighton.'

Her mum nodded and went back to pressing the creases out of one of her husband's work shirts.

'It is, it's a lovely surprise. Tell me, how is work going? What did your flatmates have to say about you calling the police?'

She bit her tongue. Hopefully that wasn't one question too many. Jessie was like a bag of popcorn that needed to be opened slowly, otherwise the contents would fly out in random directions.

'They found it funny that I panicked so much, Mum. Honestly, it was no harm done. As for work, everything is great. Couldn't be better.'

Jessie's mouth was starting to hurt from the overly stretched smile. Her phone vibrated. It was a new message from Lauren.

Hey, when are you back? Are you okay? Remember the locks have been changed and I have the new keys for you.

Shit. She hadn't thought of that. She'd have to get a new set cut from Sofie's somehow. Maybe she could go into the café and grab them off her, get them sorted in that little cobblers on the same street. It would only take a few minutes. She could wait a few days until everybody would be out at work then grab her stuff, just the essentials, it wouldn't take long. It was probably about time she did a Marie Kondo on her wardrobe anyway, decluttered and downsized. The more relaxed she felt being back with her parents, the more certain she became about getting out of Maver Place for good. This was how she wanted to feel every time she came home.

'I'll make you some toast,' her mum announced, sensing she'd lost her daughter to her phone. 'With jam?'

Jessie nodded, but didn't look up from the screen. Typical millennial. She ate the toast by nibbling off the crusts first, as she always did. Her mum watched from across the room, pretending she wasn't.

Jessie knew she couldn't ignore Lauren forever. But she also didn't want to let on what she now knew about her … friend? Her flatmate? At this point she had no idea what to call her. But given that Lauren was prone to 'unpredictable behaviour', the safest bet would be to act as normal as possible, so that she wouldn't clock anything was amiss.

My mum hasn't been all that well, so I'm spending a few days in Chesterbury with the family. Speak soon x

It couldn't merely be a coincidence that both Magda and Beth had ended up in such dire straits after living with Lauren, could it? If Lauren had a habit of forming obsessive female friendships, perhaps Sofie had only been spared because Henry was always there, acting as her heavyweight shadow. A call lit up Jessie's phone. Lauren. She couldn't answer, not yet. Not until she'd got her head in better order. Instead she switched her mobile to silent and pushed it down the gap between two sofa cushions. She'd deal with it in the morning. Her exhaustion levels were so high that she could feel drool starting to escape from the corners of her mouth. Everything could wait until the morning.

Upstairs in her teenage girlish room, left untouched by her parents, Jessie searched through the chest of drawers for a nightdress and pulled out a bobbly one with a peeling Winnie the Pooh motif on the front. It still fitted, if a little snugly. She was regressing. Being an adult had turned out to be nothing like she'd imagined it would be, when she used to lie awake fantasising about it in this same room. She practised her usual breathing exercises and tried to concentrate on nothing but the hum of the television coming from downstairs. Her parents were watching *Blackadder* again. No matter how many times her dad had seen whatever episode they were on, he would laugh just as hard as the first time.

Jessie awoke the following day just before noon, to dozens of missed calls from Lauren, Priya and Pamela. She groaned, then opened her inbox and composed an email to Pamela apologising for her absence, explaining there had been a family emergency. The message was left deliberately open-ended, saying she'd be in touch when she knew when she might be back. It was unfair to have left her in the lurch like that – Pamela and Juliette had only ever been kind to her, and even Cheryl on reception was forever popping into their corner of the office and saying hello. But there were too many other things to be dealing with right now. And doing admin full-time for the NHS had hardly been her lifelong dream; maybe getting fired would be the push she needed to look for something else. Jessie headed to the bathroom to clean her teeth and realised they were chattering, then wandered downstairs to the dining room. It was difficult to chew her Frosties. They sat in mushy clumps on the insides of her cheeks and made the milk taste far too sweet.

All she needed to do was call Happy Homes and tell them to find a replacement tenant. She could settle up the last of her bills privately with Sofie or Marcus and this would all be over. Work would be easy enough to quit too, if Pamela hadn't already sacked her; she could just drop by the office in a few days and hand her notice in. And then what? Maybe now was the time to finally go travelling, to do something entirely for herself? Why hadn't she thought of that before?

Travelling is what she should have done in the first place, rather than slotting herself back into Brighton. The whole world was out there waiting for her and the only thing stopping her seeing it was herself. Jessie turned the thought over a few times, churning it like butter, until it suddenly felt so clear, she could almost smell sun cream and feel the heat. What happened next was down to her, not Lauren or Matthew or anybody else. Just her. Her spirits started to lift a little. There were some cousins on her father's side who lived over in Australia, which could be a good first stop. A stepping stone before going totally solo. Jessie grabbed a sheet of paper out of the clunky printer attached to the family computer, which sat in the corner of the dining room. It had been there for years.

She'd hated it as a teenager, because it meant that whenever one of her parents passed through to reach the kitchen, they could see the screen over her shoulder. All her intensely personal MSN conversations with Nicole or a tracksuit-clad boy from school. Her mum in particular would always walk past at a deliberately snail-rivalling pace too.

Grabbing a biro, Jessie started to jot down a list of ten destinations she'd like to visit, feeling her excitement building with each one. She googled 'travelling bucket list', underlined Thailand several times and drew a big enthusiastic circle around Morocco. How incredible would it feel to wake up and not have to think about anything other than what mountain to trek up? There'd be no stressing about bills, ex-boyfriends, Tinder or best friends concealing an integral part of their personality. She'd never have to listen to Juliette chewing with her mouth open again. Jessie tapped the pen in a happy tune. A night at home was exactly what she'd needed to start figuring things out. Life already felt calmer, like it might be okay now. There was the start of a plan. She had hope. Jessie peered out of the dining room window, at the neat cul-de-sac of mock Tudor houses with their manicured square lawns out front. The suburbs had mollycoddled her so tightly for the first eighteen years of her life without her even realising it. Dinner had always been on the table at six o'clock sharp, dance classes were on Tuesdays and Fridays, and every Saturday morning she'd been driven to gymnastics with her hair scraped so tightly back that her scalp would ache when she later untied her ponytail. A grey old man walked past with a yappy little terrier – lots of the people who lived around here were grey, or beige. They might keep their colouring inside the lines, but she didn't have to.

Jessie's phone screen danced with an incoming call; it was a Brighton number but not one she immediately recognised. Pamela? She answered.

'Jessica Campbell?'

'Yes?'

'This is Sergeant Langley calling from Sussex Police in regard to the crime you recently reported, with the reference number C161102. We'd like to invite you to attend an identity parade.'

Jessie's heart slid down in her chest. They wanted her to point the finger at Elizabeth Holliday. A homeless woman who had nothing. Sergeant Langley paused, then added in a final request.

'We'd also like to ask you a few questions in relation to another case we have open.'

CHAPTER THIRTY-FIVE

Lauren sat at the kitchen table in Maver Place growling at her phone. Why wasn't Jessie, her supposed best friend, who she'd supported through thick and thin, messaging her back or answering any calls? If only Jessie knew about all the things she'd done to keep her safe, she wouldn't abandon her like this. It was she, and only she, who had her best interests at heart. Not Priya or Nicole. It just wasn't normal for Jessie to leave Brighton without telling her first. Something was definitely wrong. The thought made Lauren sick to her stomach; she hated being in the flat without her and felt crippled by the loneliness. Without Jessie, she just wandered around aimlessly from room to room, smoking and waiting. It was all she could do. Georgia's death had given her enough pain to last a lifetime and she couldn't stand to lose anybody else.

Burying her face in her hands, Lauren replayed some of the memories that taunted her on a daily basis. The ones that, no matter how hard she had tried to forget, with medication, therapy and anything else she could think of, she couldn't erase. The memories which coated her in a thick layer of guilt every day. They, along with the grief, were still just as raw as they had been almost four years ago, she'd just learnt to hide it better. Lauren still missed her sister so much it knocked the air clean out of her lungs. She also missed her parents, who'd become robotic ever since Georgia's death. Their perfect family of four was splintered and surrounded by shadow without her. Ever since, dinners and Christmases had turned into little more than clipped conversations, long pauses and an empty chair that nobody could take their eyes away from.

When the twins were first born, Gwen McCormack would spent hours lying next to her much longed for babies on the living room floor, stroking their identical upturned noses. She was so proud to show them off, even taking them along to audition to be in a TV advert when they were toddlers, after seeing a call-out for identical twins in the newspaper. That had been a mistake. Georgia, the elder of the two by seven minutes, had done spectacularly well – even the casting director had called her a natural – but Lauren had screamed the place down until they'd been asked to leave. On their first day of school, Georgia led the way again, whereas Lauren's insides juddered with dread at the prospect of spending a day surrounded by alien children. All the other pupils were too loud, they didn't understand her the way Georgia did – she was the only one who knew what to say when Lauren lashed out and bit another child for trying to talk to them, or when she scratched any teacher who dared try to separate them.

As the twins grew older and boys entered the equation, Lauren's confidence took a further battering. Georgia was the first to do everything, from kissing the captain of the football team to sneaking out late to stay at his house. Lauren could still remember how it felt, sitting up all night, tormented that she'd been left behind, waiting for Georgia to come home. It was the same feeling she was experiencing now, because of Jessie. It was all she could focus on. By the end of their sixth form, Lauren had caught up on the socialising front, having studied and adopted the way Georgia tossed her head back when she laughed, how she walked into a party as though everybody in it owed her their time. It had taken practice, but by the time they left home for university (the same one of course), Lauren was able to convince most people that she was charming and bright too. It had lured Jessie in, and Zach, the only man who had ever noticed her first, while Georgia was also in the room.

Her first kiss with Zach was beyond the realms of anything Lauren had ever felt before. It was hungry, passionate. She'd clung onto his shirt in the middle of the club and couldn't imagine ever letting go, so when he placed a small white pill on his tongue and gently slipped it onto hers, she let him. Her body had shuddered from head to toe. He was sharing a secret with her and she wanted more than anything to keep it. She already adored him.

At first Lauren had no idea what she'd taken, until a slow, tingling sensation crept through her body, like the relief that accompanies a yawn. Her worries and feelings of inadequacy sweated out of her skin and were absorbed into the sticky ground below. She felt the beat of the bassline vibrating the roof of her mouth, the driving need to continue dancing, even though she couldn't feel her toes. Lust for Zach, the pulsing crowd around her ... it all knitted together as though she were seeing the world clearly for the first time. For once, she didn't want to live her life through her Georgia. She wanted to follow Zach to the ends of the earth – and that night, he let her. She let him.

After that experience, Lauren found herself craving the same high, from both Zach and the drugs – which, it turned out, he sold all over the city. She laughed when he pulled the shoebox out from underneath his bed where he kept a stash hidden, but secretly felt a flash of panic.

'You're cool with it, aren't you?' he asked, not bothered about the answer.

Of course Lauren had smiled and said it was fine. Whatever Zach wanted to do, she supported. Her happiness quickly started to depend on his presence; when he took too long to reply to her continuous stream of texts, Lauren bit all her nails down to tiny stubs and snapped at Georgia until he reappeared, always full of stories about losing his phone. Then, she'd float right back up again.

'You know you're my girl, right?' Zach would whisper. And with that, her resolve to be angry would wash away.

That summer was one of the hottest on record, comprised of stifling days and late-night claps of thunder. Lauren would lie awake, listening to the rain and Zach softly snoring, watching his chest rise and fall in the gloomy half-light, tracing it gently with her fingertips. Why sleep when she could spend hours reliving the way it felt when he pushed himself inside her? She loved the noises he made. Those small, whimpering sounds that forced their way out from beneath his aloof exterior and into her ear. They were so perfect together. It didn't scare her how quickly she'd become attached to this man in her bed, who told her everything and nothing about his life. Looking back, she wished it had.

At the time, Lauren had believed that buying drugs from Zach was a double win. Not only would it show him that she suited his lifestyle perfectly, but she could also prove to Georgia and all of their friends – a party-heavy group including Beth, their flatmate, who shovelled all of her tip-jar money either up her nose or down her throat – that she was fun too. It was always Georgia who wanted to stay up with everyone until five in the morning, having deep and meaningful conversations or dancing on coffee tables, while Lauren preferred to watch the scenes unfurl from the corner of a sofa, like a surveillance camera with drooping eyelids. She had never really wanted to be involved with the clear bags of white powder or pills until she met Zach. She'd drink the right amount to feel tipsy and take the edge off, but never enough to lose control, hating the thought of not being able to react quickly enough should anything go wrong.

That Saturday, when she decided that she'd be the one to buy drugs, Zach answered quickly and said he'd only charge her £40 for the stock. 'Mates' rates,' he'd called it, filling Lauren with abject horror. She didn't want to be 'mates'. She loved him and was certain that they could stick the broken parts of one another back together, if only Zach would let her. He rode over to Maver Place on his bike and stayed only a few minutes, which added to her anxiety, before mumbling about having somewhere else to be and pecking Lauren on the cheek. She closed the front door feeling like her insides had been ripped out, holding the bag of pills tightly, before telling herself to get it together and enjoy spending the night with Georgia for a change. No matter that her hands were shaking

Georgia had offered to braid Lauren's hair for the party that evening, the way she used to when they were teenagers. It was one thing guaranteed to soothe Lauren, and it had been utter bliss, resting her head in Georgia's lap and listening to all their favourite songs from a tinny laptop speaker.

At least she always had her sister, together forever, just the two of them.

Lauren and Georgia arrived at the party arm in arm, swigging on own-brand vodka and dissolving into fits of laughter. Lauren hugged Beth, who stroked her hair and told her how pretty it looked.

'Georgia, you'll have to teach me how to do it tomorrow when we get home,' Beth had begged, raising a plastic cup to the night ahead, powder lining her nose.

Zach was in the corner drinking a beer. Lauren knew instantly that he'd seen her, but with Georgia back by her side, was able to hold off from making the first move. He could come to her tonight. She dragged Georgia to the bathroom, bolted the door and sat on the edge of the bath as her twin used the toilet.

'Can we do the pills together then?' Georgia had asked, popping her leotard shut again. 'Just me and you.'

She emptied the toothbrushes out from a glass by the side of the sink, then filled it with water. There was that hit of pride that Lauren had been waiting for, the seal of approval. She placed two tiny pink circles onto Georgia's palm, then watched as she tipped her head back and dropped them in.

'Your turn,' Georgia ordered, taking a pill out of the plastic bag for Lauren.

As Lauren drew the pill towards her lips, a banging started up on the bathroom door. Georgia banged back.

'Calm down, can't a girl wee in peace around here?' She gave a throaty laugh.

Lauren remembered how she'd bent over the sink and ran the tap into her mouth, but still, the pill sat dissolving on her tongue. She even struggled to swallow paracetamol. When Georgia turned around to bang on the door again, she spat it out and let it disappear down the plughole.

Reliving that summer now made Lauren cry out with pain into the empty kitchen. Her mind still hadn't recovered. It kept telling her to do awful things – to do whatever it took to keep Jessie close to her – unable to cope with another loss. Lauren stood up from the kitchen table and moved outside to the balcony. How could – no, how *dare* – Jessie think it was okay to up and leave like this? And without so much as a goodbye. She wouldn't let her go without a fight. Lauren pulled out her phone and dialled Jessie's number again.

CHAPTER THIRTY-SIX

Back in Chesterbury, over a hundred miles away, the phone rang. Jessie ignored it. She stood in the dining room for a few minutes gathering her thoughts: her mum had taken the bus to work, meaning the car was free for her to drive back to Brighton that afternoon. The police didn't need her until five, plenty of time to tie up all her loose ends and collect the essentials from Maver Place beforehand. The majority of her clothes would fit in the boot and across the backseat, along with her laptop and jewellery. They were all she really needed to take from the flat. Jessie glanced at the clock on the bookcase, a gilded gold thing that her parents had been gifted as a wedding present. Almost one. She pulled up Sofie's number.

'Jessie, hey? How are you, I've been worried. Lauren keeps asking if I know where you are.'

Jessie bit her lower lip.

'I'm so sorry to do this to you, Sofe, but I have to move out. I promise I won't leave you high and dry with the bills like Magda, but I'm coming to collect my stuff today, then moving home for a while. Please don't tell the others, I'm only telling you because I trust you, and I want you to know that I won't leave you all in the lurch.'

The words fell out of Jessie's mouth freely. This was the right thing to do, Sofie would understand.

'Are you in the flat at the moment? I was hoping to drop in and pick up some of my things in a few hours.'

'Oh, gosh. No, I'm at Henry's and leaving for work shortly, but I have your new key here. I'll drop it into Happy Homes on my way.'

Sofie was quiet for a few seconds.

'I'll miss living with you, Jessie. I hope that we can stay in touch?'

She was such a sweetheart; none of this had been her fault.

'Of course, Sofe. Definitely.'

It was Jessie's turn to pause.

'Lauren's not going to be in, is she?'

Once Sofie had confirmed that everybody would be out, Jessie called Priya to ask if she could meet her at the flat later on for moral support.

'I'll chat to my boss about leaving early, but it should be fine,' Priya said, grateful that Jessie had called her before going in there alone – that Lauren sounded unhinged.

Jessie programmed the sat nav to direct her back to 4 Maver Place for the final time. Her shoulders stayed tense throughout the entire journey. In a way, the thought of not saying a proper goodbye to Lauren was still gutting, given that they'd spent so much time together over the last few months. It was almost like a break-up. But she had to start putting herself first, to surround herself with people that wouldn't interfere with her own healing, people who were honest. Pulling up outside the flat just after four, Jessie sat and listened to the engine tick with heat. The phone rang.

'My last client meeting ran over, I'm so sorry. I'm on my way now.'

It was Priya.

'Don't worry,' she replied, before noticing the clock on the dashboard. 'The only thing is I need to be at the police station for five, which doesn't leave me much time to get packing. I might head in and make a start. Sofie said Lauren would be out anyway.'

Priya promised she'd be there soon, so Jessie mounted the front steps and put her ear to the door, to double-check. She couldn't hear anybody inside. Turning her key in the lock, she exhaled with relief upon finding the flat, as Sofie had promised it would be, completely still and silent, then headed to the kitchen for water. It still gave her the creeps, ever since seeing Beth ransacking it. Sipping the water, Jessie looked around the room and made a quick checklist of what to take from it. Some Tupperware boxes might be a good idea. No doubt she'd end up in another stale office job for a while, as she saved up for travelling. Bringing in lunch would help. She crouched down and began looking in a cupboard, hating having her back to the doorway.

Lauren crept down the corridor, deliberately quietly, not wanting to scare away her prey.

'What are you doing here? I thought you'd gone home.'

Jessie flinched; she hadn't heard Lauren come in at all. She turned and looked up to face Lauren, finding her looking small and lost in a hooded sweater that was far too big for her, eyes bloodshot.

'I'm just picking up a few bits before heading back to Chesterbury,' she said, trying to her best to sound normal, rising to her feet.

Lauren lurched forward and wrapped her arms around Jessie's stiff body.

'I was really worried about you, I'm so relieved that you came back. How is your mum?'

The frenzy in her voice made Jessie shake herself free and back a few paces away, feeling behind her for the kitchen counter to lean against. Lauren looked worried and moved closer too, blocking her into a corner.

'She's okay, thanks. It was just a routine operation but I still want to be there to look after her,' Jessie bluffed. 'Make cups of tea, that sort of thing.'

She silently willed Priya to hurry up. Where on earth was she? Although the heating was on, a chill was making its way through her bones.

'Well, how long will you be gone for?' Lauren asked urgently. 'If it's just a routine operation, can't you just stay here?'

Jessie shuffled awkwardly.

'Please,' she begged, grabbing Jessie's hands and trying a new tactic. 'I'll miss you too much if you have to go home again.'

The intensity with which she said it made Jessie instantly uncomfortable. She looked Lauren square in the eyes.

'Really, you're all I have.'

Lauren broke into big, gulping sobs and pulled the drawstrings of the hood around her head, showing nails that had been completely bitten down into bloody stumps. It was time Jessie knew what lay beneath her usually cool exterior. That was what *real* best friends did, they saw the murky and the ugly sides too. The frightening sides. She needed to come clean, about everything she'd done, all that she'd been hiding. All of it.

'It's more than Magda that I'm upset about.'

Jessie held her breath and waited for Lauren to continue, wishing she could move out of the corner she'd been backed into.

'Everybody I love always leaves. It's not fair, Jessie, it's really not.'

She looked at Jessie, whose face gave nothing away.

'I've never spoken to you about this, but I had a sister named Georgia, a twin, who died almost four years ago from an overdose.'

Lauren became aware of the sound of her own breath; her body and mind were drifting apart again. She drew a badly rolled cigarette to her chapped mouth and clicked a lighter at the end of it with an unsteady hand.

'I can feel her everywhere in this room, she's always watching.'

Jessie felt her throat constrict. Lauren could feel her dead sister in this room? She looked over Lauren's shoulder towards the hallway. If she tried to run, what would happen?

'Can we sit for a minute?' Lauren asked, smoke flying from her mouth as she spoke.

Lauren moved over to the round pine table, where the flatmates had all shared countless dinners, and banged on the empty chair beside her, until Jessie gingerly sat down. She had to admit, she did at least owe Lauren the chance to explain herself. Didn't she? She prayed that Priya would ring the bell any second now, wishing she had back-up. The air in the room was lacking oxygen, too thick with smoke.

'It's my fault she's dead.'

Jessie remained silent, trying to absorb the hurricane of information she'd just found herself thrown into. What did Lauren mean it was her fault? She conjured images of pools of blood, the blade of a knife cutting through flesh. Surely Lauren couldn't have done anything like that? She'd said it was an overdose? Looking at her now, she was in absolute hysterics over her twin. She couldn't be capable of that. But her file on the database at work had said she was violent, a risk, a former inpatient at a psychiatric hospital. People didn't get sent to those kinds of institutions for no reason.

Lauren thought back to that night again, where her world had irreversibly changed.

'Come here,' Georgia had said, ushering Lauren into the garden when her feet began to hurt from dancing. 'I need to tell you something.'

They walked towards the very end of it, where the shrubbery was overgrown and wild.

'I don't even know where to begin with this.'

Georgia was slurring her words, her eyes looking off-kilter. It annoyed Lauren, who despite pretending to be on a similar high, had in reality only drunk a few vodka and cokes. With Zach still not having even acknowledged her, her mood was fraught. The stupid pills were starting to burn a hole in her pocket and she wanted to throw them away. Nobody else had been interested in taking them, claiming they were 'on the powder' instead.

'Marcus and I have found a new flat – we're going to move out of Maver Place soon.'

The sound of breaking glass came from the house, followed by a raucous cheer.

'What are you talking about? You're too wasted,' Lauren snapped.

Marcus, the weird guy they'd found on SpareRoom to help pay their rising rent had turned out to be the one boyfriend who wormed his way so far under Georgia's skin that she was now wanting to move out. Lauren had never lived without Georgia before. They were meant to be together, always. What she was saying was all wrong.

'I know you don't like him,' Georgia continued, steadying herself on the fence. 'But I love him, we understand each other. He teaches me new things about myself all the time.'

Lauren spat on the floor in anger.

'He's just a boy, Georgia. Not even a particularly attractive one. In fact, he's a bit of a fucking freak, if you ask me.'

Georgia frowned, still swaying.

'He's made me realise that I'm a separate person, Lauren. That *we* are separate people, not just twins. There's more to you as well, you know.'

She was wrong about that too. So wrong.

'You're serious?'

The twins locked eyes with one another, Georgia's shone apologetically. Lauren dug her nails deliberately hard into Georgia's forearm.

'You can't do this,' she wailed, an internal fire blazing. 'You just can't.'

She wanted to lash out, like she used to at the other children in their class at school. The teachers who had attempted to split them up. The people who hadn't understood her. Why wasn't Georgia understanding her now? She was obviously too out of it and needed taking home. Her eyes kept rolling backwards.

Lauren called a taxi, then shoved her sister roughly into the back of it, hissing at her to stop groaning in case the driver kicked them out. When the car pulled up outside Maver Place, she asked the driver to wait, then frogmarched Georgia upstairs. Her legs had turned to lead and she couldn't manage the steps without help. Georgia mumbled urgent nonsense, trying to warn Lauren not to take any more of the pills, which had been cut with something that her system was struggling to process. But Lauren wasn't interested. All she could think about was Zach and wanting to get back to where he was. To get blackout drunk, to show him how crazy he made her feel when he ignored her like this. Vodka, whisky, wine, all of it. She wanted to spout about how he'd broken her heart to all their mutual friends. Kiss someone she didn't care about in front of him, even though it'd be as effective as climbing to the top of a mountain and shouting at him, hoping he'd hear her from the bottom. She slammed Georgia's bedroom door and ran back into the taxi.

'Go as fast as you can,' she demanded the driver, rolling down the window and letting her hair dance in the breeze.

Back in the flat, Georgia lay on her back looking at the crack of light poking through the heavy damask curtains that never quite shut properly. Her eyes were closing. Why was her bedroom suddenly so big and so small at the same time? Where was Lauren? She wanted Marcus. Who she loved waking up next to. A man who spoke only when he had something important to say, unlike her, who rabbited away non-stop, unable to stand any silences. If Marcus were here, he could nuzzle into her neck and hold her tight, make the nausea and spinning stop. Georgia vomited. Thick white clumps of bread from dinner earlier that night reappeared. Some of it caught in her throat. Why couldn't she move it? She tried to cough. Her mouth was coated with chemicals. The room was being played around her through an old projector. She vomited again. Then stillness.

CHAPTER THIRTY-SEVEN

'I took her home and left her,' Lauren managed to whisper. 'I left her alone to die and fucked off back to a party to chase a man who never really gave a toss about me.'

Her waxen face was starting to scare Jessie, as was the way she kept licking her chapped lips and flashing her sharp teeth. Lauren clawed at the table, frantic with her own stupidity. In the early days after Georgia's death, she would sit at the table for what felt like hours on end, clutching at the blanket Georgia had been wrapped in as a baby, unable to face going anywhere near the bedroom where she'd found her sister lying stiff and cold that sunny afternoon. Marcus and Beth would pass through the kitchen too, sometimes silently, sometimes not, equally as fragmented.

'When Beth and I came home the next day, we thought she was covered in porridge or something at first,' Lauren said flatly. 'She was already cold. It was so sunny that day and the flat was boiling, but Georgia felt like a block of ice.'

Jessie hardly dared to breathe as she listened. The thought of having to live with that guilt, getting up and putting it on each morning along with your socks and underwear. Carrying it with you to the bathroom, to clean your teeth and shower, yet never feeling clean ...

'My parents and Marcus think she got too drunk and choked to death and I don't want to tarnish their memory of her by telling them that she regularly took drugs at parties too. But everyone did, it was so normal in that scene. Marcus never liked the drugs side of things, he wouldn't touch them. Ever. If he'd have been there that night everything could have been different. It's my fault she's gone.'

Jessie was stunned; she couldn't imagine Marcus with a partner. He always seemed so vacant, so glassy-eyed. But this would explain it. She should have been kinder to him.

'Marcus was Georgia's boyfriend?'

Lauren nodded, her face still contorting with anguish.

'I couldn't look in the mirror for months afterwards, all I could see was her. That's why Beth left, it tipped her over the edge because she loved Georgia too. It's why Marcus never sleeps ...' Lauren paused to draw breath, looking as though each inhale was taking extreme effort.

That's why she had heard those strange noises in the middle of the night – Marcus's insomnia had left him wide awake, pacing around his room, Jessie realised. She watched as Lauren tore off strips from the kitchen roll sheet and let them flutter to the floor, feeling an instant urge to want to tidy them up. To try and brush them clean away along with all the horrible things she now knew. A woman had died in her bedroom. How laughable that she'd been fearful of an old locket without even knowing the half of it.

'I knew it'd be difficult having somebody else move in, but Magda and I clicked really well and, for a while, things felt like they might actually be getting better. She was so understanding and patient with me, and made me feel good about myself when I thought I never could again. I even bleached my hair to try and look more like her after she said it would suit me. I was so alone. I wanted to look like – to be like – anyone but me,' Lauren continued, her voice cracking.

She was shivering inside the oversized hoody.

'Why would Marcus want to stay in the flat?' said Jessie, finally, needing to fill the heavy silence. 'After all that?'

A tear dashed down Lauren's cheek and clung to her chin, wobbling precariously.

'He says he owes it to Georgia to keep an eye on me. He doesn't know that I was the one to give her the drugs. That I didn't stay with her.'

Jessie pictured her bedroom back in Chesterbury and wished she'd never left. Why had she bothered coming back here to collect her clothes? They were just clothes. She desperately wanted to get back in her car and drive far away from this stifling kitchen.

'We've become so close, you and I. Haven't we?' Lauren started again, rocking back and forth in her chair. 'I'd do anything not to lose you, I can't afford that, Jessie ... Do you understand? My parents were so worried about me after Georgia died, they had me admitted to hospital. They locked me up and made me take pills off a tray morning, noon and night. But you keep me steady, that's why I had to keep you safe.'

Jessie's heart was beating so hard that her T-shirt moved in time with it.

'Keep me safe?' she asked, her tongue feeling far too big for her mouth.

Upstairs, months' worth of Lauren's medication lay untouched in her bedroom. Ditching her mood stabilisers had made it even easier to do what she needed to do in order to keep Jessie close.

'I protected you from Ian – he's not as nice as he'd have everyone think, you know,' Lauren growled, stopping swaying and immediately looking angry. 'He was obsessed with you and I stopped it, I saved you from him.'

'What do you mean, you saved me?' Jessie asked worriedly.

'I made sure he never came back' Lauren replied, sounding proud.

She explained to Jessie how she'd spotted the pair of black lace knickers dangling out of Ian's pocket and what she had done the next time he had come over, with yet another flimsy excuse of needing to check the shower for leaks – that one had made her laugh at least.

'Coffee, Ian?' Lauren had asked, peering up through her long lashes.

'Love one, thanks.'

She could feel him ogling the shadow of her cleavage through her thin vest top.

'Did you want to sort the bathroom now while I make it?'

Once Ian had gone upstairs, she'd cracked open one of the spare cartridges for her electronic cigarette with a penknife. It contained a mix of toxic chemicals, including pure nicotine. Lauren knew this was unlikely to kill him – she wouldn't want that on her conscience, after all – but it would definitely leave Ian unwell enough so that the message would sink in. That he was sick. Being bedbound also ought to afford him plenty of time to think about his actions. Lauren handed over the coffee with a smile, then watched him drink, merrily stirring her own.

'I think, now that you've nearly finished, you should leave,' she had said, as soon as Ian could see his bulging eyes staring back at him from the bottom of the mug.

Her voice was level, eerily calm, confusing. Something wasn't right.

'Yes? Of course, lots to do back in the office.'

'I don't think you should come back, either.' Lauren had waited a few beats, until she could practically hear the cogs in Ian's head grinding. 'Because I know what you've been doing and I'm sure your boss would like to know all about it too. About all these unauthorised and unnecessary visits, the goodies you've picked up along the way.'

It was then that she'd sipped her own poison-free coffee serenely, enjoying watching him squirm and stammer. Ian tried to deny that he'd done anything below board, but they both knew there was no point. She had him nailed.

'Don't think I'm not serious, 'Lauren had said, swallowing down the last dregs, still smiling. 'You'll soon learn that I'm not the type of woman who does things by halves.'

Ian had pushed his chair back in a hurry and tried to exit with his dignity still intact. She was bluffing, he figured. Until he got back to the Happy Homes offices, when he started being violently sick in the staff toilet.

Jessie's face looked aghast as she listened in horror at what Lauren had done. None of what she was hearing felt real.

'I rescued you from Rob too,' Lauren boasted, smiling and covering one of Jessie's clenched fists with her icy fingers. 'It's so important that we don't ever let any men come between us. You know, it's like everyone says, mates before dates.'

Jessie snatched her fist back, eyes widening, but couldn't speak. All sense of time had disappeared. She was utterly paralysed with fear, unable to decide if she should run or carry on listening to Lauren. Her friend, her flatmate, the person she'd been living with for all these months. She couldn't believe what she was hearing.

'Hey, don't be like that.' Lauren looked cross, reaching out to grab her hand again. 'He obviously didn't care about you. All I had to do was intercept him on his way to the bathroom and tell him you have a boyfriend, then he was off.'

Jessie spotted a glint of gold on Lauren's wrist. Her old charm bracelet, the one she'd thought had been lost during her move and which Lauren had so kindly and thoughtfully replaced. This couldn't be happening.

The night that Rob had come back to Maver Place, Lauren had lain awake listening to his piglike grunting and Jessie's disingenuous moans, feeling more threatened by the second. It was exactly like being a teenager again and waiting for Georgia to sneak back into the house after her secret trysts with the football captain. The rhythmic banging of the bed against the wall felt like a personal attack on Lauren's senses. She had turned her headphones up and screamed into a pillow, but still they continued. She couldn't stand that somebody else should come between her and Jessie, the way stupid Henry had with her and Sofie. Her friendship with Jessie was something Lauren knew she had to protect at any cost. This Rob, a complete nobody, had made himself right at home, in *her* flat. He was clearly just another conceited imbecile of a man, like Henry. Nowhere near good enough for Jessie. They didn't need men or relationships, when they had each other. Luckily, Jessie had left her phone in her coat pocket that night too – and it hadn't been hard to guess the passcode for it. A few quick touches and Priya's number was blocked. Another rope tying Jessie to other people had been easily snipped. Off they went, snip, snip, snip, one by one.

'No, Lauren, no!' Jessie shook her head in disbelief.

She bent forward and began to search quietly through her handbag on the floor. Where were the car keys? Lauren lowered herself down too, to meet Jessie's eye line and give a disbelieving laugh, snorting like a wild horse.

'Yes, Jessie, yes. You have to remember that I'm half-dead myself now,' she said, a manic light dancing in her eyes. 'But I'm the most loyal friend you'll ever have.'

Little specks of spit escaped from either side of Lauren's mouth. Jessie's chest heaved. She had to get out. Why weren't her feet unsticking? The colours of the kitchen were all wrong.

'It was me who attacked you, to teach you what real pain feels like. I needed somebody I could bond with over that, someone who'd *get* what it feels like to be rejected and ground down by the world. I had to do it, so you'd need me more than ever and to bring us even closer.'

Jessie heard her heart beating relentlessly in her ears like a military drum, all senses heightened. It was Lauren who had hurt her. Matthew hadn't been involved, it wasn't a stranger taking their chances after seeing her drunk. She had been broken by one of her best friends, turned into a quivering wreck who couldn't sleep without pills or wine.

Who was too afraid to leave her room. It made sense now, of course, that Lauren would want her trapped inside. Right where she could see her, where she could never escape, the way Georgia had tried to. The way Magda almost did.

CHAPTER THIRTY-EIGHT

Jessie opened her mouth to answer, then closed it. She stared hard at Lauren, and couldn't believe that she had once looked up to her – she'd seemed so confident and self-assured when they had first met. So many questions swam through her mind, she didn't know where to begin. The betrayal was crushing. *How* had it come to this? When she left Matthew, she swore to herself, to Priya and the universe, that she'd never succumb to another's control again. Yet she'd walked right into the arms of her next predator, paying £600 a month for the privilege. Her head was spinning, the scar on the back of her skull burned.

'It really wasn't easy hurting you,' Lauren said, unblinking. 'But I had to protect you from yourself, to show you that bad things will happen when you go off alone. That we *have* to stick together.'

She was speaking at a thousand miles an hour, her words rattling off like bullets and spraying all around the room, catching Jessie in the head and heart.

'I only wanted to scare you, but once I'd started I found I couldn't stop. I thought you'd seen me so I had to keep going, until I knew you'd blacked out and … wouldn't remember.'

Hearing that, Jessie felt hot bile rise up in her throat. She thought of her limp body lying trampled on in the Pavilion Gardens, the way she'd looked up at the sky and cried out, covered in the freezing rain. All because of Lauren. Who'd then stroked her brow, made her tea, kept her locked in the house.

'It was nothing like hurting Magda – I'd do that again for you in a heartbeat. She's not the sort of person you should have been getting involved with, she's dishonest and selfish.'

After reading Jessie's Facebook messages on her phone, while she was bedbound following the attack, Lauren had contacted Magda and convinced her that they ought to meet. She claimed the locket had been passed on to her to return.

Jessie said it's best that I give it to you, it would be good to clear the air too.

Magda, kind-hearted and gullible, had eventually agreed.

Perhaps we could meet along the seafront? Somewhere public and on neutral ground, she'd said. Lauren had agreed.

Once Lauren had wrapped up a long day of shooting at work, she waited under the glow of a street lamp for Magda to arrive, watching the sea roll around in the darkness. It was a quiet night. They'd planned to head down to the promenade to where a few bars would still be open, to talk. But as soon as Lauren saw Magda walking towards her, with a wary look in her eyes, a match was lit inside. This was the woman who'd once rented Georgia's, her dead sister's, bedroom, who'd promised to be there for her, but who had then abandoned her. Magda, the woman she hadn't seen or heard from in months, was now right there in front of her. In touching distance.

Lauren remembered how much she'd looked up to Magda, admired her, and thought she'd finally found someone who could help her out of the all-consuming grief she was so deeply entrenched in. She'd thought Magda so inspiring for studying midwifery. For wanting to bring new life into the world, the total opposite of loss. Lauren had even cut and dyed her hair to look more like Magda's too, which she'd seemed to approve of initially. But then, when Lauren had started speaking about going back to university to train as a midwife too, and told her the truth about how Georgia had died, and where, Magda had upped and left in the middle of the night. Claiming in a note that Lauren was too 'intense', 'unstable' and needed 'more professional help'. The blaze in Lauren's chest grew. She didn't want to talk and clear the air after all. How *dare* Magda now try and warn Jessie away? When she knew how much hurt Lauren had already had to claw her way tooth and nail through. She'd been different this time, so careful, with Jessie too, deliberately fighting back the urge to copy her style in case it scared her off. That lesson had been learnt; and besides, she'd seen the way Jessie reacted when Sofie had tried to. She'd done everything 'right' and yet it was still at risk of going wrong. Lauren had shoved Magda towards the concrete block of stairs that connected the street to the beachfront below. She'd stumbled.

'What the... Lauren? What are you doing?'

Magda had shaken her head and gripped at the rail.

'You betrayed me, Magda, in the worst way, when I was at rock bottom. You left me. How could you *do* that?'

Flecks of spittle formed in the corner of Lauren's mouth.

'Stop it. Just give me the necklace,' Magda had pleaded. 'I've kept all your secrets, I swear. I just want my jewellery back, it's really important to me.'

It had felt good seeing her be the weaker of the two for a change, the one who didn't have a choice in what happened next. So Lauren had pushed her again. Harder. Magda had fallen backwards, lost her grip, her hands grabbing helplessly at the air looking for something to hold on to but finding nothing. She hit each solid block on the way down the steps with a loud thwacking sound, then fell silent. Lauren had laughed. A bit of power went a long way, that adrenaline rush was an easy addiction to succumb to. It was a new and welcome feeling.

'Get up Magda, stop being stupid,' she had shouted, running down to where Magda lay, nudging at her with her foot.

Magda didn't respond. She'd remained in a limp heap at the bottom of the steps. Lauren panicked, her cold breath spiralling into the air. Magda's eyes were open but unfocused, her head at an odd angle. God, no. It had been an accident. Lauren had never meant for it to go this far. She'd just wanted to scare Magda, to show her how it felt to be walked all over by a person she'd once loved. There was nobody around to ask for help and no way Lauren could call an ambulance. The wind howled in her ears, screaming that she had to keep quiet. She'd been covering up her other mistake for so long – this couldn't be the reason everything else unravelled. Magda had to stay quiet too. Lauren bent down and checked her pulse. It was there, in her wrist, but incredibly faint.

She'd dragged Magda's body across the beach and pushed her flopping head deep under the biting salty water, then watched as her arms and legs kicked out in protest. Lauren waited until Magda's limbs finally stopped moving before submerging herself in the cutting-cold sea, and swimming out as far as she could with the lifeless body in tow, silently screaming pain into the night sky. Despite being a strong swimmer, after just a minute her arms ached. The left one from making strokes powerful enough to propel a live body and a dead weight forward, the right from clinging on to said excess baggage. When they were far enough from the shore, Lauren had paused, bobbing in the waves, then let Magda slip from her grasp. The last gasps of air evacuated the vacant corpse with a low groan, as she sank below the surface. It was a sound that Lauren could never forget. She had swum back, bleached blonde hair sticking rigidly to her forehead, teeth chattering, desperately wanting to shed her red leather jacket but too afraid to do so, in case it led a trail back to the snuffed out life sinking behind her.

Freak accidents happened every day, she had reassured herself at the time. There was no reason for anybody to suspect her involvement.

Only now, she was stuck waiting for the police to publish the results of that damn autopsy, not knowing whether they might come knocking at her door again. She didn't like the way that stocky uniformed woman had looked at her. It was as if she knew something. It felt like time was running out.

Stacks of washing-up lay around the sink, where Lauren was now standing. Marcus's three-day-old saucepan with remnants of a fried egg stuck to the bottom, several glasses and plates smeared with sauces. Most tantalising of all, though, was the blade of a gleaming kitchen knife, poking out from beneath a wooden chopping board. The sharpest one in the flat. The one she used to swoosh through red peppers and dice onions into neat little squares with ease. Lauren stroked the handle of the knife tenderly, seemingly in a daze. Jessie was still struck dumb, her mind going over and over the best decision to make and coming up blank. Then her feet started moving.

'I have to leave,' she croaked, breaking into a run.

This time around, she wouldn't let the bullies win. She was so close to being able to start over.

Lauren looked up, as if seeing Jessie for the first time, and lunged at her.

She was too slow.

CHAPTER THIRTY-NINE

Sergeant Langley sucked on a boiled sweet as she drove to Maver Place. The sirens on top of the car wailed. Her boss, DCI David Tyrell, a man she'd been working hard to impress, was riding shotgun. This was going to be good. Especially as Jessica Campbell ought to be identifying Elizabeth Holliday in a few minutes too, if everything back at the station was running to schedule.

Two cases as good as nailed in one day. The results of the post-mortem had finally come back confirming that Magda Nowak had died under suspicious circumstances. It was not, as initially reported, suicide. There were several lacerations to the victim's face and marks on the body, indicating that she'd been kicked repeatedly after probably having fallen down a flight of concrete stairs. Her neck was broken but she wasn't dead yet ... She had then been held under water because her lungs were filled with liquid. Sergeant Langley had trawled through endless hours of CCTV footage and thanks to a small ice-cream kiosk, which had suffered several break-ins and turned the owner into a security vigilante, she'd found

plenty of video evidence of Lauren McCormack dragging the poor young woman – her former flatmate – into
the sea after a scuffle by the stairs. It was a brutal, animal-
istic attack. Psychopathic, almost. Inhuman.

As they wove through traffic, other cars pulling over
to allow them a clear path, Sergeant Langley thought of
how much she loved her job. She was a good driver,
despite PC Phillips teasing her otherwise. When she
rounded the corner and passed the wine bar at the end of
Maver Place, blue lights came into view. Sergeant Langley
could hear other sirens joining in with her own, a chorus
of alarm. She neared the flat and saw several of her colleagues already pulled up outside. How could someone
have beaten her to the chase? Her heart sank as she realised her radio was still tuned into the Hove, not Brighton
channel; she must have missed a call. She heard DCI
Tyrell give a small, unimpressed cough beside her. This
wasn't how it was meant to go.

'What's going on?' Sergeant Langley walked straight
over to PC Phillips, who was speaking earnestly into the
walkie-talkie attached to his vest.

He looked at her with serious eyes.

'We've had a call about a stabbing at number four, the
same flat we were in the other week,' he replied. 'It doesn't
sound good.'

The walkie-talkie bleeped and crackled. Paramedics
had stopped working on the victim. They were about to
bring the body out of the house and needed any vehicles
blocking the ambulance to be moved immediately. PC

Phillips hurriedly climbed into his car and reversed it backwards, to ensure it wasn't in the way.

Marcus didn't hear the sirens initially, as his headphones were turned up too loud, nor did he notice there was an ambulance pulled up by the kerb, alongside the police cars and vans. He noticed the blue lights though, bouncing off the front of the flat. The grip on his guitar case slackened, then he started running. Priya stood outside looking up at 4 Maver Place in horror, as two men in green uniforms carried a stretcher down the front steps and into the back of the ambulance. Strapped to it, was a woman with bleached blonde hair.

Acknowledgements

This book wouldn't have been possible without a number of people.

Thank you first and foremost to Katie Seaman, editor extraordinaire, for sending the email that changed everything and for helping me water the seed of an idea into a real living, breathing book – I'm so indebted to you. To Diana Beaumont, my brilliant agent, thank you for the invaluable support and feedback you've given along the way too.

My parents, Nick and Heather, it appears that plying me with books as a child has paid off! I'm grateful that you always encouraged me to write, allowed me to be independent and to choose my own path. You're the best.

Babette Savin, my grandma and hero – you've taught me more than you'll ever know and making you proud is my biggest motivator. To my uncle Mark and auntie Vicki, you've been my constant cheerleaders from day one and I appreciate it no end.

Benjamin Kelly, thank you not only for reading every word of this book throughout the course of it being written, and for offering your honest opinion, but for everything else that you do too. I love you.

I am privileged to have some of the most wonderful friends. Isabella Silvers, thank you for kick-starting my career. You are one of the most razor sharp, determined and encouraging women I've ever met. Hannah Cardy, Jack Coulston, Oliver Greaves, Dina Mouhandes, George Palmer and Ashleigh Ward: you were everything I hoped I'd find in Brighton and more, some of my favourite ever times have been spent with you. Adam Carter, Krista Lynch, Carina McKay, September Mead and Ellen Thomas: how lucky I was to have met you all those years ago and luckier still to have you around now.

To the book club girls, my precious Ponies, the group chat and Prosecco, interspersed with karaoke and ana-lysing celebrity autobiographies, were the perfect tonic to any writer's block. Extra thanks to Josie Copson for reading this book in draft form and giving me helpful pointers, and to Eleanor Lees for always checking in.

Thank you: Catriona Innes for all the author-related advice, you're a real inspiration, Farrah Storr for making me a better writer and Janine Pipe (plus others who wished to remain anonymous) for your insight into police procedures.

Lastly, I'd also like to thank all the terrible flatmates (and ex-boyfriends) I've had over the years. Turns out you were great inspiration.

If you enjoyed

THE WRONG MOVE

we'd love to hear from you

Leave a review online

Join the conversation on social media @JenniSavin
@EburyPublishing #TheWrongMove

You can follow Jennifer on Twitter @JenniSavin and
Instagram @savcity to stay up to date with all
her latest news